# THROUGH HER LENS

# THROUGH

## — HER —

# LENS

### A NOVEL

Melissa Clark Bacon

atmosphere press

To Miller and John

# PROLOGUE

Pablo Picasso's painting of the city of Guernica after Nazi Germany's aerial bombs annihilated it during the Spanish Revolution returned to Spain in 1981 and now hangs in the halls of Museo Nacional Centro de Arte Reina Sofia. My charge, Millicent Trayford, and I saw it for the first time with her father while it was in exile. It hung among the treasures of the 1937 Paris World's Fair. Millicent was eighteen then and believed she was every bit the adult, making my presence as a chaperon awkward at best. To be clear, she didn't aim her resentments only at me. After lunch she put on a show, stomping a step ahead of her father into the Spanish Pavilion, irritation oozing from every pore, because he had insisted on ordering her meal for her. She opened her mouth to argue, but I glared over my reading glasses, shooting a warning glance in her direction. I meant to remind her this wasn't the place to take a stand. I waited as she considered whether or not to take my advice. As a child she hung on my every word, minding a reflex. But sitting across from her then, I could make out the small voice growing deep inside her, tempting her to stand her ground, just this once. I must admit I recognized the voice. You see, I spent years coaxing it out of her. When her mother died, a bit of Millie's spirit went with her. I saw it as my job to invite it back. But in that moment it was not welcome. In less than a heartbeat, I watched my darling Magpie close her mouth as the spirited lass that took up residence in the rowdy corners of her heart retreated to her lair. I leaned back into my chair ever so slightly, pleased she remembered my lesson—pick your battles carefully. Watching her stomping ahead after the offending meal reminded me that it can take more than a second for a fire to die down.

As we made our way to the ground floor patio of the Pavilion, we passed a mural of Spanish Republic soldiers under the slogan "We are fighting," leaving the three of us confused about what to expect inside. Whatever we were about to see, it seemed unlikely that it would comport with the Fair's "technology" theme. Stepping deeper into the Pavilion, Millie instinctively rested her hand on her ever-present camera bouncing on her hip, and then she rounded the corner and took in the massive black and white mural for the first time. I watched as her eyes widened, then closed tight, and then looked away. A welcome bit of cool breeze kissed our damp skin as her father and I flanked her. She reached for our hands, as if she suddenly needed to be sure of us. She looked first to her father, who could not take his eyes off the twelve-by-twenty-six-foot painting, and then to me just as I blinked away the tears that were welling up in my eyes. After nodding at me and standing a bit taller, Millie forced herself to study the destruction, pain, and sorrow in front of her. She stole a glance at the spiral ramp leading to the second floor that offered retreat, but her father and I held her hands tight. I squeezed to remind her that with the two of us by her side, she could do anything.

Standing at the far right-hand side, Millie took it all in with her photographer's eye. If I remembered her lectures correctly, the chaotic composition was likely making her uneasy. She preached order, inviting lines, negative spaces to rest in, control. Her eyes batted to the plink-plinking of the Mercury Fountain as her eyes darted around the painting desperately searching for a pathway in. I caught a whiff of a familiar scent, her mother's favorite perfume, Shalimar, coming from one of the other well-heeled visitors and wondered if Millie's anxiety was exacerbated by a long-ago memory.

Her eyes moved from the bull to the horse and daggers and flames and lights and diagonal lines moving in all directions. They rested only when she found one of the four women. She dropped her father's hand, then mine, and lifted her camera. She stepped back and got to work; she would have to photograph the painting in sections to capture it all.

Flames trapped the first woman, and she raised her arms in terror. The second was simply a head floating into the room carrying a candle, a witness to the scene like the rest of us. The third woman staggered toward the spirit's light and the bulb hanging in the center of the room with a blank stare. Millie stopped at the fourth woman. She dropped her camera from her face. Millie couldn't tear her eyes away from the wailing mother holding the dead or dying child. The mother's head wrenched back as she cried to the heavens with her child hanging limp in her arms.

She turned to me and said, "It's like Lewis Hine said about the children he photographed. He wanted to show things that had to be corrected."

Picasso had done it here, and so had Hine. The images he took of working children came to shape America's child labor laws. I sent up a prayer that when people saw this painting, they would appreciate war for what it was—death, not a path to peace.

Millie took a few more steps back, after taking multiple shots of each woman. Standing with her legs pressed against the guard rail surrounding the fountain, she tipped back, took a shot of the entire mural, and turned to me. I smiled. Millie wanted to make photographs as impactful as Hine's work and as powerful as Picasso's. At that moment I was sure she would succeed, eventually. Things needed to change for women. Millie knew it, as did her suffragette mother. She just needed to find a way to do it without disappointing her father. I was tempted to whisper in her ear, "It doesn't matter what he thinks." I didn't. I knew it wasn't as simple as that.

Once she captured an image of the entire painting, Millie pulled me over to her father, who had left us to read the placard near the mural. As she slipped her hand into William's, creating a chain of the people she needed most, I felt the tension ease away from her. She looked up in search of her father's eyes but found them staring straight at me. I tried to shake him off, Millie shouldn't see this, but he was unrelenting.

Determined, he whispered, "So this is what the Nazis have in store for us?"

I let out the breath I had been holding and clasped the locket hanging around my neck, nodding in agreement and adding, "Then we'd better get to work."

I am not sure if I said the words out loud or not. Either way, in the years that followed, I often wondered if Millie heard or saw what passed between William and me. It would be some time before I could muster the courage to ask.

# CHAPTER ONE

Train to London

May 17, 1943

385 days until D-Day

Millie clutched her camera strap like a strand of pearls, to stop her hands from trembling; since she joined the Women's Auxiliary Air Force they often betrayed her like this. *And the work keeps coming,* she thought, staring out the train window, amazed to find herself on the Flying Scotsman speeding further away from her dreams on her way to yet another new assignment, this time at Britain's Central Intelligence Unit's headquarters. Her body hummed. She would have told the Royal Air Force pilot seated next to her it was down to the train, but the truth was new beginnings made her anxious. Especially new beginnings she didn't really want.

She had left the Royal Air Force base at Wick shortly after lunch, leaving behind a life she had accepted. She didn't mind her job as a phase one photographic interpreter at Coastal Command or her work as a part-time photographer for the Ministry of Information.

Pulling away from the station on her way to Marlow by way of Edinburgh and London, Millie realized she would miss Wick, its people, and the work she found there. At Coastal Command, she scoured hours-old images for immediate threats. For the MOI, she took photos they used for propaganda. Neither had been her first choice. She wanted to capture women's vitality with her camera before their contributions in the war effort were lost to history. But Britain was in the fight of her life, and everyone had to do their part. Enlisting had been the best way to help. She had uttered the phrase often enough. She wondered when she might believe it.

She sneaked a peek through her camera lens and took a shot of a woman in a Red Cross uniform walking down the train corridor, carrying a baby while giving it a bottle. She looked down at her once-trembling hands. Steady. She slumped back in her seat and felt her shoulders melt away from her ears and smiled, relishing the fleeting rush of satisfaction that came with an image constructed just so. The shot had everything she loved: a woman as the main subject, a sign that she was capable, and a bit of softness. *I wish I could take pictures like this all the time, not analyze them or make propaganda.* She shook off the thought with the promise, *Perhaps, one day when this is behind us. Women are always doing interesting and important things that are overlooked.*

Tucked in a compartment next to her friend Callum, a Royal Air Force photographic reconnaissance pilot, Millie craned her neck and watched the landscape fly by as the train raced toward London. After three-and-a-half years of war, the countryside looked like an old man weary from a lifetime in the mines: covered in soot, stooped with fatigue, but determined to carry on. A frightened young girl traveling alone shared the opposite bench with a young soldier on his way to help Montgomery and the Eighth Army in North Africa. The girl wore the tell-tale tag of an evacuee. *Is she going home or finding a new one?*

Millie strained at the collar of her crisp new Women's Auxiliary Air Force uniform when she noticed how its freshly dyed blue wool stood out among the tired greys and browns worn by the other passengers. It was a gift, or better put, a bribe, from her father. She didn't have any proof, but she guessed that he had a hand in her reassignment to the heart of Britain's photographic reconnaissance efforts. Her transfer had been abrupt, and the uniform arrived on its heels, adding weight to her suspicions.

Looking through the lens of her camera, Millie constructed a balanced image. It reassured her that there was at least one place where she was in control. The contrasting fabrics were lovely. They created a texture so rich Millie wanted to reach out and touch them. But that wasn't the picture Millie craved. Her right pointer finger itched to take a shot of the diminutive girl dangling her feet across from her. She hesitated. Taking a picture of a moment like this was a bit like stealing and in the small train compartment she would surely get caught. *But a photo of this reserved, frightened traveler would make the perfect companion to the one of the girl at Charing Cross Road.*

She had taken it at the bookstore the day before she gave in to her father's wishes by agreeing to become a photographic interpreter almost three years ago. Another interesting bit of symmetry. *To hell with it.* She lifted the camera and fired off a reckless shot. When the mirror slapped back into place, the girl looked up in alarm. Millie simply flexed her eyebrows and the corners of her mouth flexed up. What was done, was done.

"You're going to want this," Callum whispered into her ear, poking her side with the leather portfolio he had given her for Christmas, rescuing her from the girl's accusing eyes. Millie advanced the film before Callum said, "I added the image of the little girl in front of the blown-out bookstore. She reminds me of you."

Millie's head snapped in his direction. She looked up into his blue eyes, amazed. *Is he reading my mind now?*

"Where did you get this?" Millie snatched the portfolio. "And the photo, for that matter?" *And why did you accept a transfer to RAF Benson just when I was heading south? Did you want to be near me? Elliot isn't going to be too pleased to see you.* She had purposefully left the portfolio in her room at Teaghlach, her Grandmother Fiona's house, where she billeted while stationed at RAF Wick. If Elliot saw it, he would ask where she got it, and she didn't want to lie to him. Leaving it behind, along with Callum, or so she thought, was an attempt to keep the peace with her fiancé.

"Aggie found them when she was tidying up your room. She thought you might want them," he said, lifting a judgmental eyebrow in a gesture so small that only she would notice.

Lifting both of hers and opening her eyes wide to put him back in the box he belonged in, she replied simply and properly, "Thank you."

Sliding the photograph out of its container, Millie traced its every detail: the bundled-up girl, the missing storefront, the gold leaf decoration on the book the girl read, and the still-stocked bookshelf behind her. She had canceled her dinner plans with her childhood governess Nanna Clara to go and see the destruction herself, to record it. She was hoping to capture signs of resilience. She had succeeded. Millie fought against the satisfied smile threatening to pull across her face. She didn't want Callum to think he had been right to bring her treasures along.

When she emerged from the tube station at Covent Garden that day three years ago, her sinuses burned from all the smoke and dust, but her every nerve fired in excitement. She took a deep breath and pushed it out hard in a feeble attempt to stop her heart beating like timpani. Standing in the middle of the detritus of the nightly bombing raids disturbed and thrilled Millie. It was like staring over the cliff's edge before she jumped into the clear waters below when she was a child. She relished the anticipation even then. A cat on the prowl, she continued onward, certain of her prey. Men weren't the only ones answering Churchill's call to do one's duty, but they were the only ones on the pages of the papers. She would make the world see the ways women did their part.

She kept breathing deeply, trying to quiet the sound of her heart beating in her ears as she pressed onward, kicking rubble aside. The street signs were gone. The gas lights were unlit. All identifying marks had been wiped away to hide targets from both bombardiers and spies, but this was Millie's home; she had her memories to guide her. Her eyes darted across the landscape—searching for a public bomb shelter sign, heeding her father's advice to always know where to go when the bombs start dropping—and kept moving.

Ragged concrete boulders lined the streets, but she pointed her lens at the people, marching onward, without a smile or a tip of the hat for their neighbors. She couldn't find a single eye to focus on. *If you take pictures of people, focus on the eyes.* A rule her boss at the Ministry of Information drummed into her head. She focused instead on a group of women, baskets in hand, standing in a queue at the butcher. Grey, limp clothes hung from their bodies, washed one too many times, and their faces carried the deep lines of exhaustion. One of the women glanced her way, and Millie depressed the shutter. She waited half a second. The rush didn't come—it never did for low-hanging fruit.

As she searched, Millie enclosed her 35mm camera into its worn leather case dangling from her camera strap to protect the glass lens from the dangers that come from digging deeper.

She turned the corner to find an entire block annihilated. According to the radio reports that morning at breakfast, German bombs hit Charing Cross Road last night, littering London's streets with the words of Austen, Bronte, and Shelley as they leveled more than twenty bookstores. When Millie heard the news, she pulled the sleeves of her wool jumper down, hiding the goosebumps rising on her arms from Nanna Clara. She had precious few memories of her mother, but she had photographs. The one of the two of them standing outside of Foyles bookstore invaded her thoughts, spurring her toward her current quest.

Today, the neighborhood looked like a giant had kicked over a child's wooden block castle. She tucked her camera into her coat and shuffled through a narrow lane left in the ever-growing tower of debris. Inside the newly built fortress, Millie heard someone shout, "Be careful, miss, we haven't gotten all the bodies yet."

*Bodies?* She stopped short and shook her head yes and then no, releasing the threatening tension in her neck. Less than ten feet in front of her, she found an elderly gentleman. You might have thought he was asleep if not for the bricks mounded on his chest and the pillow of blood under his head. *Had he been shopping, or did he live in one of the residences above the stores?* Next to him was a younger woman, leg twisted backward, with blood smeared across her cheeks, underlining her open eyes. *A single daughter, perhaps, fulfilling her duties as his caregiver, quietly and without hesitation?* Warm fluid filled the back of Millie's throat. She had never been this close to death before, but she swallowed hard and snapped two photographs, capturing what was vital before it was gone. But still the feeling of completeness didn't come. Then, without a thought, she squatted low to brush the girl's eyelids shut, offered up a silent prayer for the nameless girl's sacrifice, and walked away as she might in a cemetery.

Just as she made it behind a partially destroyed wall, Millie vomited. Peter, her brother, preached that she would eventually grow accustomed to the sight of all of the destruction, but Millie did not want that. She wanted to feel and see everything so she could capture it with her camera before it was lost forever. Besides, Clara regaled her with tales of her mother, Margaret, and the battles she fought as a suffragette throughout Millie's childhood. Every story dripped with the deep feelings that drove the women. They made the women strong, not weak, as men mistakenly assumed.

The smell of iron and the sour contents of her stomach rising into her nostrils made Millie gag, so she crawled to the top of a mound of bricks and ragged concrete, desperate for a bit of fresh air and the story she was looking for. From her perch, she studied the Home Guard as they dug into the remains of the antiquarian bookshops, searching for people, dead and alive. The odor of her own nervousness dampening her underarms mingled with death. *There is nothing new to tell here.*

She went looking for more, better, perhaps just something different. Five steps in front of her lay another pair of bodies, once mother and daughter, now casualties of war. She waited a moment and let the sorrow seep in deep. When it threatened to cast a shadow on her search, she wrapped it up tight in her heart and used it as fuel to continue on—for the women's sake. Standing next to them, she looked through her viewfinder but didn't depress the shutter. Death was only part of this story. She wound through mounds of broken red bricks, shattered glass, splintered wooden beams, and confetti stripped from books, confident in her search.

When her feet found solid ground, she got to work capturing details. If she kept shooting, the feeling would come. A blood-stained wool cap. Whose head had it kept warm? A leather briefcase ripped at the seams. Did it spend its days in the British courts? A crushed golden locket. Reaching for hers, she wondered whose faces did the charm hold? With every shot and step, the anticipation bubbled up. A deflated red ball. A frayed wicker shopping basket. She crept closer, going deeper into the destruction, until something moving to her right caught her eye. Her skin tingled when the wind blew gently on her neck, in her ear. It was what she had been looking for.

A girl with a brown leather-bound book propped on her knees sat reading as if this were an ordinary day—never mind that she was seated in front of what remained of Mr. Nelson's bookstore. She wore a double-breasted plaid wool coat, a stocking cap with red stripes, and knee-high wool socks that puddled at her ankles. Two braids full of dust licked her shoulders. She couldn't have been more than nine or ten. The scene in front of her had it all: luring lines, the pages of open books cast in every direction for the eye to rest on, a dark corridor to tempt the viewer in deeper, and a girl ignoring it all. Her heart began to race again. She pushed the emotion down, holding it tightly, willing it to stay. She hadn't got the shot yet; the magical feeling was hers until then.

F-stop and shutter speed set, Millie blocked out the chatter coming from the Home Guard. She pushed away all of the chaos and slowed her breathing. She desperately needed it to be just the girl, her camera, and her now. She looked through the lens and just made out the title of the book, *Treasure Island,* scrawled across the cover in gold letters. She felt the fluttering of hummingbird wings in her chest. *A fellow adventurer.* Realizing this made the capture all the more intoxicating. Continuing forward, she forced herself to move slowly, making as little noise as possible. Something about seeing and not being seen, like a spy, added to the thrill: she took her shot. *Damn! I have to get closer.*

Sneaking forward, Millie closed the gap between herself and the girl. When she was about four feet away from the girl, she leaned back onto a mound and planted her feet to steady herself. Focusing the camera's lens on the girl's finger drawing an imaginary line under each sentence as she explored Stevenson's world, she took another shot and another. She was grasping at straws, but she didn't dare go any closer. She would surely be caught. The girl's lips moved as she read aloud. Millie smiled when she realized the girl was doing the voices.

Millie took one more shot, one that captured the entire scene. A bookshop robbed of its front window, front door, and front wall for that matter, a girl sitting on a curled-up bit of rubber tread with a shelf of books spilled at her feet, behind her a reading desk with a lamp holding a fallen rafter, to her left the side wall, covered in shelved books, still largely intact.

Next, Millie returned her attention to the girl and her chalky face. As Millie depressed the shutter button, the girl turned ever so slightly. *Bugger!* She missed her eye. She pushed on, aiming again, but the angle was still wrong. Determined, she risked standing and began pointing her lens this way and that. Looking. Shooting. Hoping. Finally, Millie checked the film counter. She noted that she only had two shots left on this roll of film. It was now or never.

Lying on her belly, she felt her heart pushing blood through her body. She took a deep breath and let it out slowly as she prepared to open the shutter. As she did, a wash of dusk's light dipped below the barrage balloons. It flooded into the broken place, magically revealing a swirling fog of fairy dust around the girl. She heard her camera's mirror lift and slap back into place. Without thinking about it, she had taken the shot. Her head shot up to see if her subject was on to her. *Still reading.* She took one more picture, this time on purpose, then her entire body relaxed, and she rolled over onto her back. It was the perfect shot. She wished she could bottle the feeling—satisfaction seemed too small a word to describe it! It was everything, all she craved. When she felt the tingle ooze out of the tips of her fingers and toes, she curled them tightly. Just one more moment. When she felt the last of it wiggle free, she stood up, dusted off her pants, and reloaded her camera—the hunt on again.

The train pulled into King Cross Station; a self-satisfied Millie tucked the image away into the portfolio for safekeeping. She had left it behind because she didn't need it with her to remember. She had memorized it. Better yet, she was likely to see it the moment she got off the train. The Ministry of Information had used the image in advertisements and posters with the headline "Books over Bombs." It hadn't stopped the Germans' barrage, but showing the world the girl's spirit was something, a start.

As Millie settled into the last train compartment of her journey to her new cage, otherwise known as RAF Medmenham, the magnificent manor house requisitioned by the British government in support of their aerial spying operation, she wondered if she would have been happier if she had stayed on at the MOI all those years ago. But after what she found the morning after taking that shot of the girl at the bookstore, there really had never been a question of what they would expect her to do next.

# CHAPTER TWO

Train to Marlow

May 17, 1943

385 days until D-Day

Millie and her fellow travelers stepped off the Flying Scotsman at Kings Cross Station, pouring onto the platform. A step behind, Millie noted with surprise that Callum had their youngest travel companion by the hand, helping her find her family. It was hard to say whether it was his American mother's influence or just his kind heart. Either way, it was a gesture rarely seen in her world.

She smiled, her heart filling, as he leaned over just a bit to keep from pulling the girl's arm out of its socket. His dark hair confessed traces of red as the light fell on it. With every break in the crowd, Callum would point in hopes that the cloistered couples would claim his self-appointed charge. They reached the doors of the station and Millie tapped Callum on the shoulder to tell him she would fetch a cab to take them to Paddington Station and the train to her final destination, Marlow. He threw her a look of apology and lifted his hand just a nudge to show her the girl's white knuckles. Just before Millie stepped through the doors, she looked back to see the child's eyes brighten when they found her parents. The once dreary girl lit up, dropped Callum's hand, and ran top speed into her mother's waiting arms. Millie lifted her camera, but it was too late. Dropping the camera, she scolded herself for not taking one of the two of them searching. It would have captured Callum's spirit perfectly.

A uniformed man shouted, "Nice camera!"

The comment took Millie back again. Back to the girl at the bookstore at Charing Cross Road.

"Is that a camera you're pointing at me?" the girl asked.

"It is." Millie walked to her side. "May I sit?"

The girl nodded, and Millie joined her on the makeshift bench, letting the girl touch her prized possession, though she didn't take the strap off her neck. The girl's hands were dirty and small. Millie's ears were flooded with her Grandmother Gertrude's constant complaints about the state of her nails when she was a child as she watched the girl's little fingers navigating the dials and buttons. Gertrude demanded Millie wear gloves everywhere she went. Before, the girl seemed, she searched for the word—magical—now she felt like a sister.

"Don't you think you should be getting home? It will be dark soon." She reached for her handkerchief to clean up the girl's face but stopped herself, remembering how much she hated being looked after when she was younger.

"Let me take a picture," the girl said, her boldness still on display. A flicker of the thrill Millie felt the first time she opened a shutter persuaded her to hand over her camera, but when she started to lift the strap over her head, the air raid sirens began to scream.

She grabbed the girl up by the wrist, determined to retrace her steps to the closest shelter.

The girl tugged against her. "I have to meet my mum at the Tottenham Court Station." She ran in the opposite direction. Millie followed. When they reached Shaftesbury Avenue, the girl froze.

"Why are we stopping?" Millie asked.

"Listen!" She pointed a finger to the sky.

Then Millie heard it—the buzz of the Luftwaffe bomber squads in the distance.

"Let's go." The girl took Millie by the hand and ran, dodging the crowd like a pro.

People ran and pushed, trying to get to the tube station for protection. Millie and the girl got caught in the flow of the crowd. Millie reached a hand into her trouser pocket to make sure her exposed film was still there. Hands pushed her as screams filled the air. Londoners, desperate to gain access to the tube entrance, crammed together in fear, the bombers so new to them then. For just a moment, they were waylaid by the wall of people. Unable to resist the sights, Millie dropped the girl's hand and lifted her camera into the air, trying to record the panic.

When the tiniest crack appeared in the human barricade, the girl grabbed Millie's arm, pulling her in and out of gaps in the horde like a needle and thread moving through fabric. They passed through an archway and plunged straight down an endless flight of stairs, crashing into one another until they reached the tunnel.

The girl jumped up on the first vacant wooden bench she saw and peered into the crowd that was settling in for the night. Some of the occupants pulled gas masks over their mouths. Reaching for hers, Millie found only her camera hanging around her neck. Her gas mask was hanging safely on the back of her desk chair at home.

Home. A twinge of guilt pinched her heart at the thought. Her father and Elliot were sure to worry if she didn't return tonight. And Nanna Clara. She checked for the film again. Still there. Relief rushed over her. Sure, the evening had gotten away from her, but the photograph, this photograph, was everything.

"There." The girl pointed down the tube where the crowd thinned. "Mum!" And before Millie could thank her, the girl ran. Clever, she thought as she realized the girl's mother was the only one down there wearing a red hat. She set a slow shutter, braced herself against the wall, and waited. The moment the girl jumped into her mother's arms, she shot, letting her breath out slowly to keep herself from shaking. If the risk worked, it just might be the best picture in the bunch.

The rank smell of nervous bodies and foul breath filled the air, something her film could never record. But there were faces everywhere. Some worn with worry, others knit with confusion, still others resigned to the new normal. They were so deep underground that when a bomb fell, the subway walls barely vibrated, and the artificial light was so dim there was little chance of capturing any of it. Without the clamor of the explosions and windows to watch the above-ground assault, the dull thud coming from overhead was the only reminder of why they had rushed to roost deep inside the earth.

People pulled all kinds of things from their bags to occupy themselves. Millie kept taking photographs. A mother giving toys to her children. A woman knitting. A businessman reading the newspaper. Then she heard a flutter, turned, and refocused. A pair of elderly men playing cards. A mother holding tight to an infant. The light was terrible, but if even one of these photos wasn't blurry, it would be fantastic.

Through her camera, she saw an RAF pilot with hair as yellow as Elliot's and a handkerchief over his nose. She shook her head thinking that it was exactly what Elliot would be doing if he were stuck in this rank place. Truth was he wouldn't recognize how offensive the behavior was to the folks sitting around him. Furthermore, he would be none too pleased that she had spent the night in a public shelter with such common people. *It's too bad we have plans for breakfast in the morning.* There was no way to keep her evening activities from him. She lowered the camera and reminded herself that he was generous in his own way. He gave his money freely to noteworthy causes and had always been so kind to her family and friends—except for Callum.

With the last frame, she photographed the man sitting on her left who read aloud with a torch. "All things will die.

Clearly, the blue river chimes in its flowing..."

Millie joined him in the recitation, and her heart slowed to match its rhythm. When he finished the final stanza, she said, "That was lovely. My father's a Tennyson man, too."

"And where is your father on this fine evening?"

"In the bowels of Whitehall, I expect."

"A military advisor or one of Churchill's men, perhaps?" He lifted an eyebrow, a glint of mischief in his eyes.

"He's pretty tight-lipped about it all."

"A wise man, indeed." He adjusted his reading glasses and lifted his book again. "And you? How are you doing your part?"

"I work for the Ministry of Information." Millie rested against the cold tile wall, showing him her camera.

He glared over his glasses, staring, but said nothing. His scowl made Millie think of her argument with her father and Peter the evening before. William had said that her images might help women get the recognition they deserved, but the real fight, now, was for *everyone's* freedom. That the work she was doing for the Ministry of Information might be interesting but would never directly help stop the Germans and was frankly beneath her abilities. She needed to put her natural talents to work. After all, she had studied mathematics at Oxford, he argued. Claimed she was the smartest of the four children. Pointed out that even Nanna Clara was doing real work, helping those hurt in the bombing raids night after night with the Red Cross. He landed his final punch when he asked, "Why educate women if they won't answer when they are called?" Peter piled on by telling her she should be ashamed. He had done as expected and joined the Royal Air Force. She wasn't doing anything to stop the Germans. Instead, she spent her days helping the government spin tales to feed the unknowing public. As Peter ranted, her father just sat looking straight through her like this man beside her now. Her father ended things with a simple statement. "Brains, not brawn, will win this war, and you know it."

When the all-clear siren rang, they marched out of their hole like a colony of ants. The crowd brushed against her as they poured into the dawn. Her fingers wrapped around the exposed film deep in her pockets, searching for heat. Holding the spools tightly, she first thought of the dead young woman's face recorded on the film within. She had paid the ultimate price. Died in service of her father as they staked their claim here in London. Thumbing their noses at the Germans instead of running away to safer ground. Then she saw the girl. Defiant. Strong. Audacious. This girl who boldly reached for Millie's camera wasn't going to sit quietly by while the Germans tried to strip her of what few freedoms she had, no matter what else she thought was important.

*And what about you, Millicent Trayford?* she thought. *Is there more you can do? Is this war and the duty it demands bigger than your cause?* It was a question Millie couldn't answer on her own. She needed to talk it through with the one person she had always trusted. A block away from Nanna Clara's flat, Millie picked up the pace, her feet carrying her ever faster. Clara would tell Millie which path to follow—her photography or a deeper commitment to the war effort. She would know what was best. She always did.

Millie rounded the corner running and stopped dead in her tracks.

In front of her stood the crumbled remains of Nanna Clara's building. She looked to the third floor, searching for Clara's window, and saw instead the inside of Clara's apartment's front door. There was nothing left but the side entrance table with the bunch of camellia flowers Millie had picked for her. Millie started wailing as she tore through the rubble with her bare hands. A member of the Home Guard tried to pull her away, but she couldn't be stopped.

"We need to wait for more help. We don't want to do more harm than good," the gentleman pleaded when he returned with more help. Millie looked up at the three gentlemen, one with a finger pressed to his lips, trying to get her to stop yelling. Her face was covered with sweat, tears, and dirt. Millie wrenched herself from the man's grip and ran. She kept running until she found her way to her family's home in Belgravia. Palms pressed to the front door, she melted to the ground in a flood of tears, as her body gave into the pain that gripped her.

"Father, Father, where are you. I need your help. Something terrible has happened to Nanna Clara, and I won't let it happen to anyone else." The words were barely audible.

Peter and Elliot found her and peeled her off the ground. When she told them her tale, Peter turned white as a sheet and Elliot sat expressionless, insisting she pull herself together. When her father finally arrived, there had been a strange sort of dance between them; but in the end, he did help her in her new crusade, fueled by either guilt or revenge—not even Millie could have said which for sure. He and her beloved brother Peter urged her to take a job analyzing photographs instead of taking them. Despite Elliot's objections, she did as they suggested. Helping with reconnaissance meant actually stopping the Germans from dropping bombs. Within months, she was on a train to RAF Wick to help with phase one photographic interpretation. *Has it really been over two years?*

The work at RAF Wick had been immediate and gratifying. The reconnaissance planes would land, and the meters of film they exposed would be processed within the hour. She was stunned when she saw the machines that developed the eight-by-ten-inch photos. It was completely automated, and the tools made her darkroom seem like it was built for fairies.

If the pilot was suspicious, which was often the case, she found herself scrutinizing damp photos to ascertain if there was an immediate threat: a new airfield, a submarine up for a look at the Scottish shore, a German battleship in the North Sea, to name a few. Often what stood out to Millie were the villages and the seaside cottages. Once, in the middle of her stack, she found signs of a festival, striped tents and all. She could almost hear the music coming from the dance floor. Water made the tops of the glossy images slimy and difficult to work with. But every time she slid a pair of images under her stereoscope, pushing them together just so until what she was examining switched from two dimensions to three, her blood began to race. At first glance, there was no way to tell if the images contained threats or not. Once a pilot was so sure that there was a battleship on the coast of France headed their way that he persuaded the commander to ready the bombers. Thank goodness he waited before sending them. The "ship" was nothing but tires lashed together. Sending bombers after the decoy was surely a trap.

Analyzing the images wasn't as exciting as being in the middle of the action with her camera, but it would do for now—or at least that is what she kept telling herself.

Steeling herself with her mantra, Millie made her way through Paddington Station. Callum stepped aside, letting Millie board the train to RAF Medmenham first. With her mind still lingering in the past, she slipped on the top step. Callum reached up to stop her from falling. Her stomach dropped, and a thrill shot through her as he touched her. *Damn! Why does that keep happening? You needed to stay back in Wick, for my sake.* "Thanks." Her cheeks flushed as she gathered herself. Since she was already standing so close to danger, she stroked his pilot's wings, sending up a prayer that he would be standing somewhere nearby when this bloody war was over, even if he was standing next to someone else. Callum let his fingers brush against hers. She jerked her hand away. *What would Elliot think?*

"You bet." Callum pushed the offending hand into his trouser pockets.

Millie found them an empty compartment. When they settled in, Callum choosing the seat opposite her rather than next to her, he asked, "Are you looking forward to your new job?"

Millie shrugged her shoulders. "I don't know what I'm

in for. The PIs at RAF Wick said the phase three interpreters gather minutiae. It could be months, if not years, before we collect any actionable intelligence. It may be tiresome, but it will please Father."

"And that's enough for you?"

"It is for now." She winked at Callum, giving him a greedy smile. *I hope no one joins us.* She liked the idea of having Callum to herself, if only for a little while. She couldn't believe he brought her photographs. She should be angry that he reminded her of what she couldn't have, but she wasn't. It touched her that he knew her so well. Nevertheless, it would have been easier to stay focused if he hadn't been so damn considerate. She would just have to make sure she didn't touch him again, else she might betray Elliot with more than just her thoughts.

"Do you have a deck of cards in that bag of tricks?" she said to cut the tension.

"I do."

"Good, because I just got paid." She rattled the coins in her left pocket.

# CHAPTER THREE

RAF Medmenham-Central Intelligence Unit

May 18, 1943

384 days until D-Day

The Central Intelligence Unit's headquarters were not what Millie expected. Instead of the Jacobean buildings that lined Whitehall Street and housed the heart of the British government, she stood in front of a grand manor that frankly looked a bit like a white wedding cake. The picturesque view inspired questions like, "Whose home was it?" and "What forces came to bear to persuade the owner to allow this invasion?" The answer was plain. It was this or surrendering it to the Germans.

"I said, are you ready?" Callum asked, the two of them standing shoulder to shoulder in front of the ornate wooden doors of RAF Medmenham. He and her brother Peter had insisted on escorting her after they got her settled at her billet.

"Just give me one more minute," Millie said.

"No more minutes, my dear sister," Peter said, draping his arm around her neck. "We are on a quest." He took a step forward, forcing Millie to do the same.

"What do you know about it?" She shrugged his arm away. Since this interminable war began, Peter's forced enthusiasm only served to irritate.

At the door, Millie lingered. She ran her fingers around and into the nooks and crannies carved into the double wooden doors. She yearned to reach for a shutter button to photograph the curves of the design and the grain of the wood, instead of the latch to open the door, but she had tucked her camera safely under her bed back at her billet. So, she took a deep breath and pushed her way into yet another new beginning.

Inside, she found a bustling foyer filled with men and women in equal measure. When her commanding officer at RAF Wick had given her new orders, she had called her father for an explanation. She knew Ramsey valued the work she did, and she couldn't think of a reason for a transfer other than her father's interference. When they spoke, he ably dodged her questions and proceeded to tell her all about RAF Medmenham, the value of the work they did, and the characters who worked there. She would meet a crew of scientists, artists, mathematicians, and engineers. He claimed they all possessed astounding intelligence and curiosity and that their curious eyes and interest in details bonded them together. Now Millie would be bonded to them, he proclaimed. He assured her it would be better than working at an airfield. Millie doubted it.

"I am Assistant Section Officer Millicent Trayford," she told the duty officer. "They weren't expecting me until this evening, but I caught an earlier train."

"And who are these two blokes?"

"My escorts," she said, thinking *captor*s, but she didn't know the man and wasn't sure how he might take the joke. "They are both pilots. This one," she pointed to Callum, "braved the train ride from RAF Wick with me yesterday, and this one," she pointed at Peter, "is my brother. He is stationed at RAF Benson. I guess they both are, come to think of it." She glanced over at Callum. He looked as tired as she felt. She wondered if the knowledge that they were sleeping alone in her father's London house in adjacent bedrooms had kept him up all night too.

"Just came over to make sure she came inside. We both fly photo-reconnaissance," Peter said.

Peter always found a way to put people at ease, and he

knew his job would ingratiate him with this crowd. With any crowd in those days, come to think of it. He cared little for his rank or station. He wanted to experience life, all sorts of life, and he had a knack for pleasing the folks who could help him.

"Spitfires?" The duty officer's eyes lit up.

"Indeed," Callum said with a smirk and nod.

"Could we please find out where I'm meant to go?" Millie pushed in front of the boys, secure in the knowledge that the pictures they risked their lives to take would be useless without people like her.

With a slump of his shoulders, the duty officer flipped through papers on three different clipboards. He detached two forms, filled in her name, and asked her to sign one. Millie then said goodbye to Callum and Peter with the promise of dinner before they reported back to work.

The interior of the house didn't reflect the outside. Temporary boards covered what could only be the manor's delicate wall coverings or wood paneling. The walls looked like a hastily built temporary building, but the exquisite plaster medallions overhead whispered the house's secrets.

Before climbing the stairs, she sneaked a peek at the disguised Grand Hall.

The room was narrow, with a bulky fireplace at one end. A photographic mosaic papered the fireplace's stone mantel, making it impossible to light a fire. Fifteen clusters of desks filled up the room, each surrounded by PIs, all with their heads down working. The images sprawled out on every surface combined into a single picture of battlefield Europe.

"Can I help you find something?" a fellow member of the Women's Auxiliary Air Force asked.

"No, thank you. I was just getting my bearings," Millie said. "I'm on my way upstairs to find Wing Commander," she paused to check her orders, "Thomas."

"All right then." Her eyes widened, brightening. "I'm going upstairs myself. I'm Hazel Witherspoon, assigned to Section L;

that's airplane factories and airfields."

"Millicent Trayford, and I'm not sure of my section."

"Technically, B, but I'll let Ham fill you in on the details. They are meeting with some higher-ups right now. Do you know your billet?"

Millie reached into her pocket and pulled out her orders to remind herself of the billet's name. The pocket stereoscope her father had given her when she left for RAF Wick three years ago came with it.

"That's lovely. Where did you get it?" Millie had never seen a girl so excited about a hunk of metal and glass before.

"My father gave it to me when I passed my photographic interpreter exam."

"You told your father what you do?" Hazel was aghast.

"He's RAF and has clearance." Millie stopped herself from saying more, not knowing exactly how much to reveal. *Do the people here know about MI6? Probably not.* The fact was she knew very little about it herself. "He recommended me for the job." She resisted saying he insisted she take the job.

The smile slowly returned to Hazel's face as her words sank in. "That's a nice bit of luck. I have to tell mine I'm a secretarial clerk. My parents don't even know I'm a WAAF officer."

The spy camera in her tunic pocket, another gift from her father, taunted her. She could take a shot of this effervescent girl in her officer's uniform and make sure that one day people knew precisely what she did to stop the Germans. But she left it, for now. *You only analyze photographs now, you fool—you don't take them!*

"Well, here we are; your new home." Hazel pointed Millie toward a repurposed bedroom. She walked on but turned abruptly. "You never said where you're billeting."

"Boyton House."

"Me, too. I'll check in before I head that way. Perhaps you will be ready to go, too."

Hazel really did have a contagious smile. It made Millie

think of Aggie, that and the warm greeting. She missed her already. Maybe there would be time to call her at Teaghlach later. Looking at her watch, Millie calculated what time Aggie was due to finish her shift at RAF Wick. *Just before dark. Perfect.*

Millie met Aggie the summer before she went to boarding school at Roedean. In the time before. Before she could even contemplate the existence of the Nazis and their diabolical weapons. Before a life surrendered to their greedy destruction. Before a dream killed on the altar of freedom.

Her father shipped her off to Teaghlach, her mother's childhood home in Wick, Scotland, after she broke her arm in a bit of mischief mere months before she was due to begin boarding school. Aggie had just started working for Millie's grandmother, Fiona. Fiona's cook, Mrs. Drummond, had broken her foot, so Aggie's mother was filling in, and Aggie was helping with light cleaning. Millie had been under Nanna Clara's supervision when she had her accident, and her other grandmother, Gertrude Trayford, wanted Clara sacked. Millie's stay at Teaghlach was part of her father's scheming.

William wanted Clara with Millie. He didn't know what to do with an eleven-year-old daughter. His interest in parenting died with his wife. He loved his daughter, but she was a painful reminder of his beloved Margaret: indelible spirit, insatiable curiosity, irresistible charm. They both sparkled in a world so full of darkness. A darkness that took root inside him the day Margaret died. Besides, he observed, lied, and contrived for a living. He was, however, honest enough to know that his crusty outer shell was bad for her. The tender heart belonged to Millie's mother. William understood all too well that Millie needed Clara, despite his mother's feelings. Margaret had loved them both, so he didn't have the heart to separate them. They had both had enough loss for a lifetime.

Because her new boarding school, Roedean, wouldn't begin until fall, he packed Millie and Clara up and sent them north—efficiently solving his problem, as far as he was concerned. Millie had a caregiver, and Clara would be out of his mother's sight. The solution didn't please Gertrude. She had very little use for her daughter-in-law's mother, either, but William forged ahead with his plan. Fiona may have been peculiar in his eyes, but she adored Clara, and so did Millie.

Millie arrived at the Wick train station with a new leather trunk. Gertrude had ordered it for school, and her father insisted she begin using it right away. She loved the drawers filling the right side, the beige silk lining, and the wooden hangers that fit perfectly over the metal strip attached on the left side, but she considered the golden monogram on the top to be the best bit. Ferguson, her grandmother Fiona's driver, made a footman deliver it to her room. After unpacking her clothes, her copy of *Peter Pan*, her camera, and a photograph of her mother, she slid the trunk out the bedroom door and toward the steps to get it to the basement somehow. She could have pulled the embroidered ribbon in her room and summoned the footman, but Gertrude told her she would have to learn to manage the trunk herself at school, so she decided she could handle it herself.

At the top of the steps, she studied the stairway. It was wide and turned in three places. As she thought through her options, Aggie came bounding up the stairs.

"Can I help, Lady Millicent?"

"If you don't mind, I like to be called Millie." She knew her grandmother Gertrude wouldn't approve, but hoped Fiona wouldn't mind. She could use a friend, and if this girl had to call her "Lady Millicent," that would never happen.

"Ma won't like it, but Pa always says what people don't know won't hurt them. What are you trying to do?"

"Get the trunk down to the basement. I could push or even ride it down. What do you think?"

"I say we ride, but we'd better hurry before anyone catches us."

The same trunk had made its way to Stellan Hall, her family home in Surrey, two days ago when she returned south yet again from Wick. Space would be precious in her new billet in Marlow. Her father insisted that rules would be more strictly enforced here at RAF Medmenham. So, she would have to manage with the basics packed in her Air Force issued kit.

Steeling herself, she crossed the last threshold of the journey.

"Hello, I am Assistant Section Officer Millicent Trayford." Millie handed her orders to a short man with glasses and a furrowed forehead. He sat in front of a large stereoscope. On each side were grey legs bent like a rainbow connected in the middle by a pair of prismatic lenses. It's a wondrous thing to watch photographs bloom into three dimensions; contours and details pop up, unlocking the image's secrets.

"A fine name, to be sure, but what should we call you? We don't have time for ceremony here," he said, going back to his work.

"You can call her Millie."

Millie looked directly into the familiar eyes of the man sitting on the stool in the back corner of the room. She started to say hello, but he interrupted her.

"And you can all call me Colonel Caldwell," said the man as he slithered to her side and offered her his hand in introduction.

Miller took his hand, perplexed. *Why had he told them to call her Millie? And why lie about his name?* She had planned on asking them to stick with Millicent. *Why does he always take away my choices?* Millie made her sound like a little girl. It was hard enough to be taken seriously as a woman. But it would be harder still if they thought she got here because she was his daughter, so she shook his hand, playing along.

"They call me Red," the man using the stereoscope said, looking between the two of them. The introductions were as strange as Millie imagined.

"It's good to see you again, Trayford." Her father slipped his hands into his pockets, fiddling with the rock, now worn smooth, Millie had given him when she was much younger. He hadn't expected to see her but smiled, thinking how well she adapted to the situation. *I was right to have her moved. If anyone can find the Nazis' vengeance weapons, it's her.*

"And you, sir," Millie replied, staying in character. "May I ask why you are here?"

"I'm not. I'm just leaving," he said as he moved back into his shadows.

Before he could turn to leave, Millie accused him with her stare. *You did this!* She hoped her father was the only man in the room who noticed her flexing jaw muscles. *Why do I need to be here?* She surveyed the room, which looked more like a cell. He tilted his head with a smirk and a barely perceptible shrug of the shoulders before slipping out of the room.

She dropped her bag rather than throwing it across the room. *Why did I come early?* She thought she would be glad to answer the question of how she ended up here. She was wrong.

# CHAPTER FOUR

---



On his way out, her father held the door for a man with deep-set eyes, a brown mustache, and lines around his mouth. He looked like most of the men she passed on her way to her new cage, except for the wrinkles. The deep ridges carved in his forehead suggested he had been in the game for a while, like her father. That and the three bars on his shoulders and sleeves.

"Millicent Trayford?" he asked.

"Yes, sir," Millie said.

"You can call her Millie," the gentleman called Red said without getting to his feet or looking up, for that matter. *What a relief. Perhaps things aren't as buttoned-up around here as Father thinks.*

"I'm Wing Commander Hugh Hamshaw Thomas, but most people around here call me Ham, and this is Neil," he pointed to the younger man in the room. "Welcome to the team. Now, let's get on with it." He motioned to an empty table in the middle of the room with chairs, gesturing that Millie should take a seat there.

Wg. Cmd. Ham Thomas started to pace and broke into a monologue using the voice of a radio announcer, deep and steady. "I've just been given this." Ham thrust a pair of photographs toward the men, who had by now abandoned their work and joined Millie at the table. They each gave the photos a look under portable stereoscopes before passing the photos around to Millie.

"What do you see?" Ham directed his question to Millie.

She took a moment to take in the 3-D image, scanning it top to bottom, left to right. Looking up, she replied, "Railroad tracks headed into the wood." She left out the obvious sights: trees, a creek, a garden wall made of stone, and a dirt road. Anyone would have noticed those.

"Nice." Ham nodded approvingly. "Trayford, our little group is in the business of searching for the unknown. The War Cabinet has asked us to find evidence that something we've never seen and can't make ourselves exists. A thing that, if real, will make the Blitz seem like a firework show to the people of London while the Germans don't risk a single man's life. We have sketchy intelligence that the enemy intends to flatten Britain with tons of explosives without the aid of airplanes." He paused.

"Our job is to figure out if and how they plan to do it."

He was a gifted storyteller, and his audience was rapt. "You all like a puzzle, have a reputation for not being able to put one down, as a matter of fact. That is why I've gathered you." He stopped just in front of Millie and lifted his right eyebrow, a move he would often deploy in their work together.

"Millie, I am going to apologize upfront for our gruff manner. For now, you will be the only lady in our midst, and there won't be much time for manners."

Millie worked to keep her eyes from rolling. "That won't be a problem, sir. I spent my childhood in my father's study and his beloved aerodromes. Besides, I grew up with three older brothers, and I was the ringleader."

Smiling, Ham slapped her on the back. It made Millie think he must have a daughter or a sister. In her experience, men were rarely so easily convinced. She would find out later that he had both. He had followed his older sister to Cambridge and was certain she was more intelligent than he. And his daughter, let's just say she wasn't the type to be outdone or left behind.

Ham continued, settling in. He shrugged off his jacket, exposing his braces. Pink paisley covered them. *Those aren't Air Force issue.* Millie's father warned her RAF Medmenham employed a peculiar cast of characters. She was beginning to believe him.

Relaxing into a seat, he continued his tale. "We have quite a task before us. First, we need to search for experimental work and production, particularly at Peenemunde, which is being photographed again as we speak. Our intel and Goebbels's speeches suggest the Germans are playing with all sorts of ideas: sonic cannons, x-ray guns, long-range rockets that carry warheads, and flying bombs, among other things. They refer to them as super-weapons or wonder-weapons." He circled Peenemunde's location on the map near the Baltic Sea. "Some say it could all be nonsense, but we have gathered intelligence since the beginning of the war that suggests otherwise. If it is true, Peenemunde is where the wretched things would be concocted and created."

Ham leaned forward on his elbows, and the youngest of the men did the same. Then, in a voice that was at once quieter and deeper, he said, "I believe they exist and that we must destroy them; our very survival depends on it."

He paused once more, giving his words a moment to take root. He let his last statement fill the room. Then he looked at each of them in turn, deeply and sincerely. When Ham broke eye contact with Millie, a chill went up her spine, and as he stared deeply into Neil's eyes, she could see goosebumps forming on Neil's forearms.

The silence and anxiety swelled, and then Ham slammed both of his fists down on the table. "Now we just have to prove it."

Millie snapped back into the moment with a start as Ham

pushed away from the table. Reflexively, she reached for his arm. She needed more information.

"If I may, sir." Millie removed the offending hand and said, "How old is the intelligence, and is any of it actionable?" Her question hung in the air for a moment before Ham answered. Millie could tell by the look on his face that he was weighing how much to tell her. There was always a risk that too much information might shape the findings of an interpreter. Ham was searching for the necessary facts. He couldn't afford to speculate. They were on a clock.

"The first bit of on-the-ground intelligence came in from a special agent in the form of a report in the fall of 1939."

Millie stopped herself from shaking her head, recalling her father's outburst after she accepted her first posting with the Ministry of Information and not his beloved Air Force in the fall of 1939. If the report came from an on-the-ground agent, she understood by now that her father had seen it. In November of 1939, she sought out her position with the MOI, using a connection from university. The British wouldn't use enlisted women as photographers, and it seemed the next best thing. Her father had suggested the Women's Auxiliary Air Force, but one of her tutors from Lady Margaret Hall College, Oxford University, suggested the MOI and recommended her for the job. The posting had disappointed her father, and in a move against type, he openly objected.

He felt she was beyond edicts, so he tried a bribe. In exchange for leaving the MOI and joining the Women's Auxiliary Air Force, he offered to get her out of her engagement with Elliot and fund her photography projects after the war. But she didn't want out of her engagement, and she had money left to her by her mother's estate. She considered his request briefly because it seemed so important to him, but Clara persuaded him to relent. The rocket search was his quest, not Millie's. Afterward, he tried to pretend it had all been a grand ruse, telling Millie he made the offer to persuade himself that Elliot was indeed Millie's choice.

Sitting in the upstairs room at RAF Medmenham, she understood it had been his opening gambit in the chess game they now found themselves in. *He wanted me to be a part of this search all along.*

"You have suspected the existence of weapons meant to be used against civilians since Britain declared war, and you are only now convening us for the hunt."

"The hunt," Ham pierced her a sideways glance, "as you call it, has been continuous. As a matter of fact, Red and Neil here have been looking for long-range weapons and flying bombs since the beginning of the year."

"What I am asking is, why expand the search now?" She knew there must be something more significant; some reason her father had her summoned.

Ham picked up the pair of images with the peculiar railroad tracks, thinking he had been right to allow her to come. Neil and Red hadn't asked that question. They just obediently kept up what felt to them to be a never-ending search. *She is special.*

"These photographs confirm some of our suspicions about the Germans' secret weapons program. They have the naysayers on the War Cabinet a bit antsy. The recon pilots took them over the Pas-de-Calais region of northern France, which just so happens to be a little too near our planned land invasion." He said the words quickly, getting used to the way the words might sound coming out of his mouth. He had only just been given permission to discuss the D-Day planning with his team.

"A land invasion of France, sir?" Red blurted.

"Yes, a land invasion. They've decided that we will try to gain a foothold on the continent by invading the beaches of northern France."

"When, sir?" Neil asked.

"They've only worked out the general location of the invasion at this point. I am afraid I cannot tell you more now, but if these massive concrete domes have the potential to launch bombs or rockets into the channel or deliver them to our shores, we must destroy them. If we don't, we'll be sunk before we've begun. And this war may be lost."

"So just to clarify, we are planning an operation—" Millie began.

"Operation Overlord," Ham filled in the blank.

Millie continued without missing a beat. "Plans for Operation Overlord are underway. A plan that, if it succeeds, could mean the beginning of the end of this war, and we need to find and destroy objects that we can't name and don't know for sure exist just in case they could impact an invasion into France."

"That's right." Ham slumped back into his chair, twisting a pencil between his fingers, hearing the absurdity of it all.

Millie concentrated on the words *are you sure about this* as hard as she could while staring into Wg. Cmd. Ham Thomas's eyes, hoping he could read her mind.

He nodded slightly, pleased she seemed engaged by the news. *Caldwell might be a slippery fellow,* and Ham was dubious about MI6, *but sending her was the right thing to do.*

"Then tell us where to start." Millie sat up straight. *The sooner we get down to it the sooner we can get back to...*She flipped the word normal around in her mind. Her world would never go back to normal. Too many had died. Too many were still yet to die, including herself perhaps, with bombs continuing to fall from the sky. But things were clearer now, and she would be a part of bringing the death to an end. This was an endeavor worth her sacrifice.

The invasion is why her father had sent for her. The end was nearer than she hoped if they could just stay ahead of the Germans, and he wanted her to know so she wouldn't lose heart. He wanted to give her hope. She picked up the images of the railroad tracks and memorized every detail. If she saw them again, she wouldn't miss them.

"The Print Library is sending everything we have from the

region. And there is this report." He passed around a fresh stack of pages, the word CONFIDENTIAL stamped in red in multiple places. "You will find our guesses to date, things concerning the size, shape—the usual. Intelligence suggests that the long-range bomb may have a range of 130 miles and that it has no navigation system, so we need to scour the French coast. The bombs will be useless without their launching system, which may simply be large ramps. But the weight of the things will be immense, so the railroad systems seem a must." He dug through the papers now scattered on the table and showed them another. "These are new-order weapons. Ones that, if made operational, will have unmatched long-range firing capabilities, killing hundreds, maybe thousands, mostly civilians. It's been four years. The Germans want to break our spirits and take our island for good.

"MI6 has ordered our friends with winged cameras to photograph every square inch of France between Cherbourg and Belgium."

Barely listening now, Millie's mind wandered to Peter, Callum, and Elliot, imagining them flying at 30,000 feet, a timer snapping image after image. No guns, just cameras, and no fighter planes to protect them.

"Millie, are you still with me?"

"Yes, sir. Sorry, sir." *Get your head in the game. All of our lives depend on it.*

"We need to build a case, and the best way to do that is to have new cover to compare with old cover. We have small grains of information, but nothing to date that could justify sending our bombers to the Baltic Sea to attack the research center in Peenemunde."

"If we know all of this," Red asked, "why not bomb now and ask questions later?"

"It's too far and too deep behind enemy lines. Plus, Peenemunde is well protected. We will lose countless men and planes when we bomb it. We need more information to justify the losses. And it must be said that there are some, mostly politicians, but some scientists as well, who don't believe these weapons exist. They think it is all an elaborate hoax. Lord Cherwell is among those who doubt their existence, and he continues to have the confidence of Churchill."

"There are a lot of inconceivable weapons on this list," Millie said, picking up one of the documents and thinking of Guernica. *If the Germans can imagine them, they can build them.* "What should we concentrate our efforts on first?"

"You are looking for the long-range rockets and pilotless aircraft or self-flying bombs, if you will. We need to know with as much confidence as possible if either of these do, in fact, exist. And we need to know how and when the explosives might make it to our shores. It's your job to make a case one way or the other."

Ham scanned the faces sitting around the table. He had gotten through to them. He knew this because they busied themselves with the precious information in front of them, handling it like it was fine crystal.

"For now, I want you looking for any odd construction in France," Ham pointed to a desk buried with photos. "The other sections will send along suspicious photos as well, though we have not briefed them as to why. This mission is considered 'for your eyes only' for now. You will receive new cover soon," he added before he disappeared.

New cover meant men risking their lives—men like Peter, Callum, and Elliot. Millie breathed a silent prayer for their safe return.

Red and Neil stood up and took a deep breath in unison. It was time to dig in. The hardwood floor creaked as Millie and the men made their way to three of the four desks occupying the corners of the room. Millie noticed the place was a mess. The ashtrays overflowed with cigar stumps and ashes. Every desk in the room had at least three empty coffee mugs on it. She had entered a boys' club, make no mistake. She hoped they weren't expecting a maid.

While they worked, Millie gleaned a few more details from Neil and Red. The most important was that, at this point, they couldn't prove that either of the weapons was real or which would be the biggest threat. The men were glad to have a bit more information and help. They had also heard that Lord Cherwell thought the flying bombs were more likely than the rockets because he doubted the Germans had the liquid fuel technology to pull off blasting into the stratosphere. The shot of the railroad tracks was new to them, but they suggested she also keep an eye out for anything that might squirt a rocket out, just in case the ramp theory proved to be a wild goose chase.

With that, Millie tucked a wild curl into her messy chignon, stuck her pencil into her hair, and got to work.

# CHAPTER FIVE

Senate House-British Intelligence Headquarters

May 25, 1943

377 days until D-Day

William Charles Trayford, Earl of Chidester, a.k.a. Wing Commander Trayford, a.k.a. Colonel Caldwell, for now, set down the latest intelligence from the MI6 offices in France, took off his glasses, and rubbed his eyes. When he reached to retrieve the glasses, he knocked over the one photograph on his desk. Personal items were discouraged in his world so full of secrets. The snapshot was of his daughter, Millie, and his youngest son, Peter. He took it the morning before he presented her to King George VI. She had insisted. At the time, it fascinated him that she entered the world through her camera, so he had obliged. He shook his head, thinking he might not have indulged her so if he had known photography would become such an obsession. But he was softer then. That was in the time after Margaret, but before the Nazis.

Peter had started her laughing by imagining, out loud, of course, all of the ways she might mess up and call the King Uncle Bertie. If he remembered correctly, at this exact moment, Peter was suggesting she offer him a muddy frog, as she so often had as a child at Stellan Hall, instead of the required deep curtsy.

The woman William saw two days ago at RAF Medmenham no longer had the same plump cheeks and giggling eyes.

She had exchanged them for protruding cheekbones and seriousness. The uniform he had tailor-made for her fit poorly. *I should have gotten updated measurements.* The circles under her eyes had darkened more since Christmas. But as she stood at attention before him, she looked the part of the dutiful daughter, because she was. William knew this work wasn't what she wanted. That its tedious nature and relative isolation took a toll.

But he believed deep in his core that manipulating her into joining his world had been the right thing to do. *Everyone has to do their part. It is the only way to stop them!* Staring into his vivacious daughter's young smiling face, he knew that his beloved Margaret would disagree. As quickly as the feeling bubbled up, he pushed it far away, storing it with all of the other thoughts and memories that made him question his current path. He knew Margaret would be disappointed with how his thorns had grown back. She had worked tirelessly to smooth them down. The shame made him admit, if only in that moment, that what he had done early that November morning was wrong.

Coming home that day, was it actually three years ago, and finding Millie composing herself in the front hall mirror had been a surprise, but he took advantage. For a brief moment, something made him hesitate, but because it had been so long since he let emotions influence his actions, he brushed the impulse away like a gnat. He had a job to do, and Millie could help. He would use her like the rest—*for her own good.* Her dream would keep.

From the front door, he saw her fussing with her unruly black curls, so like her mother's, in the foyer mirror. She appeared to be expecting someone, perhaps even Nanna Clara. If he closed his eyes, he could see Clara bouncing down the stairs wagging a disapproving finger Millie's way, armed with a clothes brush.

She would be saying something like, "Fighting a worthy

cause is no excuse for looking a mess. You may have things to do, but you mustn't forget you are the Earl of Chidester's only daughter."

He crept inside, as trained, and watched his daughter bat at her navy wool coat in vain. The dust was part of the fabric now. Defeated, she left it and moved on to her hair, twisting it into the tightest chignon she could manage without a brush or comb.

"Well, look at you," he said to her reflection.

Millie grimaced back before turning to give him her customary peck on the right cheek. She didn't twitch in the slightest, impressing her father and further convincing him that she had what it took to carry out his plans.

"A night spent in a public shelter takes its toll on a person."

"Looks like you've been through more than a night away from home." Her red eyes concerned him. He guessed she had had another row with Elliot. He understood her love of photography less than William did. William knew that most of their fights were rooted in Elliot's misunderstanding. At the heart of it, Millie was really fighting for women's rights. He was familiar with the boy's blind spots and doubted Elliot would be as pliable as he had been.

"I have." Millie found she couldn't say more. Not yet. It had been hard enough telling Elliot and Peter.

Millie pulled back and noticed the shift in her father, always a serious man, thinking a step or two ahead of everyone else. He was making plans, and she knew it. She followed him into his den. It shocked her to see him join Peter in a glass of his best whiskey before noon.

"Did you see the bus leaning against the green grocery on the high street?" He handed Millie a whiskey poured neat.

She shook her head no.

William got to work.

He pushed the heavy-bottomed glass at her. "Drink up, girl. This is no time to act the part of a lady."

Elliot grimaced at the comment. As far as he was concerned, these indulgences would never do. *How will she ever take up her role as wife and mother if they keep treating her like a man?* He didn't even attempt to hide his sigh of disgust. Millie surrendered to her father's desires, as she usually did, and took the glass. Elliot felt the smirk pull slightly at the corners of his lips when he realized she didn't take a drink.

"They were unloading bodies. Just two. The other passengers must have gotten off in time. Poor souls." He lifted his glass aloft before taking the first drink. Peter followed suit. Elliot drank his straight down.

"I saw destruction in France during the last war, but I never imagined this." As he fell into his favorite leather chair, his overcoat fell open. Millie noticed an envelope and small box peeking out of his inside breast pocket.

"Father, has something happened?" She barely pushed the words out, unsure if she could handle any more bad news just now.

He looked up with hollow eyes.

"Is it Michael? John?" She asked after her brothers.

He didn't answer the question, asking one of his own instead.

"How was your dinner with Clara last night?"

"I didn't meet her. I wanted to photograph the bombing at Charing Cross Road, so I put her off." How could she tell him that her selfishness had cost her a last dinner with Clara? And cost Clara her life. Who knows, the dinner might have turned into a sleepover, like in the old days when she visited London from Roedean. *If only I had kept the appointment.*

"You were meant to be with Clara last night? When the Germans bombed her flat?" Elliot asked. *She put me off for Clara and then for her damn photographs.* He set his glass on the table with too much force. Noticing them noticing him, Elliot rushed to Millie's side and wrapped her up in his arms, feigning concern for her safety.

Pushing Elliot away, Millie said, "Just the opposite, she was meant to be here with me. It's my fault she is dead."

"You know Clara is dead!" William jumped to his feet. Regretting the outburst, he took stock of the room. No one seemed to be listening, not really, so he took a step back to consider his next move. Emotions were high, which worked to his advantage. So, he watched and waited as the moment unfolded on its own.

"You could have stopped this!" Peter bent over Millie, yelling in her face.

Elliot stuck to Millie's side, escorting her to a worn leather armchair flanking the unlit fireplace. Noticing that Millie was shaking, he concentrated on building a fire and listened as the Trayford clan's voices raised and fingers pointed. He wanted to play the hero. He just needed to wait for his moment.

She sat, taking the verbal punches which were strangely coming only from Peter, never letting her glance glide Elliot's way. He would let her off the hook, and she wasn't ready for that yet. He barely noticed "the help." He would say she had done nothing wrong. She was just an ex-employee, after all.

Selfish. Surprised. Unthinking. Confused. Unkind. Peter continued unrelenting. And still Millie just sat, believing she had it coming.

William watched as Peter laid into her. Peter loved Clara too. When William put his plan in motion, he didn't consider how it might affect Peter. But things were underway now. All that was left was to monitor and adjust. First, William thought to put himself between Peter and Millie, but he froze, letting his son do his dirty work. William arrived believing that recruiting her would be difficult, especially when he saw that Elliot was there. But she knew about the bombed-out flat and that Clara was gone. Better yet, she clearly felt responsible.

William decided the best course of action was no action. So, he lingered at the edges of things.

When Peter delivered the knockout blow—DISAPPOINTED—he placed his hand on Peter's shoulder, demanding he relent, but Peter turned his anger toward him, so William pushed him aside before things got out of hand. He knew his youngest son was hurting, but there were bigger things at stake. Tentatively reaching into his arsenal of memories, William plucked out a promise he made his daughter long ago.

Rubbing Millie gently on the back, William carefully chose his words and asked, "What makes you think Clara is gone?"

She looked up to him with broken eyes. "I went to her flat this morning. The Germans bombed it out in last night's raid. She should have been here with me!"

Millie slammed her crystal highball into the fireplace, and the jigger of Scottish alcohol engorged the fire.

In his role as a devoted father, William took hold of his daughter and held on like he might never again let go. A small part of him was grateful that he escaped the task of telling her that Nanna Clara wouldn't be coming home. He began rocking her just as he had when he told her her mother was dead. Would she remember? His plan depended on it.

He was holding her then as he was now. The memories twisted with the present, making his hands shake. He had just told her that her mother was dead. When Millie's wailing became more than he could bear, he tried to reassure her. "I'll have to be enough now. I'll have to be enough now. She didn't want to leave you."

Shocked, Millie pushed her father away. William stayed back, finding he was relieved to have their connection severed. *Pull yourself together, man!*

"Clara didn't want to leave any of us. Clara's death is nothing like Mother's. I begged Mother to stay with me, but I wasn't enough, we were never enough. I even begged her to take me with her, but she didn't. She left. And she never came back. Clara was counting on me, and I let her down."

From across the room, William could feel the spider web of scars on Millie's heart rip wide open. He stood frozen in place willing his threatening tears to retreat. *How can she believe Margaret didn't love her? No, none of that.* He understood that

Millie needed him now—but so did the world. Something deep within him urged him to step forward, to offer conciliation. And yet he stood his ground. *Forgive me, Margaret.*

Millie stood up. Elliot and Peter were transfixed by the scene. Her father looked like a statue in Kensington Park. Cold. Still. Out of reach. She took a deep breath and muttered, "I'm sorry. For all of it."

The shift in Millie was unnoticeable to everyone but William. She was ready. He closed the gap between them and got to work. He needed her recruitment to be her idea, so she would never blame him. "I'm sorry that she is gone, but mostly that you found out before I could tell you. I wanted to be with you when you found out."

He pulled the note and small box out of his pocket. He hoped that once Millie had these precious items from Clara, she would forget to ask how he knew she was dead. Avoiding the question meant telling fewer lies.

"Clara gave me this when she signed back on with the Red Cross, just in case."

Elliot gave her a fresh drink, frustrated that he had missed his chance. He had met his match in William Trayford. This one she drank down in one gulp. Then, through blurred eyes, she opened the letter and read. William read it with her with his mind's eye.

*My Darling Millicent,*

*I keep thinking about a talk we had when you were eight years old. You seemed convinced that if you had been a good girl, whatever that means, your dear mum would still be alive. I told you then, and I'll tell you again, that's bollocks. Your mother died in a car accident headed to a fight she deeply believed in, and that's that. And if you are reading this, it means I am gone too. Knowing you as I do, I worry that you will try to find a way to blame yourself for this, but it is not your fault. I do not want to be one of the reasons you doubt your choices, because if you don't believe, you will never fly.*

*I am sending along my locket. I hope it fills you with the courage you need to do what you know is right. I have faith that we will meet again, and you should, too.*

*Always remember who you are and that I loved you most,*

*Nanna Clara*

Millie took the golden oval locket she had twisted around her fingers as a small child when it dangled freely around Clara's neck from its box. Before putting it around her own neck, she opened it. Inside, she saw a photograph of the two of them taken about a year ago and another of her mother and her when she was about five. On the back, the words "Luck favors the brave!" were engraved.

"May I read the letter?" Peter reached for it. Millie pulled it back and slipped into her pocket.

Millie looked from her brother to Elliot and then to the photograph of Peter in his flight suit on the mantle. She couldn't let him read the words *I loved you most,* not right now. But she could do something for her brother. This brother who was always ready to be her model. Who taught her to climb a tree, fish for bass, and build a fire at Stellan Hall, working with her patiently as the older boys left her behind. The one who convinced their father to teach her how to fly his Tiger Moth and never let anyone treat her like a girl. She had already considered putting her photography aside and now, armed with the love and confidence of Nanna Clara, was ready to help however Peter and her father saw fit.

As Millie reached for the note in her pocket, William wondered if it would have its intended effect. He waited as he watched Millie put her hand in Peter's instead of giving him the requested note. Something passed between them, leaving

Peter confused and stunned into stillness. Before speaking, Millie gave a look of apology to Elliot. He wasn't convinced that Peter had her best interest at heart and wasn't going to like what she was planning to say. And finally, she gave her other hand to her father. Looking at him in the eyes again, but with tears tucked away, for now, she found eyes that matched her own. Eyes fueled by anger and something deeper, longing—a longing to do more.

"I need your help," she said. "And Peter has a plan. We are going to remind the Germans who they are fighting. We beat them once, and we can do it again."

Elliot's face went white as a ghost's, but William and Peter were beaming.

Standing in front of him in the bowels of RAF Medmenham, almost three years later, his devoted daughter had looked right through him. She played along with his lies, somehow understanding that, too, was now expected, all the while twisting the gifted locket. He knew she wasn't doing it to bother him, but it had. He wanted to bark "stop fidgeting" as he so often had in her life, but he couldn't, not in front of the others. It would blow his cover. Besides, it wouldn't stop it. The deeper he drew her into his quest, the worse the fidgeting became.

Returning to his work, he reached for the file marked Paris. It contained a single dispatch explaining that the resistance group Réseau AGIR had begun their surveillance of the Pas-de-Calais region. It was signed by one of his most trusted agents—code name Bonnie Marie. He let out the breath he had been holding since the chance meeting with his daughter. He had never been a fan of chance because it left him waiting. Waiting to hear from Bonnie Marie that things were underway. Waiting to hear from Millie asking questions. He had the expected note from France, but Millie hadn't been in contact. This meant she had elected to go along for now and was also looking for the super-weapons. Everything was just as he wanted, at least for now.

# CHAPTER SIX

## RAF Medmenham-Central Intelligence Unit
## June 24, 1943
347 days until D-Day

The tedium of her work lulled Millie into such a trance that Hazel had to kick her chair to get Millie to look up from the large stereoscope taking up most of the space on her desk. Startled, Millie noticed that in her arms she carried a newspaper, a cardboard tube, and a typed report.

"You planning to work all night?" Hazel dropped her load on Millie's desk.

Millie blinked her eyes into focus. "What's all this?" she asked, flipping through a morning edition of *The London Times*. Buried deep in its pages, she stole a glance at the headline "Dutch female artists protest the Nazis" before she folded it, hiding away the outside world she craved.

"Red told me to drop the paper with you. Says you need a glimpse of the outside world for a change." Hazel picked up the abandoned newsprint and began flipping through it herself. "Why did you toss it away so quickly? It's only a day old."

Millie didn't answer. There was no point, really. The discrepancy between what was reported about men and what was reported about women didn't bother Hazel. Millie doubted she, like many other capable women, even noticed.

Instead, she moved on to the cardboard tube, ripping the

tape off one end and sliding out its contents. It was a propaganda poster of a woman flexing her arm muscles, wearing a blue uniform shirt and a red bandana on her head. Clipped to it was a handwritten note: "Never fear, the fight for women's rights continues! Love, Peter." She tore the poster in half and crumpled the note in her fist.

"What's that all about?" Hazel shuffled the strips of the destroyed poster about, trying to piece the poster back together.

"Peter thinks he's helping, but really he is just being an ass!" Millie took up the report.

"I wouldn't go tearing that one up too. I think you will find it fascinating." Hazel put down the newspaper and snagged the report from Millie's destructive hands.

She opened the report to the third page and pointed. "It says here they found a 'column' which everyone over in L sections suspects is a rocket, even if they can't say as much. It's from the Peck sortie, N/853. I think you have the images from June 2."

Millie shuffled through her "to be analyzed" pile and pulled out the images cited in the report. It amazed her how quickly she found them, her pile was so tall. In the middle of things, she saw what one of her colleagues described as a thick vertical column about forty feet high and four feet wide, which he calculated by measuring the shadow cast by the object.

"What were the pilot's height and camera focal length?" Millie asked Hazel.

Hazel surrendered the report to Millie. After skimming it, Millie picked up her slide rule and made a few calculations. "Looks right to me, but it is a bit fuzzy, and who can say for sure? The biggest rocket I've ever seen couldn't have been bigger than a cricket bat. My oldest brother built them all the time when he was home for holidays."

"Now look at this." Hazel handed her two photos. "They took them yesterday."

Millie slid the pair of images under her stereoscope and

pushed them together until the objects jumped off the page. Seeing the photographs in 3-D never got old. This time, the column pointed straight to the sky, clear as day. It looked just like her brother's toys, only larger and therefore deadly.

She passed the stereo pair to Red. "Seems like the best images we are likely to get. What will they do with them now?" Millie said to the room, but mostly to Red. He had been at this longer than she and Hazel combined. Millie had no idea how they might proceed. At RAF Wick things happened quickly. Here at RAF Medmenham—to say things moved slowly was an understatement.

"The industry section has been reviewing old cover, and so far, they have found the same object in multiple phases of completion," Hazel added. Red didn't say a word. He envied the young woman's enthusiasm, but he knew better. Here things must be proven beyond a reasonable doubt. Sometimes it felt like the test was beyond a shadow of a doubt.

"All at the same location?" Millie read the pilot's traces, answering her own question. These shots were of Peenemunde, not the sections of the northern coast of France she had been scouring in the weeks since she arrived at Medmenham. *Is this the connection to the vengeance weapons we have been searching for?* Tamping down her excitement, or was it fear, she scribbled a note to Red asking how the railway tracks and concrete works they saw in northern France might relate.

Hazel walked over to the narrow windows that filled the exterior wall of the room, pretending to glimpse a bit of the outdoors. She understood Millie and Red knew secrets she didn't and understood it needed to stay that way, at least for now.

Dropping her head, Millie mumbled, "So, the rockets are real," as much to herself as Hazel.

"At least they are still testing. We can do something about it, right? They will have to bomb Peenemunde now."

Millie gave Hazel a slight nod and took the note to Red.

And for just a moment, they all sat in silence, Millie staring at Red, unsure if she was ready to digest the news. A rocket that size carrying what could be a ton of explosives would kill hundreds of people and level multiple city blocks. And with only the lifting of a single German finger. They would get no warning. There would be nowhere to hide. And the Germans were building the launch sites in France. She was grateful she couldn't tell Hazel the extent of the Nazis' progress. It was simply too horrifying. Millie looked up at the tiny map by the door, directing them to the basements for shelter. Looking back at the image, she knew there would be no shelter from these monsters.

Red crushed his cigar in the ashtray, reading the note and examining the images. All the color drained from his face. "The rockets are indeed real," he finally replied.

"I didn't want to believe they were real," Hazel murmured. "If rockets are real, all they have left to figure out is a way to launch and navigate them. We won't be able to defend ourselves from attack, will we?" She looked from Millie to Red in search of an argument. They offered nothing but agreeing nods, keeping the launch site locations in France to themselves.

Red looked up from the stereo pair of images once again. Seeing the look on Hazel's face, he attempted to soften the news. "It all depends on if you believe this is an operational rocket." He lit a new cigar and pulled the smoke into his lungs. Millie had seen the gesture many times in the weeks they had been working together. He was working something out. "As far as we know, these things don't work. At least they may not work yet. We do know Peenemunde is a research facility. It's where the Nazis bring their dark and deadly imaginings to life. And there is no evidence so far that they are producing them. We only have an image of one object." He showed them both the Peck image, refraining from calling it a rocket this time as his Photographic Interpreter training had taught him. He understood he was expected to call it nothing at all unless he could name it with complete confidence. Millie went along with it, not only because she knew they needed to keep their secrets, but because a part of her needed his narrative to be true.

"If you think about it logically, the first conclusion must be that they are prototypes or, as some down in the tunnels of Whitehall hope, decoys." He looked into Millie's eyes. "They know we are watching them, or at least they suspect it. Too many of your mates flying Spitfires with cameras instead of guns have gone down over there to think they don't." He balled up the note Millie wrote as he skirted around their search in northern France. It would only have fueled the rumors Hazel was starting to hear around the base.

Hazel turned. "So, you think we have time to stop them?"

"That's why we are working around the clock scouring images," Red said, color slowly returning to his face.

Millie smiled, glad Red was here, thinking of the number of times her father had told her that they just needed to stay one step ahead of the monsters. It seemed her friend and trusted colleague was an optimist too, or one of the most practiced liars she had ever met. Either way, she laid a hand on his shoulder in gratitude.

"So, the next step is to bomb Peenemunde?" Millie asked. "Stop things before they have a chance to finish them."

Ham had mentioned how dangerous it would be for them to attack, and yet after seeing the rocket for herself, she understood it would be too risky not to. She pushed Elliot, Peter, Callum, and all the others from her mind, while pushing her fists deep in her pockets to hide their trembling.

"Eventually, I would think. But Bomber Command will want every detail we can find on the place first: how many people work there, where they sleep, where they work, what they are working on. I wouldn't be surprised if they build models before an attack," Hazel said in her analyst voice, reminding Millie that she spent her days identifying targets. She wasn't a scared citizen anymore. She was a woman on a mission. For now, the dark shadow had passed for her.

Millie looked to Red for reassurance rather than dragging her friend back into her fears. Red said nothing in reply. They talked around things at RAF Medmenham anyway. Hazel understood that. None of the interpreters ever said outright what they were looking for or why. Everyone kept their secrets well.

"You have a nice view," Hazel said in retreat.

"Can't say I noticed." Millie rubbed her eyes. It had been a long day. Truthfully, it had been a long three years and then some. The new cover of northern France trickled in these days like a dripping faucet. But as she feared when she received her new orders, investigations of this scale crawled. Stationed at Wick she had been the hare, but here at Medmenham they were all the tortoise. She walked back to her desk thinking *at least these new images may be of some use.*

"We can see the river from our windows, but I'd say your view is better. At least at the moment."

Millie went to the window and saw a gravel courtyard. Hazel pointed to a man sitting on a bench to the left. In the dusk light, Millie could make out his pilot's uniform, jet black hair, and his cigarette smoke. She remembered the first time she saw him smoking and smiled, welcoming the fond memory.

All she could see was a pall of darkness as her train pulled into the station in Wick, Scotland—the location of Coastal Command sealed the deal she made with her father to become a photographic interpreter the day after she discovered Clara's bombed-out flat. She might not love analysis work or being stuck inside and away from things day after day, but she knew she would love the people. Elliot had been angry. He tried to talk her into standing up to her father. He told her to insist on a different placement, something closer to him, but she didn't. *I couldn't.* She expected that Elliot would forgive her spinelessness. Elliot backed down, sure in the knowledge that once they married, she would comport to his will. He believed it was her way.

Snug in her train compartment, Millie smelled the picture and the letter her grandmother Fiona mailed welcoming her to billet at Teaghlach—cloves, lemon and soap. They had taken on two evacuees, but as she would remember, there was still plenty of room for her beloved granddaughter. She would have her parents' old room, and everyone, Mrs. Drummond, Ferguson, Aggie, and even the neighbors, the ridiculously wealthy Blairs, looked forward to her arrival. Rereading the names brought back so many good memories, and she snickered out loud, thinking of how long her grandmother had been describing the Blairs as "newly" rich. They had lived in Wick since before Millie was born.

She hadn't pulled into the one-room station in a few years, but she could still feel the cool water lapping at her feet in the winding river flowing behind it and the tug of sleep brought on by the crashing waves of the North Sea to its left. If she were taking a picture, she would use the smallest aperture to make out the girl with wild black curls and the blue-eyed boy playing in the waves. They were a matched set. She only remembered him being there one summer. Sometimes she wondered if he was real.

Millie tightened the green and pink floral silk scarf around her neck as she trudged down the abandoned platform to the agent's office, lighting the way with a torch. She banged her leather-clad fist on the glass service window. No one answered unless you counted the owl screeching in the distance.

"There isn't anyone in there." The man's voice gave her a start. Reeling around, Millie found a pilot in a Royal Air Force uniform with her torch. He would have made a perfect portrait with his head tilting just so and his chin slightly lifted, but there was no light, and she didn't have her camera.

He lowered the light with his ungloved hand, saying, "All out herding sheep."

"It's a little cold for that." Millie tossed the reply in the air like a shuttlecock.

He returned with an admiring and raised eyebrow.

With a flip of her hair, Millie won the point and took a seat on a nearby bench, discreetly taking another mental portrait of him as he ran his hand through his thick black hair, expertly flashing his cloudy blue eyes her way. His face belonged on the pages of *Hollywood* magazine, and the sparkle in his eyes confessed that he knew it. But there was something else about the eyes—something familiar.

He slid next to her on the bench. "As you may know, Wick's a whistle-stop, and the agent is the only one here in the evenings. He'll be getting the train ready to be on its way back to Inverness before he comes back to his booth."

"Are you part of the welcoming committee?" Millie said.

"Oh no. I'm posted here at Coastal Command." He contorted his body, trying to show off his pilot's wings.

When Millie shipped off, she hadn't given much thought to the fact that Wick would be full of pilots. Pilots were always up for a bit of fun. She bit her lip to stop from smiling. She didn't want to give this charmer the wrong idea. Elliot wouldn't like her flirting, especially with a rogue.

"And how does an American find himself in the Royal Air Force?" He could be Canadian, but his rascally nature suggested otherwise.

"Nice. You have a good ear. Most people assume I'm from Canada."

"At least if you were Canadian, joining the RAF wouldn't have been illegal." She looked him straight in the eye. There was something; she just couldn't place it.

"Beautiful and smart. My kind of girl. But you are wrong on all counts. I'm as English as Winston Churchill himself. Just spent most of the last ten years in the good old U. S. of A. with my mother's parents." He slouched against the wall, crossing his outstretched ankles.

"Is that so?" Millie noticed traces of a Scottish accent now that he mentioned it, but she had tired of their game, so she changed the subject. "Tell me, how do you find things at Coastal Command?"

"Now, why would a girl as lovely as you wonder such a thing?"

She gave him a pressed-lip smile, wishing she had worn her uniform. He would never have asked a WAAF officer that question. Something had changed about his look, his tone, a spark of recognition on his part too, perhaps, but she was done.

"It was lovely meeting you, but I really must be going. My grandmother's driver will be waiting."

Before she took a third step, he was on her heels. "Wait a minute. Are you back in Wick long or just a visit to Teaghlach?"

"Long enough, I suppose. Do we know each other?" His shift to a more familiar tone perplexed her. There was something about his eyes, but she couldn't put her finger on what. Frankly, it irritated her. She prided herself on remembering details as minute as the pattern of freckles on a person's cheekbone. *And he said, "back in Wick," hadn't he?* She was sure she heard him correctly. She glided a few steps toward the exit, sure he would follow but unsure if she wanted him to.

He avoided her question. "Smoke?" He held up both hands; one gripped a silver cigarette box and the other a box of matches.

"No, thank you." Elliot smoked. Of course, she had tried it before, but she didn't see the appeal. Judging by this familiar stranger's hoarse voice, Millie decided he'd been at it for a while.

He put the cigarette to his lips and struck a match to light it. The smell of sulfur filled the air, but the wind blew out the flame. He lit another match and tried to block the wind with his free hand. It didn't help. Millie knew she should be looking for Ferguson, but the scene unfolding before her was getting funnier by the second.

Five matches in, the man said with a chuckle, "You could help?" He handed her the box of matches.

"You need a lighter against this wind," Millie said as she slid open the box, took out a match, and struck it. She had been doing it for her father's pipe habit since he saw fit to let her play with matches. The blue-eyed pilot wrapped his hands around the flame and led Millie's hand toward his mouth. He drew in a deep breath, and the end of the cigarette ignited. Millie breathed with him in spite of herself. *This rascal is good.* Lighting a cigarette had never been so grand.

"Lady Millicent?" The agent tipped his hat. "Ferguson's waiting at the end of the platform."

"So, no more Millie?" The pilot smirked as he dropped the next bread crumb, daring her to remember who he was.

*He does know me, but how?* "I'll ask again, sir, how do we know each other?"

By now, the couple was standing at the end of the train platform. From the top of the stairs, Millie saw the old Bentley parked in the curved drive with a small, old, capped man leaning against the bonnet. She turned to the pilot and waited, determined to get her answer this time.

"Can I help you with those, Ferguson?" The airman spoke directly to the driver, dodging her question yet again, pointing to Millie's trunk and bags.

"Certainly," Mr. Ferguson answered. "I'm getting too old to lug around a lady's luggage."

While the airman loaded the boot, Ferguson gave Millie a tentative embrace.

Millie tightened her arms around his neck, remembering their rainy-day games of hide-and-seek from her childhood.

Ferguson slapped the airman on the back in appreciation when he finished loading Millie's things. "Do let Lady Blair know Lady Millicent is home for the duration of the war. She'll be working at the base with you and Aggie."

"That's an awful lot of ladies to keep informed." He lifted a scarred eyebrow and winked. "I think I'd prefer to call her the Duchess of Abberly." He took a deep bow, lifting his cap.

The moment he said the words "Duchess of Abberly," Millie heard his taunts at the beach all those years ago. It was the sprite from her memories. The boy who had disappeared. The boy she could never quite be sure truly existed.

"Callum?"

He took her hand and kissed it. "So, you do remember?"

"I do now." She pulled her hand back and stuck it into her pocket, desperate to reveal nothing, knowing the night air hadn't caused the chill traveling down her spine.

"Well, Lady Millicent Trayford, I hope I see you around the base soon. But I must be getting back. They'll be needing this at the base." He lifted the package that had come by train and flashed his blue eyes at her.

"Perhaps," Millie said, already looking forward to their next meeting, in spite of herself.

Looking out the window from her room at RAF Medmenham, Millie wondered how over a month had passed here at CIU so quickly and with no progress to speak of. Callum was there for their promised monthly dinner with Peter at the Hare and Hound in Marlow. From the look on Hazel's face, staring down at him, she wanted to join them. Millie stopped herself from offering an invitation, feeling a bit like a child who didn't want to share a toy even though they weren't playing with it themselves.

"Wonder if he is stationed at RAF Benson?" Hazel asked.

Millie turned to her desk to put on her tunic and buttoned it up to the collarbone. She needed to hide the pins holding up her trousers from Callum and Peter. Elliot made a game of counting her ribs the last night they spent together, relishing how small her wedding dress would be. He would be the envy of all his mates, or so he said, but the other men in her life might find the weight loss alarming.

"He is."

"So, you know him?" Hazel squinted her eyes to get a better look. "I see; he's the gentleman who brought you to Medmenham. There was another bloke with you too."

"My brother, Peter," Millie said, looking at Callum, wishing, and not for the first time, she was the cigarette and hoping Elliot would never find out. *It is just a schoolgirl's flirtation. Harmless, really.* Millie waved the thought off. The two of them were too much alike, plus her family would never approve. Plus, she was happily engaged.

"How well do you know him?" Hazel couldn't read minds, but she read details as well as Millie, and Millie's face said a lot.

"We were childhood playmates at my grandmother's home in Scotland." Millie gathered her things and continued, sure she had revealed too much without meaning to. "We became reacquainted when the WAAF sent me to RAF Wick as a phase one interpreter."

"So, I ask again, how well do you know him?" Hazel's eyebrows reached for her hairline.

"It's not what you think. I'm engaged." Millie flashed her platinum set sapphire in Hazel's direction.

"Whatever you say."

"Really. He is truly a scoundrel. His family made all their money in banking and bought their titles. His father, Sir Blair, is fond of saying he was born in a house with a number but planned on dying in one with a name." Millie made a move for the door, anxious to get out of the conversation. "We are going to Marlow for dinner. I promised Callum and my brother a monthly reunion. Care to join us?"

"You bet I would."

# CHAPTER SEVEN

RAF Medmenham-Central Intelligence Unit

June 24, 1943

347 days until D-Day

Before Millie and Hazel made their way to the door, a clerk with a devilish grin stepped in and handed Millie a note. It read, "Join me on the terrace at seven o'clock." It was unsigned.

"Who's this from?" Millie spoke to the retreating form. He didn't answer. *Callum or Peter wouldn't send a note. We already have dinner plans.* She reread the typed message. *Perhaps it's Elliot?* It was her birthday after all. She hadn't invited him to dinner because they had already made plans to celebrate in London in a few weeks when they both had some time off. *He might have gotten away tonight to surprise me. It's unlikely, but it could happen. Besides, who else would it be?*

She looked out the window to see if Callum was still there, but she didn't see him. He had tucked himself behind a massive tree. She caught her reflection in the window—she looked a mess. Her clothes were a bit musky; her hair was tied back into a rat's nest. She could go to her brother and Callum looking a mess, but not Elliot. He liked her to look the part, especially when his friends were about. Her watch said six-thirty. She had plenty of time to freshen up and work out an excuse for canceling dinner with her brother and Callum. *Unless...*

"Do you have anything I can use to freshen up?" Millie handed the note to Hazel and made her way back to her desk, pulling out her drawers, looking for something that might help. All she found was a stale bit of scone and a comb. "Elliot is coming, and I stink. I'll take anything; powder, lotion, perfume." She cupped her hand over her mouth and let out a breath. "A little toothpaste wouldn't be a bad idea either."

Hazel's head shot up. "Wait a minute; this isn't signed. How can you be sure it's Elliot? Why not Callum?" She lifted her eyebrows, teasing. "We're supposed to meet Elliot in London in a few weeks to celebrate your birthday. Is it like him to make an unexpected visit?" She walked to the window and looked out and found no one. "What if the note is from the lonely smoker?" Hazel fanned herself with the mystery letter, not mentioning that he seemed to be gone.

Millie reached for the stationery, but Hazel hid it behind her back. "Can we get back to the original question? Look at me. I'm a disaster, and I'm meeting him on the terrace soon."

Hazel surrendered the note. "I don't have a thing here. Too bad you don't have time to go home and change." Then a thought struck Hazel. "Try Bridget? She always keeps a few essentials on hand in case someone wants to go dancing."

Millie grabbed her satchel and zig-zagged through the corridors to the other side of Danesfield House. "Bridget, do you have anything I can freshen up with?"

She reached into her desk drawer and handed Millie a small tote without a word.

In the cramped toilet, Millie took off her tunic, shirt, and pants, glad the mirror was the size of a postage stamp so she wouldn't have to see her bony body. She washed her face, neck, and underarms and used talc powder to dry off. She wished now she had brought her own things to freshen up. She had dinner plans after all, but she hadn't wanted Callum to think—what? What didn't she want Callum thinking?

The fine powder filled the room with a fresh, clean smell. *Thank goodness for Bridget.* She sprinkled a bit of the white dust on her shirt and shook it out, blinking away the tiny particles landing in her eyes. She let out her hair and stopped.

If it was Callum, she should leave it down, but Elliot liked to see her neck. She knew all this fretting was nonsense, so she re-twisted her hair and poked it back into place with three hairpins. She stood in front of the mirror—one last detail. The lush cherry lipstick glided across her lips. She puckered and blotted it on the flannel hanging next to the tiny sink. It would have to do.

Millie returned the tote to Bridget with a hug as a thank you and hurried out the back glass-paned doors onto the grand terrace. The sun was beginning to set, making the sky the loveliest shade of pink. In the distant garden stood a man in uniform. He turned and approached her, carrying an illuminated fairy cake, and right away, she knew. He had been moving—no, gliding—with that sense of ease since the day they met. She should have been deflated, but she wasn't.

The man's dark hair shone, and the content look on his face eased the tension in Millie's neck. Her body relaxed—all of her banal work and pressure forgotten. She closed the distance with a swagger of her own. Standing toe-to-toe with her visitor, she said, "What are you doing here, Callum? We're meant to meet at the pub at eight."

"With the world crashing in around us, we can't forget little things like birthdays."

Millie blew out the candle. "We're celebrating my birthday in London in two weeks."

"Who cares? My flight was canceled, and I needed a reason to say hello."

"You never need a reason." Millie took the cupcake, gently grazing his hand. "Where is Peter?"

"Back at the base. He's in the middle of a high-stakes poker game, but he told me to tell you he will see you at dinner for your not-birthday."

She should have known Peter had a hand in this. He had been against Elliot from the start and pushed her toward Callum since her arrival at RAF Wick. "In that case, sit, tell me all the gossip from the airbase. Start with anything you've got on Peter." Pilots were fearless and shameless creatures. Callum's tales were always entertaining, if not a little scandalous.

"There is nothing I would rather do, but first, I have to ask you one thing." He swiped a loose curl from her forehead, resisting the urge to pull it all down, and the warmth of his fingers sent a thrill through Millie.

"Sure." Her cheeks flushed.

"Why are you wearing that awful lipstick?"

Millie shoved him like they were children once again. In response, Callum took the cake out of her hands and took a bite, just before Millie pushed it into his face. When he dropped the smashed confection to the ground, a peal of laughter that could wake the heavens broke loose from the two of them.

# CHAPTER EIGHT

War Cabinet Rooms

June 29, 1943

342 days until D-Day

William arrived first and took a seat in one of the wooden chairs that lined the walls nearest the door. He wore a wool tweed suit. The men in attendance all knew him, and other costume would have elicited questions. Today the scientist had the floor.

He took attendance as the others arrived. Prime Minister Winston Churchill sat at the head of the table, with Anthony Eden on his right and Deputy Prime Minister Clement Attlee on his left. The other politicos included Home Secretary Herbert Morrison, Minister of Aircraft Production Stafford Cripps, and Duncan Sandy. The military had their representatives: three chiefs of staff and Churchill's chief military assistant, General Ismay. That left the scientists to fill in the empty chairs surrounding the table: Lord Cherwell, R. V. Jones, Sir Robert Watson-Watt, and Dr. William Cook. Lord Cherwell and Jones sat opposite each other, which seemed appropriate to William. The battle lines lay between them. Cherwell thought the rockets were an elaborate German hoax. Jones understood they were real. *Jones has his work cut out for him.*

After Cherwell laid out his theories supporting the hoax, the men took a moment to look at his documentation. William knew that the greatest threat to Britain was not in Germany but sitting around this table. The hubris of men like Lord Cherwell—who believed if he couldn't make a rocket fly, no one could—was going to get everyone on their island nation killed.

Next up was R.V. Jones. William wasn't a fan, but he was all he had, so he had turned over every stone, looking for evidence of the rocket program and the pilotless bombs to give him a fighting chance. In addition, he sent his son and daughter to help procure the most trusted form of intelligence—aerial photography. After all, seeing is believing.

Jones started, as one does, at the beginning of the story. They had received the Oslo Report just two months after declaring war on Germany. It described the Germans' dreams and aspirations for their super-weapons development program. Combing through its pages, William and every man in this room read words like gliding bombs, aerial torpedoes, pilotless aircraft, long-range guns, and rockets. It also pointed to Peenemunde as the research and development center.

Next, Jones moved on to the countless signals received from secret agents in Germany, France, and Denmark, and the recorded conversations between high-ranking POWs held in London. Finally, he tied the MI6 intelligence to the aerial photographs by explaining that the information from the agents informed where and when aerial reconnaissance pilots flew. He passed out enlarged pictures and a report compiled by RAF Medmenham.

Duncan Sandy handed a copy of the report to William. Skimming through it, he could see Millie's fingerprints. No detail was left out, including the two torpedo-like objects that measured thirty-eight feet long found among the images taken by Sergeant Peck.

Jones ended his argument with crystal clear images of rockets taken at Peenemunde during the same sortie that captured the photos of the torpedo-like objects. It made no sense for this to be a hoax. It was too elaborate, and it left the British no option other than bombing Peenemunde. Jones asserted the Germans wouldn't intentionally invite such an attack.

After careful consideration and a lot of argument, they decided they would bomb Peenemunde, despite the risks.

William slipped out of the room unnoticed as they drew up orders for Bomber Command. He had won the battle, but not the war. It was time to shift his attention to the concrete structures Bonnie Marie kept sending dispatches about. His gut insisted they were connected to Peenemunde. They would lose the element of surprise once they bombed, so they needed to gather information as quickly as they could. He crawled above ground. As the first beams of sunlight hit his face, he began to calculate the German response to the bombing of their treasured research site and how the British would remain just one step ahead in this game of cat and mouse.

All of their lives depended on it.

# CHAPTER NINE

West End Pub

July 6, 1943

335 days until D-Day

Photographs of fallen pilots covered the walls of the Angel and Crown, haunting the fun. Peter and Callum comforted themselves by regaling Hazel and Millie with stories of being alone in the cockpit of their Spitfires while they waited for Elliot. They flew at 30,000 feet and shot photographs instead of other planes, making their work less catastrophic but no less dangerous. The tales went on and on. Locations included the coasts of France and Norway, Danish Fjords, Germany's major cities, and even a few places on the edge of the Baltic Sea.

Millie thought back to her days memorizing every inch of the photographic cover MI6 ordered of the Baltic Sea and northern France coastline. *Did Peter or Callum, or perhaps even Elliot risk their lives to take the photos?* Elliot didn't talk much about his work, which was proper, so Millie almost forgot he flew out of RAF Benson with Callum and Peter.

"What are your pilot numbers?" Hazel asked.

"64G76," Peter said.

"73B78," Callum said. "Why?"

"When I analyze images, it's nice to know who risked their lives getting the intelligence. It reminds me that I am part of a bigger mission. When you are stuck in the middle of nowhere in what amounts to an old larder, never seeing the impact of your efforts until the next batch of images finds its way to your desk, it makes it easier to cope."

"Makes what easier?" Peter drank down the last of his ale and waited to hear her answer before getting the table another round.

"The fact that, sooner or later, my discoveries will warrant sending bombers to those places, killing people on the ground, if not losing the bomber crews themselves."

Millie sat unmoving after Hazel's answer. She expected her to say she felt disconnected, drained, not at all a part of the whole. Being connected to the pilot-photographer reminded her that time passed, moved on, even if it moved on without her. But clearly, her feelings about their work weren't universal. She had no idea Hazel felt the weight of the deaths like that. A sense of responsibility didn't drain Millie; it was the isolation, the lack of tangible contributions, and the absence of connectivity.

"Are you always so cheerful?" Elliot arrived a bit late, as usual. Millie wondered what kept him this time, but she didn't ask. Elliot wouldn't like it, not in front of so many people.

"Hello, Elliot." Millie sprang out of her chair, which may have been just a tad too close to Callum's.

"Why dwell on the bombings?" Elliot kissed Millie on the top of her head. "Don't we get enough of that on duty?" Elliot stole a chair from a nearby table and pushed it between Callum and Millie before taking a seat.

"Millie doesn't," Callum said. Millie's eyes begged Callum not to start in with Elliot. Ever since Peter had recruited Callum to his new life's mission of alienating Elliot, the barbs came from every direction. Callum, and Peter for that matter, never missed a chance to let Elliot know they understood Millie far better than he did. She kept staring at Callum, desperate for him to see that she simply didn't have the stamina for any more tension. Not after the tedium of the last month. But she could tell by the look in his eyes that he had dangled the hook and planned on setting it. She took a deep breath, resolved to be the one to reel the story in.

"How do you mean?" Elliot said.

Callum reached in front of Elliot and took Millie's hand. "Our girl here craves action. As for me, I can't wait to get her back in a foxhole."

"A foxhole?" Hazel asked. Elliot leaned back in his chair and wrapped an arm around Millie's shoulder. Millie jerked her hand back from Callum's and took hold of Elliot's.

"It was nothing. Just a strafing back when I first arrived at RAF Wick," Millie said.

"Oh, do let me tell it," Peter said. "I just need to get a few refreshments first."

"You won't tell it right. You weren't there," Callum said. "I'll tell it."

"No, I'll do it. But only if Peter is buying and he gets me a shot of whiskey," Millie said.

Elliot drank down the last of Millie's pint. He had heard this story one too many times.

Millie drained the whiskey and started to tell the tale as succinctly as possible. She could feel the hostility permeating from Elliot's pores, and she wanted to be quick for his sake. But something came over her as she spun her tale.

She began the story the way the morning had, with a walk outside Wick's local paper, *John O'Groat Journal.* Her mood immediately lifted. Her heartbeat, which had been stuck in adagio, jumped to allegro in seconds as images unfolded in her memories, highlighting the tiniest of details as if she had jumped into a chalk drawing with Mary Poppins.

"Mr. Graham, the paper's owner, had a photography assignment for me from the Ministry of Information." She turned to Hazel to explain. "My old boss at the MOI said he might need me from time to time, even though I enlisted with the WAAF. This was the first time he had reached out.

"Orders in hand, I picked up the pace and headed for the

Bentley, which was parked in front of Mrs. Layla's, to meet Aggie. Before I made it to the car, the anti-aircraft guns started hammering. I pasted myself to the haberdasher's front window, taped to keep it from shattering, took hold of my camera, and pointed it to the sky. Aggie caught up with me and peeled me off the display window, reminding me, 'This isn't London. It's only a German weather plane.'

"'How can you be so sure?' I asked her. The memory of Nanna Clara's burnt-out flat was still fresh in my memory. I could barely hear my voice over my pounding heart.

"'The German weather plane comes at the same time, every day. He waves at the Territorial Army. The TA fires off a few shots with their anti-aircraft gun to remind him he isn't welcome, and he goes on his way.' Aggie sashayed down the road to prove her point."

Millie stole Peter's pint and took a sip before continuing. Elliot excused himself and headed for the loo.

"Before Aggie took a third step, two squadrons of fighter planes in formation darkened the sky, like a murder of crows. I yelled, 'Weather plane?' and ran to the nearest solid wall. Tape and glass won't stop bullets." Millie looked around the table to be sure her audience was still with her. "Screams came from every direction, and people dodged whizzing bullets and shards of flying brick, glass, and wood.

"'Aggie?' I expected her to be at my side, but she wasn't."

"Where was she?" Hazel blurted out.

"Just listen." Peter put a reassuring hand on Hazel's arm. "Go on."

"I scanned the pandemonium and found her. She was hunkered down in the middle of the sidewalk with her hands covering her face."

"Dear God!" Hazel said, covering her mouth with both hands.

"I started to run to her but was pulled back by a strong arm. It was this guy," Millie pointed a thumb in Callum's direction, "assuring me it was fine. I said something like, 'What are you talking about?' trying to shake off his grip, 'Aggie's frozen with fear. She is going to get killed if she doesn't move.'"

Callum interrupted and continued telling the tale. "She wanted to go to Aggie herself, but I told her I couldn't let her and proceeded to wrap my arms around her waist and pin her against the wall." He paused to see how Elliot might react, but he wasn't back at the table. It was a shot wasted.

Millie's face was flush with life for the first time in weeks, and she couldn't stop herself from jumping back into the role of storyteller. Even the sight of a returning Elliot didn't deter her.

"I stomped on his foot, expecting him to drop his arms. He didn't, so I elbowed him in the ribs and yelled, 'Let go of me!' Finally, his arms loosened, and I made a break for it." Out of the corner of her eye, Millie could see Elliot smile at the thought of her fighting Callum off.

"When I reached Aggie, Callum was just a step behind, and she was still screaming, 'They're going to bomb us! They're going to bomb us!'

"Callum said, 'Millie, this is too dangerous. You have to make her move. I need to know you're safe before I report to the base.'

"All I could think to say was, 'Who cares what you need,' so I ignored him and squatted beside Aggie.

"'I'm serious, Millie. You need to go. Those Messers are coming back. If she won't move, you need to leave her. I'll make sure she's all right.'

"'Don't you get it; I'm not going anywhere without her. And if you need to report to the base, I suggest you do it.'

"Aggie's face was ashen, and her eyes fixed on the sky, following the planes as they turned about, preparing for the next round of strafing. Every muscle in my body tightened, and the urge to run for cover pulsed through my veins, but I wouldn't leave Aggie. We, and by that I mean Callum and me, tugged at her once more, trying to lift her dead weight, and a shot ricocheted off the wall over our heads. I pushed Aggie to the ground and covered her with my body, waiting for the barrage of bullets to stop.

"When the planes started to make their turn, I got up and changed tack. I jerked Aggie to her feet, nearly pulling her arm out of its socket. 'That's enough.' I was prepared to slap her back to her senses if she didn't move. 'We have to get inside somewhere.'

"Her eyes were wild, but she followed along to the haberdashery, the crowd pushing desperately to get inside. The next public building was the paper up the street. Dodging people, bullets, and shrapnel, we sprinted to the top of the hill. Callum followed along, yelling, 'Those planes will be back.'"

Millie stopped for another drink, but Hazel urged her on.

"We barged into the paper and found Mr. Graham huddled under the composition table in the middle of the room. Eldon was still working the linotype in the back of the room, unaware of the chaos outside the building."

"You expect me to believe he didn't take shelter?" Hazel put a hand on Millie's arm.

"My apologies." Millie patted her hand. "I forgot you don't know these people. Eldon works the linotype machine at the paper, and he's deaf," Millie said.

"That makes more sense." Hazel finished off her beer, and Peter offered to get another round, assuring Hazel he knew the story.

"Callum rushed to him and pushed him off his stool just as lead pierced the back window. Eldon swung at him, but Callum caught his arm with ease." Talking directly to Hazel, Millie added, "Eldon must be about sixty years old. As you can imagine, he began fighting as if his life depended on it with a mix of fear and fury on his face.

"Callum grabbed Eldon's face and turned it toward the shattered glass. Eldon looked back with wide eyes and nodded with understanding. I melted into a heap on the floor, grateful to be inside."

"That sounds worse than the bombings in London, or at least as bad," Hazel said. "How long before you got to go home?"

"Oh, that was just the start of it," Peter said. "I would have given my fortune to see this one's face when she went back out into it." He was pointing to Callum, of course.

"You went back out?" Hazel said.

"Yes," Elliot said, arms crossed in front of his chest. "She did."

"You don't know me well, Hazel, but before all this, I was a photographer."

"You are still a photographer. I just didn't know that about you then," Callum corrected Millie, glaring at Elliot.

"The truth is, my camera is all the excuse I need to be in the middle of things, which I love, so, after a few deep breaths, I checked my film count. I had twenty-eight shots left. And there was no way I was going to miss out on the action."

"It's true," Peter interrupted. "When we were kids, she always took the biggest risk and was the first one running toward trouble."

Millie smiled at her brother before she continued. It was the nicest thing he had said about her in years.

"Callum was camped out at the door, and I checked in with him. He told me he thought there were at least twenty armed German planes and that it looked like one of the squadrons was doubling back to hit the town again. In the distance, we could see retreating planes. It looked like a swarm of bees.

"I reached for the door, and Callum grabbed my arm again. He told me I couldn't go back out, and I reminded him he wasn't my boss or my husband." Elliot tossed a wadded-up napkin in the center of the table and leaned back in his chair.

"You said something like, 'You'll get yourself killed, and for what, a few photographs?'"

"I did say something like that, right before I went out to get myself killed," Callum said.

"Camera ready, I pushed past Callum and crouched down against the brick wall so I could survey the chaos, searching for my picture, the most vital image out there, before it was lost to history forever.

"Callum and I dodged bullets, shattered glass, and flying hunks of concrete as we ran north toward the river. Callum suggested we might be able to lend a hand to the anti-aircraft gunners. The bullets themselves were invisible, but they announced themselves with a violent whistling, distant at first, that got faster and straighter and sharper until the shells lacerated their targets. It set the hair on the back of my neck on end, but I didn't stop running.

"When we reached the Station Road, Callum made himself one with a door in a small vestibule. Mimicking him, I panted, 'Where to next?' Callum shook his head in disbelief at me and pointed across the street. I saw the sandbag fortress of an anti-aircraft gun in the distance, guarding the south end of one of Wick's bridges. I knew immediately it was my story—a man defending his home. The only thing that would have made it sweeter was if the person at the gun was a woman. It wasn't likely, but a girl could always hope."

Peter reached out in the emptying pub and took hold of his sister's hand. He noticed the loose-fitting engagement ring and nails ripped to the quick. He thought of all the boxes of photographs stacked in her bedroom back in London. Before letting any guilt settle in, he vowed to himself that he would help her get them published when this was all over.

"With a break in the shooting, I moved closer with Callum, my back skimming the buildings that lined the main road, keeping an eye on the temporary bunker. Blood exploded into the air when a bullet hit one of the defending gunmen. I cringed, watching the other gunner struggle to reload his massive gun alone. I looked up and noticed the fighter planes turn, trying to take the gun once and for all. I pointed toward the sandbag wall. Callum nodded. He ran in their direction, and I was right behind him. I held my camera tight to my chest and ran, bent low, toward the bunker. I have to say the cocktail of anger, fear, and excitement was intoxicating.

"Within seconds, Callum jumped into the bunker, strapping on a helmet, and helped the stranded gunner. Two planes laid down an artillery barrage between the anti-aircraft bunker and me, so I tucked myself into a nearby doorway. I inhaled to regroup.

"I lunged at my chance to move, but a bullet pierced the sidewalk, inches from my foot. I jerked myself back to the wall, sweat dripping from my forehead. I told myself to be patient. Just breathe and wait. Lifting my camera to my face, I searched for the humanity in the mayhem.

"A few feet away, Callum and the uninjured gunner loaded the ack-ack gun with a fresh string of shells, took aim on the retreating fighter planes, and sent artillery hammering into the sky. I released the shutter of my 35mm camera and advanced the film. Four more planes ran for home. But the dicing planes kept coming in quick succession, sending bullets whizzing, making it impossible for me to move close enough to the bunker for a better picture. I punched the wall, bloodying my knuckles. I needed options. That's when I saw them."

"Saw who?" Hazel asked.

Millie held up a finger and waited. It was a bit dramatic, but she was getting to the best part.

"In the corner doorway on the opposite end of the block, two young children clutched each other in front of a now chipped red brick wall, looking in my direction. I checked the sky. There were no planes coming for now. I dashed for the huddled children, stopped two feet before I reached them, stepped out, and took two pictures, focusing first on the girl's wide eyes and then on the boy's. A returning plane fired, sounding like a drummer boy in a battle, and I charged at the children to shield them. 'Ready to get out of here?' They shook their wet, dirty faces yes. 'Good.' I smiled. 'When the plane passes, we run.'

"After the last drumming of shots, I took their clammy

hands and retraced my steps, back down the hill to the *Groat*. The little girl couldn't keep up, so I swept her onto my back. I burst through the front door, the children flanking me, and handed them over to Aggie hiding behind the desk with Eldon. A natural-born mother, she inspected the charges at my side. She knew their names, of course. Penny and Liam."

"Aggie knows everyone in Wick," Peter told Hazel and Elliot.

"She waved them under her wings, pushing her anxiety away now that she had someone depending on her. They nestled into her sides. I took a photograph. She looked to me and asked, 'What's it like out there?'

"'The planes keep coming back.' I noticed Mr. Graham still frozen under the table, though he somehow managed to fetch and empty a whiskey bottle. 'Never mind him. He's useless.' Aggie pulled me down near her nest under Mr. Graham's roll top desk. 'Why are they here at all?'

"'I have no idea. When I find out, you'll be the first to know. Maybe Callum or the Territorial Army fighters have some idea.' Her grip crushed my hand. I peeled back her fingers, telling her I had to go.

"Outside, the remaining planes retreated, and I pumped my fist in the air. I hoped we riddled them with holes. Fueled by adrenaline, I raced to the anti-aircraft gun. 'You gentlemen all right?' I dropped down into the shelter, happy to be off my feet.

"'I am.' Callum looked to his partner on the gun.

"'I do believe that's the first time I've ever been called a gentleman by an actual lady,' the middle-aged man said, lifting a box of cigarettes from his shirt pocket.

"'Any fellow who sends the Germans running has earned that rank in my estimation.' I leaned back against the wall constructed of sacks and sand. 'Did you hit the last few planes?' I snapped a photo before they could object. Then another, before Callum put up his hand and blocked the lens."

"Did any of the photographs turn out?" Hazel asked.

"Of course they did," Peter said, beaming with pride. "And I'd bet next month's wages they are in a box under her bed back at your billet."

With Elliot's eyes piercing her, Millie let Peter's words be the only ones on the subject. It would break his heart if he found out that the one of Callum, after the fight smoking a cigarette in the bunker, held a special place in the leather portfolio Callum had given her for Christmas. Looking at Callum, smug as ever, having stolen the show from Elliot, she was sure he was the most frustrating and interesting man she would ever know.

"Well, that was a nice trip down memory lane, but I didn't come all this way to hear about your adventures in Wick," Elliot said. "May I escort you to the Dance Hall? We have some birthday celebrating to do."

Millie's heartbeat slowed, and she offered her hand to her fiancé. She noticed Peter's look, pleading with her to stay, but dancing had been the plan all along, hadn't it?

# CHAPTER TEN

Paramount Dance Hall

July 6, 1943

335 days until D-Day

Elliot kept a tight grip on Millie's waist as he led the way to the Paramount Dance Hall. He could hear the rest of their group rabble-rousing behind him, and he wanted them all to know she belonged to him. It had been bad enough having to share Millie with Peter all these years, but now this Callum was on the scene. He knew he would have to whisk her far away from them both if she was to ever be entirely his.

He had never really approved of her photography but found himself wishing that she had stuck with it these days. He might use it as an excuse to get her away from both Peter and Callum, without her noticing his possessiveness. The work made her a solitary creature and a bit too assertive for his liking, but back in the day, it captured her attention. At RAF Medmenham she had too many distractions.

Picking up the pace, he shrugged off his concern, glancing Millie's way. His friends envied him and why shouldn't they? She was a beauty: dark hair, smooth porcelain skin, sky blue eyes. Her family name was the pinnacle of prestige. And though Callum and Peter's conniving ways concerned him, given his family's wealth and position, he didn't really believe she would ever leave him; despite the fact that she was part Scottish and stood to inherit a tidy sum when her grandmother, the Lady

Abberly, passed. He couldn't conceive of a woman of independent means.

Millie squirmed as he pulled her closer, reminding him that she was—what did his friends call her—oh yes, feral if left to her own devices. He didn't blame her. After all, she had been without a proper mother for most of her life. His friends taunted him by questioning whether he could ever tame her. He held her firm, and she relented, willing enough to go along to avoid a fight in front of the crowd. She was always quick to please everyone. He smiled, knowing he could always use her tendency toward self-sacrifice to win the day. Now he just needed to get her to set a wedding date.

Elliot saw a few fighter pilots from RAF Benson at the front of the queue, so he led Millie onward. Millie turned and overheard Callum and Peter discussing whether or not they wanted to brave the mob. She held her breath, hoping they would go looking for a quiet pub somewhere nearby. Standing near the closed doors, they heard the muffled sounds of the practicing band whose horns promised a rambunctious evening. Elliot introduced Millie to the fighter pilots. She noticed his broad smile as his new mates admired her.

Millie finally got him to loosen his grip and turned, looking for Peter, Callum, and Hazel. She dropped Elliot's hand and skipped toward her brother when she saw them coming their way. She tugged at Hazel's hand, leading the three of them back to Elliot, and made Elliot repeat all the pilots' names. She giggled as she watched Hazel put them in rank order on the invisible dance card in her mind.

Trumpets sounded the moment the doors flew wide open. Two clear, quick notes invited them to the party. As they passed through the double doors, the doorman asked if they needed a number for the dance-off. Elliot declined, without asking Millie if she was interested, offering her a wink. The tallest boy in their extended group turned to Hazel.

"How about it?" He offered her his hand. Smiling, she took

it and a number as they bounced inside.

The scene inside was a cacophony of sights and sounds. Millie's shutter finger twitched. The way the flaring skirts of the competing girls kept time with the music captivated her. But before the sight invited her deeper into the scene, the drummer tapped *ta-ti-ti-ti-ta* on his cymbals, insisting she move. The sounds and sights were infectious and instead of watching, Millie wanted to play. The smell of sweet perfume mixed with cigarette smoke. From the minute Elliot pulled her to the dance floor, her body ached to keep moving. Too many long days just sitting and looking. She looked back before they got lost in the fray and saw Peter and Callum invite a pair of girls to join their emptying table. She lost track of them when Elliot found them a place in the middle of things and gave her a twirl before pulling her into his chest.

Peter, already bored by the company, surveyed the room. The band played on an elevated stage on the wall opposite the doors. Girls stood along both sides of the room, wearing work suits and tight curls, tapping their toes, and waiting for an invitation to dance. On the right side of the dance floor, a buffet was set up, with a punch bowl and sweet treats. Peter finally relaxed as the band finished up their rendition of "Boogie Woogie," making way for a bow-tied man who grabbed the silver microphone and broke into "Don't Get Around Much Anymore."

"Quit looking around and dance, you silly girl," Elliot yelled into Millie's ear, a bit too loud for the quieting music. "This is our time." He pushed her hair aside and kissed the side of her neck, and whispered in her ear, "I wish you had worn your hair up."

Callum shuffled his partner nearer to Elliot and Millie. When they were within reach, he noticed Hazel's feet in the air. The toss didn't sync up with the music, but everyone stepped back out of the way. They were warming up for the competition.

Millie watched, too, and caught Callum's eye, sending him a plea which he knew meant *don't interrupt us tonight.* Elliot had had enough, and she wanted to get lost, if only for the night. Callum nodded, answering the message—*very well*—wondering if she was getting everything she needed.

As the beat revved up, lovers and friends alike peeled themselves apart and formed a circle around Hazel and her pilot to make room for their routine. They twisted and shimmied, pitched and rolled, and even wagged a finger or two at the crowd. The room was electric.

With the warmups finished, the music shifted to another slow dance, and the crooning resumed.

Elliot took Millie in his arms, resting his hands on her low back. Millie watched Hazel and the pilot gallop to the punch bowl in search of libations before the next rowdy dance, wishing she had a camera to capture the fun. But she didn't, so she surrendered to Elliot. They swayed to the rhythm and absorbed the smooth sounds of the vocals. She rested her cheek on Elliot's chest and relaxed.

The leader sang about always loving you as Elliot coiled a stray curl around his finger and whispered, "I want you" in Millie's ear. They moved like one. Millie looked up, wanting to get lost in him too. She kissed him on the cheek—an invitation to leave. In an unusual move, he turned his face toward Millie's and kissed her on the lips, softly saying her name. His breath was sweet and warm. There wasn't a tingle, but it relaxed her. Elliot's embracing arms felt familiar, dependable. *This is how things are meant to be.* The only people who seemed to disagree were Peter and Callum. She tried to pull back to ask if he wanted to go, but Elliot held tight. *Is this another show for Callum?* Elliot was rarely this tender and never this passionate in public. *Stop worrying. It doesn't matter if Callum sees.* She hungered for escape, so she searched for his neck. Kissing it, she whispered, "It's time to go."

Callum watched as Elliot dragged Millie back out into the

night. Peter had told him that the sex was perfunctory at best, but the thought of Elliot having her to himself sent his pulse racing. He picked up his jacket and moved toward the door. Peter grabbed hold of his arm.

"This round goes to Elliot, mate. Let's go find a card game."

# CHAPTER ELEVEN

House in Belgravia

July 7, 1943

334 days until D-Day

Walking to her family's London home after her night with Elliot, Millie fished her camera out of her satchel, pleased she had thought to store her things with him yesterday rather than leaving them at Hazel's. She pointed her lens at her deteriorating neighborhood as she walked toward home, heartsick at the scene, exhilarated by the occupation. When she depressed the shutter, a spark lit through her entire body. A feeling she had felt only once since transferring to RAF Medmenham, though in that case her camera was nowhere in sight. It was as if she were full of warming helium and becoming lighter with each step, reminding her of the heaviness she had learned to live with under the constant Nazi threat.

Through the lens, she saw a world hidden under a pall of grey. The pock holes decorating the buildings and sidewalks of her childhood neighborhood made it look diseased. Her old world could be added to the list of dead. She wondered if things would feel more alive when the streets began to fill with morning goers, many of whom would be pouring out of the city's underground bomb shelters, or if the grey gloom would engulf them too. A film of dust hung in the air, mingling with the morning fog, adding an eerie quality to every picture. These shots were more about atmosphere than people. The shrouded early walkers felt like ghosts, and she couldn't help but watch for her mother and Clara coming back to haunt their old stomping grounds. *Will they see anything they recognize?*

Unscrewing her lens and replacing it with a telephoto, she explored the faces of her early morning company. As she turned the final corner toward home, she made out a dark-headed man in uniform halfway up the block. She felt the spark again. She dropped her camera, letting it dangle just above her waist. Her step quickened. Then a bit of sunlight broke through the haze, revealing the green hue of the man's uniform. Her shoulders stooped as if someone had let the air out of her. And her mind drifted to Callum.

He glided more than walked through life, and she imagined that sex with him would feel less like a sporting event and more like a ballet. Elliot was the only man she had ever been with. There had been boyfriends, of course, who had stolen a kiss or a touch, but by the time she left for university at Oxford, she and Elliot were a matched set. It didn't seem fair that they could be so well suited but have no spark between them. Being with him wasn't nearly as exciting as simply looking into Callum's eyes.

With her thoughts betraying her, she looked with her mind's eye at the two of them, backs leaning against the bar, tolerating each other over a pint. Standing there together the similarities weren't hard to miss. Both wore a pilot's blue. Both stood tall and proud. They shared the easy posture of a man born to privilege, the naughty and inviting glint of the eye that told the world they understood they belonged in every room they entered, and a crooked smile that was at once mischievous and tantalizing. But Millie could see the difference. If she took them down from their esteemed shelf the differences emerged. Elliot was a first edition—admired but unread. His cover was pristine, but if one tried to open the pages the spine would creak. Callum fell open straight away—his spine supple and his pages stuffed with treasures: letters, ticket stubs, pressed flowers, receipts, insect wings, and perhaps an errant snapshot of a wild-haired girl.

Elliot never left home with a strand of his blond hair out of place. His every seam was pressed, and she had never seen him without his golden pinky ring engraved with his family's seal. Often, he folded a few pounds and slipped them into his front pocket, not wanting a wallet to ruin the fall of his trousers. The precision of his exterior mirrored his personality perfectly. He sought control in everything. He loved all of the gauges and dials on his plane's dash telling him what step to take next with precise accuracy. Elliot never left anything to chance.

Callum, on the other hand, wore a mop of dark wavy hair and his clothes had never met an iron. Rather, the fabric was worn in, and he was most himself engulfed by an easy wool sweater and a pair of trousers three seasons too old. Where one might forget the color of Elliot's eyes, the ice blue of Callum's was unavoidable. Millie found she often looked down to avoid their fierceness. He was a man of passions, of endless curiosities, and his eyes told her that both extended to her. He was a flame and Millie feared that if she got too close, she and all her dreams would burn up. With Elliot, she would live a quiet life near, but not too near, together. A life with Callum would be one lived in tandem. Climbing the steps to her front door and pushing through it, she thanked God that things were settled with Elliot. Pursuing photography after the war would simply have to be enough. *Best to not get too greedy.*

Walking down the entry hall, Millie noticed the door to her father's study stood open like an invitation at the end of the hallway. Millie's shoulders dropped from her ears, and she let out the breath she was holding as she crossed the threshold. She sat down in her father's desk chair, tipping back to stare at the ceiling. The perfect posture for thinking. How many times had she found her father sitting just like this?

Mountains of papers surrounded her. Instinctively, she reached out and began sorting them into piles, as she had as a child. One stack was for household receipts, one for donations, and one for her father's pursuits.

Putting them in order from biggest to smallest took her back. Deep in the recesses of her mind, she unearthed a conversation between her father and mother when she was five and the perfect size to hide in the window seat behind the velvet curtain.

"William, I've taken care of these, but you need to give this bill for the aerodrome your attention. I don't know why we're still paying them. You haven't flown that old Tiger Moth for years."

She heard her father get to his feet, walk around the desk, and the swish of her mother's skirts as he took her into his arms. "Just give those to me. I promise to see after the plane." The papers fluttered down to the desk. "Now, why don't you dance with me?"

Through a crack in the drapes, Millie spied an intoxicating smile spread across her mother's face, and a familiar glint of playfulness sneaked into her eyes as she let down her hair. Millie barely breathed, afraid if she rustled in her hiding place, she would break the spell. The dancing prince and princess captivated the little girl as the fairy tale sprang to life right before her eyes.

Picking up an image taken the day she got engaged, she wondered if she would ever have the same transforming effect on Elliot.

Millie continued with her digging and stacking, until she came across a type of document she had never seen at home before—a folder hiding pages with the word "confidential" marked in red. She slipped out a single piece of onion skin paper headed by a crest with the unicorn and the lion. She learned during her first week at RAF Medmenham that the mark belonged to MI6, the British Secret Intelligence Service her father worked for. *What are these doing here?*

Under the first memo was another and another, mostly

from an agent code-named Bonnie Marie in the Paris Station. She guessed it was one of the special agents or resistance fighters funneling information out of France to help with the Allies' cause. As she reached the bottom of the stack, a telegram slipped to the ground. It was from Stockholm. They sent it to inform MI6 about a conversation between Professor Fauner from Berlin and an engineer, Stefen Szenassi. The telegram described a giant rocket with a range of one hundred and twenty-five miles and a five-ton payload. They claimed the Germans were testing rockets near Swinemunde on the Baltic coast.

Just one of the many clues they were collecting in the effort to prove or disprove what was going on at Peenemunde. She thought, and not for the first time, that if the weapon had an accurate navigational system, it could take out Parliament and Westminster with the single push of a button and wondered if they were ever going to get around to bombing Peenemunde.

A book dropped on the desk. Millie flinched, dropping the telegram.

"I hope you make a better analyst than spy," William said. Millie saw the same charming smile on her father's face as she had all those years ago.

"I had no idea this is what you've been up to." She picked up the stack of papers marked with the MI6 emblem, working to steady her breathing and quiet her panicked heart.

He scooped up the folders with one hand. "Let's be clear, my doting, or is it nosey, daughter," he paused to survey the orderly stacks on the leather desktop, sorted and stacked with a loving hand. "You haven't the foggiest idea what my contributions to this war have been or are still." Sternness and weariness stole the brightness from his eyes in this rare confession. William could only hope she would never know the extent of his manipulations, his deceit. He told himself it must be done to secure victory for the Allies, to protect and preserve their very lives, but he knew if she ever learned even a nugget, he might lose her forever.

Millie waited in the silence, calculating. Her father put her on this search. There had to be space to discuss it without setting him off or pushing him inside himself.

She decided on a parallel track.

"Why don't we get those reports?" she asked. "It might help us understand the aerial photographs better."

"Some members of the War Cabinet believe the PIs need to discover peculiarities on their own, blind to other intelligence." William's voice grated with irritation. The tug-of-war between the factions who believed the advanced weaponry existed, and those who did not infuriated him. They wasted his time and cost others their lives with their debates. They needed to make forward progress, and arguments certainly weren't going to help them regain the foothold in France they lost when they fled from Dunkirk. "They hope your findings will confirm these tidbits of information, not be informed by them. They need too many reassurances." Her father walked around the desk and stood by Millie's side. He tucked a loose curl behind her ear. "They aren't brave like you."

Millie took his hand, smiling. "And luck favors the brave."

William squeezed her hand, nodding as his beloved Margaret's favorite battle cry slipped from his daughter's mouth.

"It does indeed." He may just be forgiven his sins someday, after all.

"And this Bonnie Marie in Paris, who sends intel about the northern coast of France, is that a person or an organization?" The moment the words reached William's ears, Millie saw a storm return to his eyes. She didn't know what lay beneath this particular stone, but her instincts yelled that there was danger in lifting it. It was time to retreat for both their sakes.

Holding a hand up, she said, "Forgive my curiosity. I can smell cinnamon. That means there must be oatmeal on the stove. Let's go."

She took her father by the crook of his arm, and they made their way to the dining room.

He asked, "What are you doing here anyway? I know the food is bad in the mess, but this is a long way to travel for a bowl of oatmeal with no butter or sugar."

Ladling the greyish porridge from a silver tureen, Millie answered, "We all went dancing last night, and this morning I took a walk with my camera. I wanted to process the film and see if anything turned out."

"I thought you had put your project aside for now," William said. He had noticed a bit more color in his daughter's cheeks and had hoped she was settling into her new work. It baffled him to think that a simple early morning walk with her camera could be so therapeutic. He hoped the intrigue and rush that came from solving a puzzle and saving the day would come to satisfy if not thrill her too. She didn't love it like he did and possibly never would. And deep within him, the pesky voice that served as his conscience pleaded, "Why have you taken her dreams from her?" He barely heard and quickly dismissed its concerns. *When the Germans are back in their cage, she can get on with things—if she still wants to.*

Millie lifted the roll of exposed film. "Not a well-meaning woman anywhere to be found on this film. These are just shots of the—" she quickly substituted the word *neighborhood* for the phrase the *walk from Elliot's*. "I just wanted to disappear in my own world for a change."

"In that case, have at it." He wiped the corners of his mouth and placed the monogrammed linen napkin on the highly polished table. "I'm just here to clean up a bit. I have to head back to the War Rooms shortly."

"Is it about the plans to bomb Peenemunde?" Millie asked, pushing back her chair.

William lifted an eyebrow. "What have they told you at RAF Medmenham?"

"Nothing much, just that they will bomb sooner rather than later and to keep searching for the heavy sites on the coast of France." Millie knew her father had more information than she did, and that Bonnie Marie was the one supplying him with intelligence. "But we don't know what we're looking for. Railway tracks and large concrete installations aren't much to go on."

"No one does. We've never imagined these kinds of weapons before. But they are out there—the Nazis are inventing them. I have every confidence that you will crack this thing. Just keep at it. We are all counting on you." He hesitated before getting out of his chair, letting his words of praise settle in. He had to do something to keep her on his hook. Her greatest vulnerability was that she hated to disappoint. His plan depended on exploiting it.

"We see things, but they don't add up. And frequently, the images are too old."

"I'm working on that." He stood, looking his daughter in the eye. "Just remember the real trick isn't to destroy them all. It's to stay a step ahead. Everything depends on reclaiming the Continent. Don't lose focus of that."

Millie nodded in understanding.

"What time is your train back to Marlow?" William said.

"Tonight, at eight."

"Then enjoy your time in the dark." He kissed her on the cheek and went on his way. Millie thought to herself, "*I spend my days at Medmenham in the dark.*" A day spent in her darkroom would lighten her.

# CHAPTER TWELVE

RAF Medmenham-Central Intelligence Unit

July 24, 1943

317 days until D-Day

Millie, Red, and Neil circled the scale model of Peenemunde. The details were extraordinary. They scrutinized the minutiae for something that resembled the peculiarities they saw in the photographs taken over the Pas-de-Calais region of France: barracks for the scientist, research building, roads, train tracks, and strange earthen works.

"Will they really bomb it directly? The people who work there are noncombatants, after all." Millie thought of the weekly, sometimes daily trips to bomb shelters here and at RAF Wick. She wondered if their work was all that different from that of the scientists at Peenemunde.

Red answered before she could finish. "Are they? They are conceiving, designing, and building prototypes for the most dangerous weapons ever known to man." He pointed to the mosaic of photos affixed to the wall of their office.

Pinned to the wall next to Millie's desk was a copy of an image that matched parts of the model perfectly. In it, two perfectly formed rockets lay horizontally on a vehicle in the confines of an elliptical earthwork, waving at her with the three radial fins at their bases. In the middle of the ring, a long shadow crept to the ellipse's edge. It was cast by another rocket standing on end. A large concrete pad supported it. The higher-ups told them to look for a hole of some kind from which the rocket might squirt. From the images they collected, it appeared all the Germans needed was a flat, hard bit of ground.

"Think of the day one of these rockets makes it to London. One of those so-called scientists will likely be the one who pushed the button. The place needs to be bombed, and the masterminds with it."

"Maybe this is something." Neil, always uneasy with tension in their little group, took an image off one of his many stacks and showed an enormous concrete dome near a known chalk quarry in France to Millie and Red, adding a piece to the puzzle himself. "What do you think this might be?" He traced along the railroad tracks leading into the structure.

Millie went along with the diversion, grateful to Neil for giving her a way out of the conversation. Of course, the place had to be bombed and the scientists with it. If not, they would just begin again deeper in the belly of the Nazi machine.

"I have no idea. Could it be part of the Nazi defense works?" Millie said.

He pointed to a pin he placed in the map of France on the wall beside his desk. "It's too far inland."

"You think it has to do with the rockets?" Millie felt an energy building between them.

"I do. Look at this." He took out his ruler and slide rule and made a few calculations. The concrete pad in Neil's photograph from France matched the one in Millie's photograph from Peenemunde and the one built to scale in the center of the model of Peenemunde.

Millie and Red grabbed rulers of their own and double-checked Neil's math. The pads were indeed the same size.

"This could be how they plan to store and subsequently launch the rockets," Millie said, circling the emerging dome and adjacent launch pad. "The construction looks nearly complete."

"I know, but it's the only one I've found." Neil went back

to the map. The dome stood in the northern tip of France, and the only thing between it and London was the narrowest bit of the English Channel. "There should be more in this area. It's within reasonable firing distance, but this dome won't hold a catastrophic number of weapons, and they wouldn't put them all in one place. Right?"

Looking at the map with Neil, Millie thought back to the notes she found while sorting papers on her father's desk. She had seen the words Wissant, Marquise, and Watten written in Bonnie Marie's correspondence. They hadn't meant anything to her then, but skimming the area around Neil's finger, she realized they were towns in northern France.

As if Red had read her mind, he put a hand on Neil's back and said, "It's as good a place to look as any. I'll fetch coffee from the mess. Millie, you get to the print library, and let's see what else we can find before we send our weekly update to Ham."

# CHAPTER THIRTEEN

RAF Medmenham-Central Intelligence Unit

August 17, 1943

293 days until D-Day

Three weeks had passed since Churchill ordered strikes on Peenemunde, but still it stood. Of course, an attack of that magnitude required planning and good weather, but their continued research had shown Millie the extent of the destruction the Germans imagined there, and now she wanted it razed to the ground.

While her team waited for news, the search for the domes, or what they now called heavy sites, continued. After digging through thousands of photographic pairs, they identified six sites that seemed complete and had marked five other construction sites as places of interest for continued photographic cover.

After her shift, she biked straight to Marlow's phone booth. The watching and waiting were wearing her down. She decided to call Aggie in Wick for a moment of escape. She had the necessary change in her satchel. She only hoped she didn't have to wait too long in the queue.

To her delight, the booth stood empty. She fed the phone with a tuppence to connect the call. She propped her feet on the phone booth door, glad she had decided to wear trousers, while Mrs. Drummond checked to see if Aggie was in the Servants' Hall. Aggie had been going to Teaghlach to help with the evacuees when she could. Millie crossed her fingers and waited.

"I'm so glad you caught me here." Aggie always talked a bit too loudly on the phone, but tonight Millie had to hold the phone away from her ear.

"Why are you yelling?" Millie said.

"Ferguson has the wireless turned up too loud, and the boys from London are making a fuss."

"What are they reporting?"

Aggie listened for a moment. "Something about successfully bombing a German town on the Baltic Sea. I think they said Peenemunde."

"Are they saying why?" It surprised Millie that both the War Office and her old stomping grounds, the Ministry of Information, allowed the target's name to be released.

"No, just that we took a large lumber of losses. Why?" Aggie said.

"No reason," Millie said it like a shrug of the shoulders. Aggie worked the telephones at RAF Wick and didn't have any idea what Millie actually did for the Air Force. "You know I like the news."

"But usually only when it involves women."

"Fair enough." Millie slipped another coin into the phone just as Aggie started yelling again.

"Mr. Ferguson, please turn the wireless down. I'm trying to talk to Millie."

Aggie must have put a hand over the mouthpiece halfway through because all the sounds started to muddle.

"Millie? Are you still there?"

"Yes." Millie got to her feet, anxious to find a radio while wondering how to get off the call without raising Aggie's suspicions. "What was that all about?"

"The wireless is reporting that two hundred and ninety of our boys didn't make it home from the raid," she said. "Ferguson thinks I should go over to the base. He saw the bombers fly out earlier. He offered to drive me."

Millie knew bombing Peenemunde meant risking lives, but almost three hundred men were gone. *Will there ever be good news again?*

"He's right—you should check in." It was just the break she needed. *Thanks, Ferguson.* "And Aggie, keep your head up. The Germans know where RAF Wick is."

"I remember."

She rode straight back to RAF Medmenham. If the BBC had the news, they would have assessment photographs soon. She needed to keep busy to keep her mind from wandering to Peter, Callum, and Elliot, any of whom might have been sent to take pictures of the damage.

At the back door, she found Peter leaning against the wall smoking a cigarette. There was a pile of butts at his feet. He had been waiting for a while and, it would seem, anxiously.

Millie tipped her back to the wall, scooting so close to her tender-hearted brother no light could have shown through.

"Bad day?"

"Just a bad wait."

Without looking Peter's way, Millie forced herself to ask a question she didn't want the answer to, so she skirted it just a bit. "What are you waiting for?"

Peter laid his head on her shoulder. "Not what, who."

Millie swallowed hard. If Peter was here, it could only be one person. "Have it your way, who?"

"Callum. He's been sent to photograph Peenemunde."

"Okay." It was all Millie could manage. She forced herself to stay composed, though inside she began to shrivel. There was no acceptable reason for her to overreact.

"Will you be okay?" Peter squished his last cigarette under the heel of his boot.

"It was going to be one of you, the way my life is going." She stepped in front of Peter and stood toe to toe. "I am glad it wasn't you."

"Aren't you going to ask about your beloved?" Peter pressed his forehead to hers just before the jab.

"Is Elliot flying?"

"He is, but I didn't ask where."

"You really can be a shit." She punched Peter in the arm.

"Will the two of you knock it off?" It was Neil coming back to RAF Medmenham, presumably for the same reason Millie had. "Peenemunde has been bombed. Red is going to need us."

Millie hugged Peter and whispered in his ear, "Let me know when he gets home."

"Will do. Sorry for the news, but I thought…"

Millie cut him off. "You were right. Now off with you."

Walking up to their nest of an office, Millie felt the weight of Peter's news with every step. Her life had been filled with loss, but this was one she wasn't sure she could bear. She continued onward. Every time her foot hit the ground, she told herself, *Callum will be just fine.*

"The news of the bombings is out." She busted through the doors of her group's little corner of the world. She feigned excitement, unwilling to let them see what she felt was inappropriate concern. She needed to ask herself where her worry for Elliot was, but she wasn't that brave. At least not yet.

"Yes." Ham's face looked grim. "And the death toll is high."

She walked over and rested a hand on his shoulder, glad to have an occupation. At times like these, he resembled her father. "What can I do, sir?"

He handed her a box of photos. "Let's see if we have to send the boys who lived back."

Millie opened the box to find damp photos, here, at RAF Medmenham. That means they came from RAF Benson. She checked the traces and found his number, 73B78. Callum was back! Her knees threatened to give way, so she rushed to the nearest chair. "Why didn't the phase one interpreters look these over?" she spat out, but on the inside, she was shouting for joy.

"They did, but I want us to decide what we hit and what

we didn't, not those kids at the airfield."

"Hey, I used to be one of those kids." Millie took the chance to lighten the mood so it matched her own.

"Get to looking, young lady," he said, as if he were swatting her with a switch. It was just the spark they needed to get through the work. Things came at them so fast, there was never time to rest, just to keep going.

Millie began poring over the images, fighting the urge to go to RAF Benson and see Callum for herself. Red and Neil joined her. The three of them rarely kept to their official schedule. She could go if she wanted to, but they needed her here, just as the Royal Air Force had needed those bombers and Callum flying over Peenemunde. Knowing he was safe would have to be enough.

They examined the once pristine and exacting structures in three dimensions with their stereoscopes. Some were left jagged, others leveled. Pock marks covered the earth. Allied bombers had succeeded in decimating the launch testing sites. The bombardiers must have dropped thousands of tons of explosives perfectly on target—ensuring they wouldn't have to go back.

Red looked up from his work. "A chap from Bomber Command told me they threatened to send them back if they didn't get the job done. Looks like the threats improved their aim."

"Red's right. There's not much left, sir." Millie said to Wg. Cmd. Thomas.

"That, at least, is good news."

"What's the bad news, sir?"

"Hitler knows we've been watching now. The rockets won't be so easy to find next time."

# CHAPTER FOURTEEN

RAF Medmenham-Central Intelligence Unit

August 23, 1943

287 days until D-Day

Carrying a plate filled with what could barely be described as food, Millie scanned the dining hall for Hazel. She found her sitting alone in the far back corner of the room, taking deliberate bites of her lunch. She joined her, and at first, they sat in comfortable silence.

"We had the strangest order today," Hazel finally spoke. Millie stirred her tepid tea and waited for her to elaborate. Hazel worked in Section L and concerned herself with aircraft and aircraft factories. As her tea got cooler, Hazel said nothing. She was considering if breaching protocol to have a work discussion was worth it.

Millie broke the stalemate. "Strange in what way?"

"The note was from your boss Wing Commander Thomas and said that though it wasn't a priority, we should be on the lookout for any odder-than-usual—actually, the note said peculiar—aircraft."

Millie thought back to Lord Cherwell's claim that the pilotless aircraft were sure to be more of a problem than the rockets. They had been looking for them too. To be honest, she and her crew found it difficult to decide whether the intelligence they received, aerial or otherwise, pointed to the self-flying bombs or long-range rockets. It was as if they were working with pieces from two different puzzles with no system for sorting them apart, but they kept at it day and night.

"And why is that strange?" Millie knew she couldn't discuss the matter, so she elected to listen.

"There is nothing to go on. What does he mean by peculiar? This whole business is peculiar."

Millie couldn't admit Ham had told her all he could, and practically all he knew, himself. "They never give us anything to go on." She clinked her tea mug against Hazel's, raising it in the air, and said, "Here's to third phase interpretation!"

"But surely there's more to it than that. I hear the rumors like everyone else. Especially after we bombed Peenemunde. They say they were building hideous weapons there. Plus, Ham works closely with the War Cabinet, and they get information from every direction. Who knows what they know? We have ears and eyes, and for what it's worth, feet and hands scouring the Continent for intelligence. So why don't they tell us what they want us to look for?"

Millie thought again of the dispatches from Bonnie Marie and others in her father's study. She hated that she couldn't tell her friend what she knew. That the weapons were grave. That they did exist. But that was all they knew for sure.

"I'm sure they will tell you what they can when they can." Millie put a hand over her friend's. This war took things from everyone. Right now, it toyed with Hazel's peace of mind.

"But will it be in time?" Hazel snatched her hand back, sending a fork spinning to the floor.

"In time for what?"

"In time to destroy the disastrous devils before the Germans use them to attack." Hazel's hands trembled.

"Are you really so frightened?" Millie slid her chair closer to her friend. She needed her to calm down and to lower her voice.

"Aren't you?"

Millie put a finger to her lips as a quiet warning.

"If you believe the talk, these weapons are unimaginable. Everyone I love lives in London, and you just know she will be the target. We killed forty thousand civilians this summer in Hamburg with Operation Gomorrah. Why did they wait so long to bomb Peenemunde?"

"Taking out Peenemunde was risky for our bombers. It was too deep behind enemy lines, and it was well fortified; plus, the attack killed thousands." Millie hurried to add, "At least that's what the papers say." She put a gentle hand on her friend's slumped shoulder.

Hazel sat up. "They're planning to send those things over here to kill innocent people, Millie. I say better them than us."

"If this job has taught me anything, it's that there are no easy solutions. Someone, or perhaps lots of someones, is going to pay a price no matter the choice."

As she spoke the words, a man on the opposite side of the room sat up a bit taller. He could see their ill-fitting clothes and the dark shadows under both the women's eyes. He wondered who the blond gal was and what section she worked in. As for the other one, the one with the wild black curls, he hoped she would have the fight to finish this task he had assigned her.

# CHAPTER FIFTEEN

---

**RAF Medmenham-Central Intelligence Unit**

**August 23, 1943**

287 days until D-Day

William sat alone in the back corner of the mess hall like someone who wanted to blend in. The trick of an old spy. He saw a room filled with worn spirits with fires that still burned deep within. It reminded him of his time spent in the halls of the prisoner of war facility during the Great War. Not a day passed that heads weren't smashed together, plotting and planning ways to escape, to find materials and information they might steal, or how many Germans they might kill on their way out. He had the scars to prove it. They had managed to beat them last time. He prayed they would do it again.

"This is a surprise." Millie joined him. He pretended to be engrossed in some typed report. No one could know their connection.

"Do you happen to have a copy of the *Times* or the *Daily Telegraph* in that ancient briefcase of yours? I will give you a week's wages in exchange for them," Millie said. "It's been weeks since my hands have smelled of newspaper ink."

William reached into his tattered leather bag and pulled out both newspapers, hiding his smirk. She always was the most curious of his children—his favorite and most painful to be around since the loss of Margaret. If he had stayed close to her, would he be doing this to her now?

"Keep your money." He pushed the papers across the table along with a small brown paper sack. Millie peeked inside to find sugar. She looked up to see her father's tender eyes. Millie wet her pinky finger and stuck it into the white granules loose on the bottom of the bag. They melted on her tongue, filling her mouth with sweetness for the first time in ages.

"Thank you for that. And for these." She put the morning edition of the *Times* to her nose and took a deep breath. The smell of the ink and dust combined with leather and cigarettes reminded her of easier times.

"Anything in there you don't already know?" William said, eyes averted, not trusting his audience even here on friendly ground.

"These days, I only know about rockets, flying bombs, and would-be launchers." She dropped one of her precious sugar cubes into her full cup of tea and took a sip as she scoured the paper for photographs. There was a picture of Allied soldiers fighting to liberate Sicily. The photographer didn't take time to compose a story, so his images only showed chaos. And, of course, there wasn't a single image of a woman, apart from the propaganda images placed there by the Ministry of Information.

She folded up the pages and began using them as a coaster. "Is it that bad?"

"I don't suppose. It's just disappointing. Look at all of the women here. Why can't the world know how amazing they are and how they will help bring this war to an end?"

William lifted her tea mug and put the paper back in his briefcase, buying himself a moment to think. His concerns were immediate and she, like her mother, was always fighting for a faraway victory. Where was her sense of urgency? He needed her to focus. He needed her at her best, worrying as much about the threat the rockets posed, if not more than who will ultimately get credit for the find. He understood from Margaret that his was a convenient position as it was as likely as not to be a man who got all the glory, but how could that possibly matter now. German bombs didn't care whose head they dropped on.

Since there was no purchase in making his argument, he side-stepped the question as he usually did. And unlike her mother, Millie willingly followed him. One day he would have to let her off his leash, or all that he loved about her might be lost.

"Are you on duty?"

"Just got off my shift."

"Isn't there somewhere else you can go?"

"Why?"

"Because from the looks of you, anywhere else would do you some good."

William got to his feet. He wanted to kiss the tenacious creature in front of him on the top of her head and insist she go outside and play like he had when she was a child. But...

"Are you going to tell me why you're here?"

"Nope. Now get out of here. That's an order."

# CHAPTER SIXTEEN

RAF Medmenham-Central Intelligence Unit

August 23, 1943

287 days until D-Day

William left Millie and entered the ground floor office of Wing Commander Douglas Kendall, the conductor of all interpretation at RAF Medmenham, just as the meeting started. Wg. Cmd. Thomas, his daughter's supervisor, sat in front of Kendall's desk in one of the chairs. William took a seat in the other.

"You summoned me?" William said.

"We did." Kendall didn't call him by name, and neither did Ham. They had played this game for a while and weren't exactly sure what William called himself these days.

"Sandy filled us in on the Bornholm wreckage. Do you think it's the weapon they found at Peenemunde?"

William pulled his chair closer and picked up a pen. He drew a torpedo-like object with wings on a ramp. "The reports I'm receiving from the ground are that this isn't the rocket you've been searching for. Instead, they think it may be the self-flying kind." He was loath to admit Lord Cherwell may have been right about the greater harm.

He pointed to the drawing and continued, barely speaking above a hush.

"According to witnesses."

"Can they be trusted?" Ham, who needed to see a thing to believe it, interrupted.

"May I finish?" William peered at Ham over his glasses, the constant doubting growing tedious. He had been at this since these boys were in nappies. They needed to trust that he knew what he was doing. Though he never trusted anyone.

"You may." Kendall walked around his desk to get a better look at the drawing.

"According to witnesses, a pilotless aircraft approached Bornholm from Peenemunde at considerable speed. The aircraft found at the crash site had no motor or propeller, nor was there room to carry anyone. Where the pilot's seat would normally be," William pointed at the drawing, "there was a complicated apparatus which resembled the inside of a radio receiver. An eyewitness reported a humming sound before the crash."

It was then Ham's turn to point, this time at the ramp. "My folks are seeing miniature runways aimed at London on the film we are getting out of France."

"Why have you drawn wings?" Kendall took the drawing in hand.

"We hear chatter out of Denmark about a winged rocket."

Kendall tore the drawing to bits and dropped them in his ashtray before burning them.

"And what do you hear from your gal in Paris?" Kendall asked, taking his seat.

"The report from France mentioned a Colonel Max Wachtel is reportedly in the process of creating a regiment that would have its headquarters in Amiens. They plan to operate one hundred and eight catapults located in the Pas-de-Calais region. The Germans expect the sites to be fully operational by November—when the catapults will be capable of firing a bomb every twenty minutes."

"How do you keep it all straight?" Ham walked to the cupboard on the back wall. "May I?"

Kendall nodded, and Ham poured them all a drink.

William took a sip and shuddered. Even the quality of the

booze was affected by the war. "I just take it as it comes. Word is we will start bombing the heavy sites soon."

"I don't see how we are going to make a dent. Those domes are massive," Ham said.

"Well, maybe we can at least slow them down. Kendall, how are plans for Operation Overlord coming?" William said, keenly aware that these men saw things in absolutes rather than in degrees. He understood that victory in this marathon would be measured in inches, not miles. He just needed to keep them all moving forward.

"Fine, I guess. But if these catapults of yours or the rockets Bodyline found start firing, all the planning in the world won't help," Kendall replied.

"Has a date been set for D-Day?"

"I couldn't say."

William knew he wouldn't or at least shouldn't say and wondered why he had tested him. As far as he knew, the date and location had yet to be determined. There was still time.

"Very well. I'd better get back to it. Unless you need something else." William was on his feet.

"Until next time." Kendall and Ham finished their drinks. William left his glass half full on Kendall's desk.

# CHAPTER SEVENTEEN

Boyton House

August 30, 1943

280 days until D-Day

Caffeine and sugar coursed through Millie's veins as she made her way back to her room. The day was dreary, and she had planned to spend her day off back in bed catching up on much-needed sleep, but she was wide awake. She found Hazel just waking up. She was staring under Millie's bed.

"What's all that?" She pointed to the boxes lined up against the wall under her bed.

"Mostly photographs."

Hazel pushed up and sat on the edge of the bed. Millie handed her a mug of tea sweetened with one of the cubes her father gave her the week before.

"Like the ones you took the day of the strafing."

"That's right."

"May I see them?" Hazel set her tea on the bedside table and stood up on her bare feet.

"I can't see why not."

Millie reached past the boxes and fished around for her leather portfolio; she stored her best shots safely within its folds. Across her bed, she laid out an image of a girl in a bombed-out bookstore reading a book, the same girl jumping into her mother's arms, a close-up of Callum smoking a cigarette with an anonymous member of the Home Guard in Wick, women working in a laundry, women tending the victory gardens in Kensington Park, and nurses tending the wounded one morning during the Blitz.

Hazel shuffled past the impromptu gallery. She stopped in front of the one of the girl reading. "Haven't I seen this before?"

"Probably. I worked for the Ministry of Information before I joined the WAAF. They used the photograph for a poster in the early days of the war."

"Why did you quit? You're very good." Hazel said, showing Millie her own work.

"My father and Peter pressured me to do more. I put up a fight for the first few months of the war. Taking pictures is like breathing to me."

"So, I ask again, why did you quit?" Hazel picked up the recognized shot and reached for her tea as she studied it.

"My nanny, her name was Clara, was killed in the Blitz. I was the first to find her bombed-out flat. I missed a chance to have one last dinner with her because I wanted to take pictures of the wreckage." Millie reached for her locket. "It felt frivolous doing what pleased me when I could be doing more to stop the Germans from attacking us. If I had kept our dinner date, she might not have even been home when the bombs crushed her flat."

"You can't blame yourself. War equals death. My brother died in the Battle of Britain." Her words were little conciliation to Millie's guilty heart. "She gave you the locket?"

Millie looked down to see her fingers working her precious possession, dropping her hand. "Yes." She wanted to say more but the words stuck in her throat.

"May I have a look inside?" Hazel reached a hand gently in Millie's direction.

Opening the locket, Millie nodded yes.

Hazel looked at the two images. In one, Millie was a child held by a woman with whom she shared a striking resemblance. In the other, she found Millie, the young woman, with an arm draped around the neck of someone who looked to be a true friend.

"This is your mother then?"

"Yes, she died two weeks after Clara took that photograph."

Hazel read the words engraved on the back aloud. "Luck favors the Brave!" Watching the drained woman sitting with her now, Hazel didn't see the spirit required to take the images spread out around her. The doubt Clara wrote about in her last letter to Millie had spread to her eyes. Millie began to question if she had enough courage after all.

Remembering the message Clara left behind for her, Millie wondered, for the first time, if Clara had meant for her to put down her camera at all. *Perhaps she wanted me to continue with my work, not the work Father and Peter wanted me to do. Standing up for what I wanted might have been the braver move.* She began to worry that she had, in fact, forgotten how to fly.

"And so, pictures of women," Hazel opened one of the boxes and flipped through the stack of images of women doing perfectly ordinary but essential tasks. "Except, of course, this one of Callum from the day of the strafing."

Millie nodded. "I wanted to tell their stories." Millie picked up the shot of the nurses. There were four in a line wrapping bandages on the wounded, and in the upper right-hand corner, another pair loaded an elderly man into the back of an ambulance. Their billowing sleeves seemed soft against their heavily starched cuffs. Blood, soot, and grime stained their once white aprons after a morning spent in the crushed streets. "Women amaze me. They work quietly and without complaint and never get any credit." She turned the photo to show Hazel. "I wanted to show the world how vital they are." She reached for her loaded camera and took a shot of Hazel before she could object. "How vital you are."

Hazel threw what passed as a pillow at Boyton House at Millie. "Please!"

"What did I say?" Millie tossed the pillow back, a hint of a blush growing on her cheeks. "As I said, women never want any credit."

"What's going on in there?" The matron of the house barged into the room without knocking.

"Just a bit of fun," Hazel said, hiding the pillow behind her back.

"You remember fun," Millie said.

Mrs. Clerie rolled her eyes. "Barely. There is a call for you."

"Thank you." Millie bit at the inside of her lip. The only thing worse than an unexpected call these days was a telegram.

"Remember," Mrs. Clerie followed a running Millie down the hall, "Don't talk too long. There's a payphone down at the pub for that."

Millie nodded, picked up the heavy black receiver, and forced out a hello. A familiar voice responded, "Everything all right there? You sound strange."

Elliot! Relief flooded over her. "All's well here. I thought it might be someone calling to say—"

Elliot interrupted her. "You know better than that. If I get in a mess, I'll put the Spitfire down. I've heard the French resistance is sneaking pilots out through Spain. If I do go missing, look for me there."

Millie took a seat on the floor to give her shaking legs a rest.

"I was hoping you would have time for a spot of lunch before my next flight. I could meet you at the Hare and Hound in about an hour," Elliot said.

They hadn't seen each other since London. Millie couldn't believe it had been almost two months. Truth be told, the only people she had seen since her belated birthday trip were Hazel and the men in her section. The search for rockets and pilotless aircraft was relentless, but today she would put it aside.

"You bet." Millie wanted to say more, but Mrs. Clerie loomed just two feet away, making a circle in the sky with her finger. Her way of telling Millie to wrap up. "See you in an hour?"

"Sounds like a plan to me."

Elliot hung up the phone and rolled over in bed, his arm draping over the redhead he met last night. Peter and Callum had been playing cards at the same pub Elliot found her in, and they both took a keen interest in the fact they had left together. He had planned to spend the day with the exotic American but decided to cut the affair short in case Callum or Peter tried to talk to Millie first.

Millie bounced back into her and Hazel's room and shared her news. Hazel began stacking up the images carefully, treating them like the precious intelligence she handled every day. "These are great. Did you have to stop?"

Millie began changing clothes. "I need to concentrate to do a thing well. I'm glad I put it aside to contribute." Millie hoped Hazel didn't notice the hint of regret in her voice.

"Are you?"

Millie shrugged. Any more talk, and she might drop the mask she had been wearing since she enlisted in the WAAF. Or had she put it on when she said yes to Elliot?

"But you will go back to it, won't you?"

"I hope so. Now braid my hair, so it isn't such a mess when I see Elliot."

# CHAPTER EIGHTEEN

**Boyton House**

**August 30, 1943**

280 days until D-Day

Callum approached Boyton House torn. He wanted desperately to tell Millie that Elliot had taken that American photographic interpreter to bed last night, but it would only cause a fight. Her blind loyalty made her all the more attractive, but it cost her so much. It pained him to watch Elliot manipulate her need to keep everyone happy. She never could stomach a loss. That summer they spent together so long ago, she drove him crazy, saving every bug, bird, and snake they found.

He knocked on the door, resigned to keep his Elliot news to himself. He decided he didn't need to be the bearer of bad news. Besides, he didn't want to ruin his surprise. The gal worked at RAF Medmenham. Millie was bound to find out eventually. Since none of them could talk about their work, personal gossip spread like wildfire.

Mrs. Clerie answered the door. "May I help you?"

"You may," Callum leaned in just a nudge, cocked his head slightly to the left, and laid it on thick. "I'm looking for Millicent Trayford."

"You must mean Millie. May I tell her who is calling?"

"What would you think of keeping it a surprise?" He smiled, showing all his teeth, bouncing his eyebrows up just once. He had used this choreography with great success for years now.

Mrs. Clerie blushed. "I suppose that would be all right. Just wait here."

"There is a young man at the door for you." Mrs. Clerie met Millie coming down the stairs.

"Young man?" Why would Elliot come here when they planned on meeting at the pub?

"Yes, and if you ask me, it isn't proper." She fiddled with her keys, the flush in her cheeks exchanged for a sour mood. "I came to tell you because this one's in uniform, and I thought it might have something to do with your work."

Millie slowed, thinking.

Mrs. Clerie pushed her along. "Don't keep him waiting. It's too early for visitors. I don't want the other girls coming down in their nightclothes to find him at the bottom of the stairs."

From the bottom landing, Millie spied Callum through a front window. She snickered, impressed that Mrs. Clerie made him wait outside. She would die if she knew she had left the son of one of the richest men in Scotland standing out on a damp, hot day. Callum kicked at the gravel in the drive. *He does fill out his uniform well.* Millie bit her lower lip. The RAF blue brings out his eyes.

"What are you doing here?" Millie said, trying to act nonchalant, all the while looking about for Elliot just in case. She hadn't actually seen Callum since he was sent to photograph Peenemunde. Peter had called to tell her he was safe, and she told him she had seen the images. But seeing him, now, standing in front of her worked to soothe her heart like a salve.

Callum hadn't seen her since that night back in July when they went dancing for her birthday. Their plan to have monthly dinners hadn't panned out. He had never seen her so wrung out. "Peter mentioned last night that they were making you take a few days off."

"Wing Commander Thomas insisted we honor the work schedule for now. While there seems to be a break in the intelligence." She checked her watch for the third time and scanned the driveway as if someone might catch her doing something wrong.

"In that case, come with me." He took her by the hand and pulled her toward a parked army jeep.

Millie resisted, planting her feet firmly in the gravel drive. "I'm meeting Elliot for lunch."

*Of course she is. Elliot must have seen me last night at the pub. He wanted to get to her before me and Peter.*

"Surely you can give him a call?" Callum swallowed his rage in disgust. "I have an adventure planned that you don't want to miss." He lifted both eyebrows and smirked, inviting her to come along for a bit of mischief.

"Where were you planning on taking me?" Millie tipped her head, pointing at the jeep parked next to the wall of bikes in Mrs. Clerie's drive.

"I guess you will have to come with me if you want to find out." Callum stepped so close to Millie that she could feel the warmth of his breath on her face. That lighter than air feeling started at her curling toes and began to rise, quickening her heart and blushing her cheeks.

"I can't." She pushed Callum back, letting her hand linger on his chest. She checked her watch, wondering if there might be a way. Releasing a sigh, she said, "I'm sure he is already on his way to the Hare and Hound."

"Couldn't one of the gals," he motioned to the house, "take him a note? I did go to a lot of trouble." It wasn't a lie. He had been on the phone all morning making arrangements.

"I suppose," Millie said, fighting the urge to scream. "RACE YOU!"

His toothy smile returned, "What was that?"

She punched him on the arm. "I said yes. Just promise you will get me back before I need to report for my shift."

Callum wanted to say *forget about work*. He knew she didn't belong there. She belonged behind a camera. But he took the victory. That day, her priorities were work, adventuring with him, and then Elliot, and that was enough.

"Promise." He winked.

Callum waved to the house, and Hazel walked out the door with an overnight bag and Millie's camera.

"You have been busy." Millie couldn't believe he had gone to such trouble and hoped it wasn't written all over her face.

Hazel winked. "I have indeed." She gave Millie a peck on the cheek and slipped her spy camera into her front trouser pocket. "Have a wonderful day, you lucky girl."

"Will do." Millie squeezed her friend, baffled by the fact that no one, at least not Hazel or Aggie or Peter, especially Peter, thought it odd that she would stand up her fiancé in favor of cavorting off to who knows where with Callum. A thought rushed in. *Should I really be with Elliot?* But it slipped away as quickly as it had emerged when Callum honked the jeep.

"Times a-wasting," he yelled.

Millie jumped in the jeep, and they were off.

At the airstrip, they climbed into a waiting plane, engine purring, and motored down the runway for takeoff, but to where? If this was a photo-recon plane, Millie could have made a lovely image of the aerial view. The midday light warmed the terrain, and from this vantage point, the ground looked like a giant quilt. Millie searched the landscape for clues, some landmark that might help her decipher where they were going. Callum remained tight-lipped, looking straight ahead at the soft white view and his gauges.

They flew through a cloud bank which prevented her from seeing the terrain, so she just shouted names over the hum of the propellers. She started with London, but they had been flying too long now for that. *Maybe the beaches near Whitby?* As minutes became hours, she knew every guess was wrong. Callum's face gave nothing away, and he sure wasn't talking.

As they began their descent and left the cloud cover, the jagged edge of Wick's North Sea shore came into view. Millie squeezed Callum's arm, immediately glad she had come. He had brought her to her mother's home. She wouldn't have been able to stop smiling if she tried.

Callum smiled himself, a closed-lipped, crooked smile—his best and truest smile—happy to see Millie coming back to herself and that he had a hand in it. He let down the landing gear expertly and they touched down with a slight bump—effortlessly, as usual.

"Does anyone know we're coming?" Millie watched the young, enlisted man on the field marshal in their plane, her heart pumping with excitement.

"Only Aggie. I called her from the base before we took off. She's meeting us at the guardhouse with a picnic." Callum stepped out of the plane and saluted his fellow airman.

"If she has a picnic, I'll bet all of Teaghlach knows too." Millie skipped to keep up with him. Watching her, happy and light, made Callum glad he hadn't told her about Elliot's indiscretion. He knew it would keep for another day.

"I made her promise not to tell. We don't have enough time for a full-fledged reunion."

He waved at Aggie, who was jumping up and down and waving both arms in the air. It surprised him to see Peter at her side. He hadn't mentioned his plan to whisk Millie away to him last night. They had discussed Millie's wellbeing. She seemed to be wasting away right before their eyes. Someone at RAF Benson must have mentioned it to him when Callum agreed to transport the repaired plane to RAF Wick on his day off. Callum only hoped Elliot didn't find out; it would make things harder on Millie.

Millie broke into a run at the sight of her old friend and her brother, beating Callum to the guardhouse gate. They joined hands and spun around as they had as children so long ago, singing *Ring Around the Rosie* at the top of their lungs. Callum just shook his head. *So much for a quiet arrival.*

They jumped into an old lorry. Millie sidled next to Callum, and Aggie sat on her lap. Callum and Peter shut the doors, and the lorry sputtered to life.

Looking around at the planes, a wave of guilt spread over Millie. She hoped Hazel had delivered her note and that Elliot believed that she had been called back to RAF Medmenham. She wrapped her arms around Aggie and hugged her tight, fortifying herself, refusing to regret coming with Callum. They hadn't had a day like this, well, ever. It was just the kind of day she needed to lift her spirits.

# CHAPTER NINETEEN

Wick, Scotland

August 30, 1943

280 days until D-Day

The crisp green grass of the new lawn at the Old Wick Castle was the perfect place for a reunion. Aggie and Millie walked hand in hand while Callum and Peter hauled the hamper, blankets, thermos, and champagne out of the back of the lorry. Peter pointed with his chin to the wool blanket tossed over his shoulder, indicating that one of the women should take it and spread it out for their luncheon. Aggie and Millie skipped along the cliffs ignoring him, giggling like a pair of school-girls, recreating moments from their childhoods. In an act of pure childishness, Callum dropped his load, tagged Aggie on the shoulder, and yelled, "You're it!" With the game afoot, the four of them ran, bobbing and weaving out of Aggie's touch until she finally managed to graze Peter on the shoulder. Peter scooped her up and ran toward Callum and Millie as if playing a game of rugby. When they finally ran out of steam, they collapsed in a heap and laughed until they wept, grateful for the easy company of old friends.

"How did you explain the picnic to Mrs. Drummond?" Millie asked.

"She didn't pack it. Callum's mom had her driver bring it to the base. I took a peek. I haven't seen oranges or kippers in years."

"And champagne!" Peter exclaimed, popping the cork, taking a slug, and passing the bottle around.

"I'm sure the cook remembered to put glasses in the hamper," Aggie said when the bottle reached her.

"Don't be a party pooper," Callum said. Aggie tipped the bottle in the air and took a swig.

Callum began unpacking the hamper of delights.

"Where did your mother get all of this?" Millie said.

Callum didn't answer. Instead, he twisted an imaginary key in front of his mouth and threw it away.

Millie had her fill of the treats. Between the sunshine and the food, she felt a long-forgotten energy flow through her veins. It felt foreign to her. She slipped off her tunic and rolled up her shirt sleeves, craving more. Callum stretched out on the blanket like the head of the clan, soaking up the summer sun himself. Peter and Aggie followed suit.

After her food settled, Millie rolled over for a nap and felt the Minox in her front pocket.

"Aggie, scoot over closer to Callum and Peter so I can take a picture." Millie's spirits soared when she peered through the tiny viewfinder.

"That's a camera?" Aggie asked. The four-inch by one-inch by half-inch grey metal rectangle box didn't reveal its secret.

"Sure is. Father gave it to me. Spies use them." Millie hadn't felt this high since the day she saw the girl reading near Charing Cross Road. She wondered why she hadn't taken any pictures at RAF Medmenham. It occurred to her that it might be the only way to avoid shriveling up and disappearing before the war ended.

They leaned close to each other and smiled. The light bouncing off the North Sea was perfect. They made silly poses for the next few shots, and then Callum got up and took the camera from her.

"How does this thing work?" he said.

"Just look through the viewfinder to make sure we're in

the shot and push this button." Millie ran over to Aggie, and they stood cheek to cheek. The loose curls framing Millie's face flapped in the wind. Then Peter stepped in between them. Millie looked up to see his beautiful smile, grateful he had come.

"Give someone else a turn, old mate." Peter took the camera from Callum. "How about one of you with Millie?" Everyone noticed the smirk on his face. The matchmakers were up to it again.

Callum wrapped his arms around Millie's shoulders, and she leaned back into him.

"Surely you can do better than that. She's not your grandmother."

Callum shot Peter a glare in reply. Then, with a twinkle in his eye, he swung his arm under Millie's knees and cradled her. Millie held on to his neck and planted a kiss on his cheek.

"You two look perfect together!" Aggie said as Peter took the last shot on the roll. The words set Millie to wiggling, trying to get down. Callum dropped her flat, and the moment was lost. Aggie wished she had kept her mouth shut. Callum was just so easy to love.

Millie started to get up and give him a pop when she got a better idea. She stretched out and rolled down the hill. Following her lead, Peter, Aggie, and Callum joined her. About halfway down, Millie's hair came loose, picking up every loose twig and blade of grass.

They ran and rolled and skipped and just plain frolicked for as long as they could stand it. Their laughter urged them on, and for a brief moment on that summer afternoon, Britain wasn't at war.

Exhaustion overtook them, and they headed back to the blanket for the last few bites of food in the hamper. They lounged like kittens, using each other as pillows. Millie fell asleep to the sound of the crashing waves and the smell of the rich soil.

When Millie woke, her companions were still asleep. Above

the waves, Millie thought she heard the buzzing of a propeller. She jumped to her feet, ran to the cliff's edge, and looked out onto the horizon. Sure enough, in the distance, a plane was approaching. She woke Callum. Wick was no stranger to aerial bombing.

"What is it?" He sat up, rubbing his face.

"A plane is approaching. Do you think it's one of ours?"

Callum fetched a pair of binoculars from the lorry and checked. "You can relax. It's a Spitfire." He handed the glasses over to Millie.

Millie sat down. "Thanks for all of this. I am as happy as I have been in a while."

Callum sat next to her. "This war can't go on forever. You'll be back at this," he handed her her camera, "before you know it. Where will you go first?"

*What a question? And why is he the first person in my life to ever ask it?* Sitting next to him like this, Millie felt effervescent, like the champagne they popped earlier. The feeling gave her the courage to give words to her dreams.

"I'd like to follow the Red Cross nurses through the Continent after we invade."

"That's amazing. How are you going to get out of the WAAF?"

She couldn't believe she was having this conversation. She twisted at her ill-fitting engagement ring, hiding her torn-to-the-quick nails. "I could go ahead and get married. They would have to let me out then."

"And Elliot would be okay with you heading into a war zone?"

"That's the weak link in my plan. If I try to free myself from the Air Force, I will tie myself to Elliot's wishes. Of course, I could go, but he might never forgive me, not to mention my father and brothers." Millie walked over to the cliff's edge.

"Who cares what they think?" Callum said, wishing he had said, "*You could marry me.*"

"I do." How could she explain what it felt like to be left behind? As far as she knew, he had never lost anyone who mattered to him. Millie noticed Peter had opened his eyes and was listening. He gave her a half smile filled with understanding and a touch of guilt.

"Quiet, you'll wake her." Callum pointed to Aggie, who looked like an angel sleeping.

"She is always so innocent." Millie reviewed her laundry list of sins.

"That and content." Peter sat up and wrapped his arms around his knees. "All she ever wanted was to find a young farm boy to marry and have a brood of laughing children like her mum."

"Is this new world all you hoped it would be?" Millie asked Peter, glad to be talking about someone else.

"By and large, but no one gets everything they want," Peter said, peering off into the horizon.

"And what about you, Callum?" Peter said with a knowing, or was it a teasing, glance?

"I'm with you, mate. No one gets everything they want."

"It's hard to think of you wanting," Millie said.

Callum didn't answer her. Instead, he remembered Peter telling him that Millie suffered under the illusion that men have complete freedom—translation: they have everything they want whenever they want it. While that may be true from her point of view, all Callum could think was, "*I can't have you.*"

"What do you want, Callum?" Aggie asked from behind them.

"Yeah, old chum, what do you want that you can't have?" Peter taunted.

"I want to go home, sleep in my childhood bed, and hide from the war a little longer."

Millie didn't know what was happening between Peter and Callum, but the magic of the day had worn off. They loaded up and drove back in silence. When they hit the South Road, Aggie reached for Millie's hand. "Just tell me we're all going to make it through this mess."

"Safe and sound, my sweet friend. Safe and sound," Peter said, reaching his arms around them, squeezing them tight.

# CHAPTER TWENTY



Wick, Scotland

**August 30, 1943**

280 days until D-Day

Peter headed back south straightaway, but Callum and Millie weren't due back until the following day. Callum dropped Millie off with Aggie. She had decided to spend the night with her so as not to cause a fuss at Teaghlach.

Aggie's childhood home was tight and full of children, so she and Millie spent the early evening out in the small but meticulous garden in front of the five-room stone house. The roses' heavy buds weighed down their stems, full of hope and promise. Aggie's younger brother and sisters scattered to their afternoon chores and games, laughing with delight in the hot summer air. The older one tended the piglets while the smaller two played a clapping game near the garden bench where the ladies sat. Millie took a picture, thinking of Peter and the days they spent together on imaginary adventures. She couldn't stop herself singing along with them, "Was the bottom of the deep blue sea, sea, sea."

"That's not right." Aggie stood behind her youngest sister and took hold of her hands, moving them as if she were a puppet.

"I can do it myself." The four-year-old wiggled to free her limbs.

"Do you remember the clapping part?" Aggie said to Millie.

"I think so."

"Then let's show them how to do it."

They stood face-to-face and started the rhyme with their palms together, giddy as the little girls. "A sailor went to sea, sea, sea, to see what he could see, see, see..." Aggie's sisters matched them clap for clap.

And then, out of the corner of her eye, Millie saw a bomber with a yellow engine cowling break through the low-hanging clouds on the horizon, followed closely by an entire squadron. Unlike earlier that day at the picnic, Millie knew immediately they were Germans, and they meant to release their bomb. She picked up one sister. Aggie swooped up the other. They ran for the garden wall. Millie threw herself over the youngsters like a blanket while Aggie sprinted to her brother behind the pig pen.

Millie could hear the bombers above them now. Most of the bomber squadron turned in the direction of the airfield at Wick. She watched, holding her breath, hoping the wayward bomber didn't open its doors and drop its load. But the bomb doors cranked open, and the nauseating whistle of the falling bomb interrupted the plane's hum. She held onto the girls for dear life.

The explosives collided with the ground, shattering all the house's windows simultaneously. Dust and smoke engulfed them, making it difficult to breathe. Large hunks of rock and soil flew through the air. Millie saw flames licking the drive. The girls screamed and cried, grasping at Millie. She held them tight. Rechecking the sky, she watched the lone plane turn for the open water of the North Sea and remembered to breathe.

A thick haze rose from the burning, wet grass, making it hard to see. The bombs didn't hit any buildings, but a truck fell headlamps-first into a pit left by the bomb at the end of the drive.

"Run!" Millie pushed Aggie's siblings in the direction of the house.

The smallest one stumbled into her mother's arms at the

door as Aggie and her brother ran for the fence. They nestled next to Millie before continuing. Millie helped Aggie check the boy for shrapnel wounds.

"You need to get inside." Millie pointed toward Aggie's mother.

The ashen boy sprinted to the door.

"You need to go too," Millie told Aggie, hugging her and pushing her toward the house before taking up her camera. Excitement mixed with terror pulsed through her veins, invigorating her. She was elated.

"That's my dad." Aggie pointed down the lane to the main road. "We have to help him and my brothers."

Millie stood, took two shots, and pulled Aggie forward by the hand. They closed the quarter-mile gap between them and the truck, zig-zagging through the obstacle course of rocks and holes created by the blast, veiled by the slowly lifting cloud of dust.

At the edge of the forty-foot-wide hole in the ground, they heard Aggie's slightly younger brother yelling for help as he tugged at their father. Luckily, the bomb had dropped in front of the truck; it wasn't aflame. Millie sat on the edge of the pit and focused on Aggie's dad through the windshield.

"MILLIE! Put that camera down and help me," Aggie shrieked from the bottom of the hole. She shifted the camera onto her back and lay down on her stomach, offering a hand to Aggie's brother. He waved her off, moving to the other side of the hole to help push his father out of the cab of the truck.

They all managed to crawl out of the pit. Aggie's father struggled to breathe and had a deep gash on his forehead, but they were all alive. Millie took a shot of Aggie tending to her father's head, then lifted her camera in the air.

Aggie had known Millie for years now and had been with her on the day of the strafing. She knew exactly what she was asking. "I know. You need to get to town. Go! Go!" She blew her unlikely friend a kiss and sent up a silent prayer, whispering, "Please, do be careful."

Millie lifted Aggie's bike but hesitated.

"GO!" Aggie yelled.

Millie pedaled as fast as she could, legs aching. She couldn't fathom why this little town remained a target. But today, she wasn't an analyst. Today, she would be the one who showed the world what the Germans could do.

She slid to a stop at the edge of RAF Wick, but there was no sign of an attack there. She continued, confused, her satchel heavy with her camera, bouncing as she pumped the pedals. She patted her hip pocket, assuring herself that her spy camera was there if she needed it.

Just before she reached the bridge to town, a column of thick, black smoke rising from Wick's Bank Row came into view. A cold chill spread down her spine—in this war, civilians had become fair game. Her mind went to the children she used to see playing in front of the newspaper when she was stationed at RAF Wick a few short months ago and still did some photography for the Ministry of Information.

The roads were unpassable, forcing her to run down the river embankment and hide her bike under the bridge. Back on the service bridge, she looked down at Wick. The sky joined her as she wept at the horrendous sight. At the end of the bridge, she saw a police officer standing over his mate, sprawled on top of a pile of rubble, not moving. She shook her head against the reality. *Why attack the town and not the base?*

When she stood a few feet from the officer, the policeman took shape in her viewfinder. His face was damp as his hands worked a pearl rosary. She turned away from his grief for a moment. Then, taking ten steps forward, she continued but stopped, reconsidering. It may have been an unforgivable intrusion, but she had to capture his pain, preserve it as a reminder. So, she walked back and took up her camera, breathing deeply to steady her heart, her breath, her mind. She stepped in as close as she dared; she didn't want him to compose himself. Not yet. This was the story of the day—heartbreak.

Transformed from a victim into an observer, Millie grew numb to the sights, but the inhuman wails struck at her core, making each step further into the dusty, blood-stained street excruciating. All she wanted to do was stop and cover her ears, like a child, but instead, she pushed onward because she needed to make a record.

A pall of black smoke lingered just above the gutted buildings shrouded in fire, and the setting sun left her little light to work with. She checked the light meter. To get a crisp picture would require perfect stillness. She steadied herself on a stoop outside the greengrocer, capturing its dazed owner's wife picking up an onion and putting it back in a crate of potatoes. Squatting, she took a shot of a mother clutching her crying daughter outside their destroyed home. A half a block away, a still, lifeless child, dirt smudged on her cheek, lay, but Millie couldn't bring herself to push the shutter. She stood still, heartbroken and strangely grateful. At least here in the middle of all this horror, Millie felt something. She knew she was alive. She knew her being there mattered.

She coughed to clear the dust and smoke from her throat and composed herself before moving forward, camera ready. Water rushed down the streets from the firemen's hoses, and all around her, people sprang from pile to pile, desperate to answer the prayers for help coming from the souls buried alive. The groans unnerved her, tightening the knot in her stomach.

She tripped over a cast iron skillet and barely caught herself from falling. She should slow down, but she was running out of sunlight fast. *What next?* The buildings closest to the impact burned. The Territorial Army doused the flaming cars and smoldering buildings with water from the river, mixing more smoke with the clouds. But they weren't the only ones working to save the buildings. The women of the town had formed a bucket brigade, throwing water this way and that, doing their part. Millie stepped in, flames warming her face, sending her heartbeat into a full sprint. When she took an image of the woman passing water, she caught the smell of burning flesh. She finished the roll of film but didn't reload. She couldn't.

During her three years billeting in her ancestral home, she came to know these people. They accepted her and did her the favor of not taking her position as the Duchess' heir too seriously. Wick was one big family, indeed. Her shoulders shuddered, and she gave into the sorrow. A high-pitched scream alerted a nearby fireman, and he ran to her, thinking she was the source of the heart-wrenching peal. Millie shook him off, along with her crippling emotions, and followed him into the fray. She simply couldn't record the horror any longer. She had to help.

# CHAPTER TWENTY-ONE

---

Wick, Scotland

August 31, 1943

279 days until D-Day

Millie meandered down Union Street and surrendered to the exhaustion born of digging for people for more than three hours. The echo of the church bells ringing when everyone was accounted for pounded in her ears. Fifteen strikes, ringing over and over again for the fifteen members of their town killed by the German assault—eight of them children. All Millie could think of was the amount of damage that would have been done if one of the rockets she looked for day and night had come. Wick would have had no warning. She knew then if the rockets found their way to Great Britain, the death count would be unimaginable. She needed to see a reassuring face, so she stepped carefully in the darkness, feeling her way down the wall-lined street to the newspaper office.

Despite the wreckage, she could hear the chatter of people mingling in the streets. The door to Mrs. Lyall's, the best spot for fish and chips in town, opened as she passed. Millie was grateful that the place fared so well. The shop was only two blocks away from the worst damage. Millie's shoulders eased away from her ears when she saw the *John O'Groat Journal* sign still swinging from its hooks. The *Groat* had been spared, too. Across the street, she noticed a figure slumping on the wall. It was Callum come to check on her.

Millie wanted to fall into him and have him wrap his gentle arms around her. She leaned next to the wall beside him instead, afraid, or at least unsure how he felt about her and the fact that she was engaged. There were rules about such things, after all.

"Looks like you've been in the thick of it." He offered Millie a stained cotton mechanic's rag to wipe her face, neglecting his own.

"I helped dig for survivors." She waved off the rag. "You?"

"First, I helped search for missing children and then transported the wounded to the hospital." He looked down at her white-knuckled hand clenching her camera. "Are you all right?"

He asked the question instead of taking her in his arms and reassuring her he would keep her safe.

"Fine." Millie didn't dare look up into Callum's face.

"Is that so?" He stroked her gripped hand, sending a charge down her spine. She jerked it back reflexively, looking him straight in the eye. He held his hands up in surrender and slowly reached for her hand again. She kept a close watch as his soft, gentle fingers pried the lens cap out of her hand and secured it on the uncovered lens.

Millie let the camera hang freely about her neck, rubbing her eyes, and tipped her head onto his broad shoulder, allowing the tension to slip from her body. "I can take the sights, Callum, but I'm going to have to learn how to block out the sounds. They're excruciating."

As expected, he said nothing. Instead, he put his face up to the moonless sky, closed his eyes, and just sat, content to be with her. Millie rested beside him until her breathing matched his. *Why was he so good at simply being with her?*

"You're so composed," she said.

"I know we will survive this." He looked down at her.

Millie whipped her head around. "How can you possibly say that after what happened here today? They intentionally killed civilians. This town has no strategic value."

His eyes found hers in the darkness, and he stared for a moment before speaking. "Because I've survived worse."

"What could be wor—" she tried to speak, but he shushed her and patted his shoulder—an invitation.

"There will be time for war stories later. I bet you've got a picture on that roll of film for Mr. Graham to print." He pointed to her camera. "Aggie says it's why you came to town." He got to his feet and offered her a hand up.

"Is that why you're here?" Millie's face was close to his, too close, but she didn't step back.

Callum stroked her hair, imagining thrusting his fingers into her mane and closing the gap between them, but he stopped short. He needed her to be the one to lean in. He waited for the moment to pass and tilted her head forward, brushing a kiss on her forehead, before taking her hand in his.

As they walked side-by-side up the hill to the lorry, Millie noticed a limp in his gait.

"Are you all right?" She turned to him again.

"I will be."

"But your leg?" Looking into his eyes, her heart raced again. *Why won't you just kiss me?* But the real question was why she wouldn't just kiss him. Fiddling with the ring on her left finger, she found her answer—the damn rules.

"I can make it home. Mother is going to kill me when she finds out I didn't come to see her first. Guess stopping by to see the boys at the base was a bad idea."

"I think I'll stay here. A little work will do me good." Millie pointed to the newspaper offices.

"But no one is there."

"I know where Mr. Graham hides the key."

# CHAPTER TWENTY-TWO



The image of the police officer and the one of Mr. McLeod's truck, tail end to the sky, were the best on the roll. Millie worked through the night making plates large enough to fill the top half of the front page, leaving room for two short columns of copy. The Ministry of Information wouldn't let publishers like Mr. Graham report many details, so the images would have to speak for themselves. The *Groat's* readership's home became a battlefield last night. It deserved a moment of attention.

"I took these yesterday." Millie handed a drunk Mr. Graham her proofs. After three years of using his newspaper offices as a part-time photographer for the Ministry of Information, she understood better than most that its surly editor/publisher wouldn't want to print them, but she stood her ground. Persistence was how she coaxed her nanny Clara into taking her to the science museums rather than fancy teas, her tutors into teaching her calculus instead of how to balance family books, and Mr. Graham to print a few of her images in the *Groat* over the years. Persistence was the only way she would get this image in the paper—so she didn't budge.

He didn't yell right away. He and Eldon were considering the proper placement of a Ministry of Food leaflet titled, *What's in the Larder: 12 ways to use leftovers.*

"What do you expect me to do with those?" he grunted around his soggy cigar after taking the paper images.

"I expect you to print them." She attempted forcefulness. "The Germans leveled our home and spirits yesterday. It's our job to report that fact. These images will do it better than volumes of words." She fought the urge to bite the inside of her lip, bracing herself for his legendary fury.

"That is why women have no business in a newsroom." He had said something along these lines the day he came searching for Assistant Section Officer M. Trayford and discovered that the MOI wanted him to use a female photographer for a piece they expected him to print in his paper.

"Excuse me?" She hated that her voice was shaking.

"Women are too passionate. The news is about facts."

Millie waved the proofs in his face. "It is a fact that Officer Smith was weeping as he surveyed the home he loves in pandemonium. It is also a fact that Mr. McLeod's lorry was set on end when it fell into a chasm created by a German bomb."

Mr. Graham grabbed the dangling photographs. His eyes began to well up, taking them in for the first time. He stepped too close to her, but Millie held her ground. He snarled and tore the proofs down the middle. "That's what I think of your work." He stormed to the door and flung it open. "Aren't you supposed to be headed back to wherever they sent you last spring?"

She collapsed in a nearby chair. Mr. Graham was going to hold off publishing the candid images out of spite. Aggie told her that her departure upset him, which was hard to believe, but she had no idea it made him this angry.

Eldon placed a consoling hand on her shoulder and handed her a note. "His best friend was killed yesterday. He was Smith's father. Plus, he's missed you."

She dropped her head in her hands. "It's just too awful."

Eldon gently lifted her chin, and she realized she needed to repeat herself so he could read her lips. He scribbled another note. "There will be time for tears later. We have a deadline."

Millie pushed out a cleansing breath and spoke clearly, looking right at a waiting Eldon. "What's next?"

He rolled the heavy drum over her plates, pulling two new proofs, and scribbled another note. "We need to unlock the front page and reset it."

He held up each image in turn, his way of asking which photo to use. The weight on her chest lifted, and she hugged Eldon, crushing the images. She pointed to Aggie's father's truck. She wanted to make peace with her old friend, Mr. Graham. The image of the officer, his friend's son, had undoubtedly set him off.

Eldon unloaded the type galley and began rearranging the lines of type. With a composition stick in her left hand, Millie picked up sixty-point serif letters, building a new headline, before helping Eldon with his tedious task.

Mr. Graham returned to find them locking in the new front page and pulling a proof. He reeked of whiskey and grief. His eyes scanned the headline, *Bombs Miss Target,* and continued over to the two columns of type bookending Millie's photograph.

He looked up and patted Eldon on the back. He picked up a composition stick and set a subheading: *A small town survives.* He removed two wedges to make room for the typeset and pulled another proof, handing it to Eldon for his approval.

He was going to run the photo. Millie stood utterly still on the outside but on the inside jumped for joy. Then, without a word to Millie, Mr. Graham sat down at his typewriter. He swiped his fingers over the keys and then pulled them into a fist.

"Run down to Lyall's and get me a pot of strong coffee," he said. Millie had a quizzical look on her face, so he added, "It will sober me up faster than any breakfast tea."

Millie returned to a room filled with the clacking sounds of the typewriter. Mr. Graham's fingers moved so furiously, it was a wonder the typebars didn't tangle. She poured a cup of the rich-smelling brew and set it on the desk, but Mr. Graham didn't stop writing. She stepped back and joined a waiting Eldon.

Finally, he ripped the article from the platen, removed the piece of copy paper sandwiched between the white pages, and offered the fresh story to Eldon and Millie.

The paragraphs of his editorial revealed a new man to Millie. Mr. Graham wrote poetically of pain, loss, friendship, and resilience. He described a tenacious people who would emerge victorious from this hideous chapter of human history if they could keep hold of their humanity, even if they were learning to speak German.

Millie bit at the inside of her lip, choking back tears, unwilling to show him her *female frailty*. Before she got to the bottom of the page, he barked, "We'll run it on the back page with your other picture."

Before she could explode with words of fawning appreciation, Eldon threw the clutch of the linotype, filling the room with the deafening sound of the machine roaring to life. Millie hit the composition table with her fist with a tight-lipped smile.

She had done it! She stood up for what she believed and won—and it felt better than she could ever have imagined.

She lifted the stack of freshly printed papers, still damp from the press, to her nose and took a deep breath. She belonged to this smell now: the ink, the paper, the melted lead. She wanted to bottle it, so she could wear it like perfume. It radiated from Eldon, too, as he swung his truck around the loop at the end of Teaghlach's drive and put the car in park. Millie leaned over and hugged him before sliding out of the lorry.

"I'll get your bike, Lady Millicent," Mr. Ferguson greeted her. "I'm glad you decided to stop by before Callum took you back to Marlow." Millie knew they all knew she was here. Wick was simply too small to keep that kind of secret, especially from Fiona.

Ferguson had been waiting for her. Eldon made her promise to let him take her to Teaghlach so her grandmother Fiona could see for herself that she was in one piece. She tucked the newspapers under her arm and made the sign for thank you, almost dropping her load. Mr. Ferguson closed the ancient wooden door and turned on the vestibule lamp. He was a stickler for the blackout rules. "Callum is waiting with the others in the kitchen. He says you need to get back tonight."

Millie's heart lifted.

"Did you finish the paper?" Fiona stood in the doorway to her rooms. Millie ran into her grandmother's outstretched arms, crying. Fiona gave Millie a moment before guiding her into her rooms and putting her in a chair by the fire. Walking to the grand piano, she picked up an oval blue velvet box. After handing it to Millie, she sat down herself.

"Well, go on, open it," she urged.

Millie unlatched the thin box to find that it wasn't a box at all but a picture frame holding three pieces of faded fabric. Embroidered on the silk was the date June 1862. She tilted the image under the light. Looking back at her was a young girl with rosy cheeks.

"That's my mother, Marcia Lucia. She craved adventure too. Perhaps it's genetic." She wrinkled her nose before she looked at the photo. "Those are samples from her wedding outfit. She met her husband, my father, on the day of her wedding." Fiona's eyes sparkled. "She always had a cause. The last was the fight for women's suffrage. Sadly, she didn't live to see us get the vote. Thankfully, your dear mother did."

Millie reached for the locket hiding under her blouse.

She returned the fabric to its home and closed the box. "Why are you telling me all of this?"

"Because she always found a way to pursue her dreams. But even doing what you love comes at a price."

Fiona took one of the papers from Millie and looked at the images on the front and back. "You're sad now, and the night was horrifying to be sure, but was it worth it?"

Millie's brain pounded from exhaustion. It had been worth

it. She wondered if her great-grandmother or mother would say the same. She also wondered why there was always some trade-off. *This photo was taken eighty years ago. Why is it still so hard, especially for women?* Millie extended her arm, attempting to return the box to Fiona.

"You keep it. As a reminder."

"Of what?"

"That you have her tenacity and pluck."

The question remained; would she remember that when it mattered most? Moreover, would she remember that standing up to Mr. Graham had worked, and it hadn't cost her anyone that genuinely mattered to her? Quite the opposite.

# CHAPTER TWENTY-THREE

Teaghlach

**August 31, 1943**

279 days until D-Day

The rustle of turning newsprint greeted Fiona and Millie as they walked into the Servants' Hall for tea. They were all reading the *Groat*, bookended by Millie's photographs of the bombing. Millie felt sick thinking on the losses but felt proud to have been there to tell their story.

"You look a little better than the last time I saw you." Callum put down his copy of the paper as Millie approached him and Aggie. "Well done, you." His words alerted the room to her presence, and everyone jumped to their feet, applauding.

"The miracle of it is reading a heartfelt article from Graham," Ferguson said. "He hasn't written like this since before the last war."

"I'm not going to tell you how many cups of coffee I siphoned down his throat in the process." Millie sat down with her friends, and the staff got back to their reading. "The pictures are good, aren't they?" Millie said.

"The standing ovation wasn't enough praise," Callum said. He hated that she worked so hard for others' approval.

"I think I deserve a little of the credit." A cheeky smile grew on Aggie's face as she pushed Millie a bit. "I was the one down in that pit helping my dad while you held back taking the cover shot."

Millie lifted an imaginary glass of champagne and cried, "Three cheers for Aggie," her equilibrium restored now that the attention had shifted to someone else.

"That'll do." Aggie pulled Millie's arm down. "Isn't it time we get the two of you back to the base?" Aggie wasn't any better at being the center of attention than Millie.

When they arrived at RAF Wick, a crowd was milling about. Callum dropped Aggie off at the main entrance because her shift was about to start, and Millie rode with him to the hangar.

"The Faithful Annie you're taking back is fueled up and ready to go," an airman Millie didn't recognize told Callum. "It's not nearly as nice as the two-seater you flew in yesterday."

Millie shuffled toward the hangar, looking forward to the nap she planned on taking on the flight back to RAF Benson, but stopped in her tracks when she heard Aggie screaming behind her.

"Millie, Millie. Oh my God, Millie!" Aggie ran as fast as she could.

The last thing a person wanted to hear in war times was someone yelling, "Oh my God!" Millie steeled herself for what was sure to be bad news. When Aggie reached her, she took Millie into her arms and squeezed the breath out of her. Millie tried to pull away, but Aggie wouldn't let go.

"You have to let go of her and tell her what has happened." Callum was instantly at Millie's side.

Aggie pushed back but still held on to Millie. "Elliot didn't make it back from his sortie." She gasped for air between words. "Peter called ahead." Another breath. "For now, he's classified as missing in action." Another breath. "So, there is still hope."

Millie broke Aggie's hold and fell to the ground as everything began to spin. This can't be happening. Not again. "I should have stayed behind. I should have had lunch with him. I shouldn't have lied to him." She looked up at Callum accusingly. "I should never have come with you."

Callum knelt beside her. He reached out to stroke her hair, but Millie slapped away his hand. Callum put up his hands in surrender, a move he seemed to be perfecting, and spoke. "Elliot was flying last night either way. Night flying is riskier, and you know it. But now that the bombers go out at night, we have to follow with our cameras."

Millie got to her feet, ready to blame Callum for it all, but found she couldn't breathe. She bent over and tried to catch her breath, but it didn't help, so she collapsed back down to the ground. She should be crying. *Why can't I cry?*

"Millie!" Aggie said.

"I can't breathe."

"Someone get her a bag." Aggie joined her on the ground. "She's hyperventilating." Callum ran to the cockpit of the Avro and pulled out one of the bags the boys used if they needed to vomit.

"Breathe into this," he ordered.

Millie grabbed the bag and took in one breath after another with the bag covering her mouth. With each inhale, the air traveled further into her lungs, and she began to calm down. As the lightheadedness faded, she started thinking clearly. Looking up at Callum, she could see the worry on his face. She should never have blamed him. *It was my fault.* When was she going to learn that breaking the rules came at a price? She hated herself for hurting the people she loved.

"When did they discover he was missing?" Millie pushed Aggie away. Everything was too close.

"He wasn't with the bombers when they arrived back just before dawn, but none of the crews saw him go down." Aggie tried to give her friend some space but wouldn't let go of her hand. Callum took a chance and knelt by her side.

"I'm not going to faint if that's what you think." Millie stood up and started walking to their plane.

"Where are you going, Millie?" Callum said.

"Back to RAF Benson. I need to talk to Peter. He has to know more than Aggie does. I need details." She hugged Aggie, promised to call when she had news, and climbed into the cockpit.

Callum strapped himself in beside her. "What more do you think Peter can tell you?"

"For starters, they can tell me where he was when the other pilots lost sight of him. If it was France, then we may find him yet." She left out the fact that after seeing Peter she would be going to London. If anyone could find Elliot, her father could.

Callum trod lightly. He didn't want there to be any trace of the fact that for him this wasn't entirely bad news. "Listen, Millie. Elliot is one of the best pilots I've seen. And he can talk his way out of just about anything. With Polish and French resistance out there looking for our boys, he stands a good chance of being found. We just need to keep calm and wait for more information."

Millie gave him a sideways glance. "Who are you trying to fool? You and Peter both hate Elliot. I am stunned that Peter didn't send the note with a bottle of champagne." Her words cut, and she knew it. For some reason, she had no problem standing her ground with Callum.

"I don't hate him. I just don't have much use for him." If he were brave, he would have said, I don't hate him, but I want you, and he is in the way.

"He told me to look for him in Spain." Millie couldn't help thinking of their last telephone conversations. She closed her eyes and began shaking her head. She pushed all emotion aside and tried to apply logic to the situation. For now, she didn't want to admit, especially to herself, what she was feeling.

"What's that?" Callum kept looking to the horizon.

"Never mind." She shook her head. "Please just get me back to London in one piece."

Compassion, or was it love, shone in his eyes. He pulled up to a higher altitude and increased the thrust, doing exactly as she asked.

# CHAPTER TWENTY-FOUR

Senate House-British Intelligence Headquarters

September 3, 1943

276 days until D-Day

The walk back from the War Rooms always left William with more questions than answers. This time, he pondered over what a debacle the Schweinfurt-Regensburg Mission had become. They had sent some 376 bombers deep into German territory to strike at the heart of German aircraft production. If they had any hope of Operation Overlord succeeding, they would need to curtail the Luftwaffe. How had they missed Schweinfurt entirely, and how had they lost over sixty bombers and their crews? It seemed to William that they had done as much harm to themselves as they had their enemy. Proving yet again that war is a messy business.

His aide greeted him with final casualty numbers from Schweinfurt-Regensburg, the photographs taken after the raid, a note from RAF Medmenham concerning the heavy sites, and a note from his son, Peter.

"When will we strike the aircraft manufacturer again?" his aide asked.

"We took a lot of losses ourselves." He handed the numbers, now out of the envelope, back to his aide. "I don't imagine the Americans will be in a rush to get back over there anytime soon."

William looked at the report concerning the bombing of Watten. It was much more encouraging. "This looks better."

He pushed his glasses back in place to get a good look. "They knocked the concrete dome over. The folks at RAF Medmenham think it will delay the heavy site by at least three weeks. They are scouring the area for more targets like this one." William flipped through the stack of papers, passing them off to his aide after reviewing them. "Still nothing on the pilotless bombs." His frustration manifested in an audible sigh followed by a struggle to shake off his coat as he entered his interior office saying, "Just knock if anything needs my attention," and punctuated with the slam of his door.

Sitting behind his desk, William picked up a brass letter opener and cut through the seal of the envelope from Peter. Dumping out its contents, William found a handwritten note saying simply that Elliot was missing in action and a copy of the *John O'Groat,* the paper from his wife's hometown. Unfolding the newspaper, he saw the image of the bombed truck on the front page with the byline *Millicent Trayford.* The old bastard Graham finally printed one of her images, was William's first thought. The next was, what was my daughter doing in Wick just, he looked at the date, four days ago?

He went to the door and spoke to his secretary. "Please phone RAF Benson and ask my youngest son to join me here in London as soon as possible."

"May I say why?" She knew it wasn't likely. Her boss wasn't one to explain himself, but she felt she needed to ask.

"No," William said with his back to her. "But please find out all you can about Flt. Lt. Elliot Harrington's last sortie."

Back behind his desk, William looked over the special edition of the *Groat.* She was a fine photographer. Thinking of her running through the streets, putting herself in harm's way for others, reminded him of his wife and her damn suffragette marches. One day he would have to tell Millie all about them and give her Margaret's medals. If only she could be here to see that Millie was made of the same stubborn stock as she. No matter how hard he tried to hold her back, to find ways for her to fulfill her duty far from danger, Millie always seemed to find a way into the fray—not unlike her mother.

There was a knock on his door.

"Yes."

His secretary opened the door, holding her pad. "Peter is currently flying, sir. His commanding officer will get him your message when he returns. As for Elliot, they will send a report over, but the basic details are that it was a night flight, and the bombers lost sight of him over France."

*Perhaps that's just the bit of luck we need to find him. If he's in France, I can get him home.* William reached for a blank sheet of stationery and his fountain pen, composing a letter to Bonnie Marie. If anyone could find a needle in the haystack that was occupied or Vichy France, it was she.

# CHAPTER TWENTY-FIVE

House in Belgravia

September 3, 1943

276 days until D-Day

William slipped into his favorite leather chair in his study. Setting down his briefcase, he reached and turned on the lamp. He began to relax into the supple leather but stopped suddenly. There would be no rest for him.

Millie, or rather a shadow of Millie, sat across from him. She had been staring into the darkness. Now she was looking through him. A fleeting thought passed across William's mind. It might have been a bit of a concern, but he didn't take hold of it. Instead, he got to work.

"How long have you been here?" William said, easing back into his chair without as much as a flinch.

"I don't know exactly, but it was daylight when I arrived."

"You don't look yourself." He let himself relax, at least for the moment.

"Elliot is missing. Probably dead." She spoke into the void. "Mr. Graham put my picture in the paper. I mean one that the MOI didn't order him to print. It's not of a woman, but, taking it, I felt more myself than I have in years. Who knows, the very moment I took the image on the back page, Elliot may have been plummeting to his death." She reached for the locket and began fiddling, still staring off into space. William gripped the arm of his chair. The monotone of her speech unsettled him, but still he sat and listened. "We bombed the heavy site at Watten. But they have managed to pick up the pieces and begin rebuilding the place as if it were an erector set. I just spent the day verifying it. They say it might take three months for them to rebuild." She turned and looked her father dead in the eyes. "Is there a way for me to do that with my life?"

William could have handled tears, outrage, or even collapse, but nothing could have prepared him for his once vivacious daughter's detachment. The calm was unnerving, bordering on frightening. William prided himself on being comfortable with silence, but each second that passed felt like a countdown. He had to respond.

"How did you find your way to Wick last week?" William finally spoke, but in a whisper, afraid to startle the fawn before him, as he pulled the copy of the *Groat* from his bag.

"Callum surprised me with a picnic." She still clung to the locket, but she maintained eye contact. It felt like a small victory to William. He leaned forward slightly in his seat. He would win the day one battle at a time.

"Callum?"

"I know what you are thinking. That I've been unfaithful to Elliot." *He doesn't know the half of it.* She stood. Truth was he was thinking no such thing. He could never conceive of Millie as unfaithful, disloyal. His mind swirled with possible ways to get out of this conversation with his daughter intact and without blowing his cover.

William could feel the defensiveness grow in his daughter. He proceeded carefully, hoping his words would act as a soothing touch. "I thought nothing of the sort. I was simply unaware that the two of you had become friendly."

"We spent quite a bit of time together when I was stationed at Wick. We became reacquainted the day I arrived for my posting at the airfield." She thought of the cigarette and how she had envied it, suddenly craving one herself. "Do you have a cigarette?" Millie saw her father's brow knit but didn't rescind the request.

Perplexed, William eased over to his desk and grabbed a silver cigarette box before stopping at the cart to pour himself a whiskey. Millie asked him to make one for her, too. With a cigarette in one hand and her drink in the other, William's daughter became a stranger to him. It was time for a change of tack.

William slammed his drink down on the side table. Millie blinked back to the present, and he demanded, "Why are you here?"

"I thought I should ask you to look for Elliot." Millie's eyes began to fill with tears.

"You thought you should?" The evening kept getting stranger and stranger. He began to think Millie wasn't concerned for Elliot after all. Now that he thought of it, the note about his disappearance had come from Peter.

"Yes, the thought crossed my mind the moment we got the news. I thought if he went down in France, maybe some of your contacts there, isn't there one called Bonnie Marie, in any case, I thought you might be able to help."

She stopped rambling and took a drag on the burning cigarette, flicking the ashes into the fireplace. William sat transfixed. She didn't cough after pulling the smoke down into her lungs. She had smoked before and often. He wondered what else he didn't know about his daughter.

"But when I got back to RAF Medmenham, there was work to do, and..." she trailed off for a moment, but William waited.

He didn't want to finish her sentences for her as he so often did to get his way. He needed information. He had to risk letting her say anything.

"I thought of him again this morning. Who waits four days to think of a lost fiancé?"

When Millie admitted she had forgotten about Elliot and fallen back into her work, tears began to flow. She didn't want her father to see her shame, so she buried her face in her hands.

William fell to his knees in front of his daughter, relieved.

He told himself that her rambling could all be about grief and guilt, an entirely rational reaction to the war taking yet another thing from his typically tough-as-nails daughter. Before the tears he thought she might quit on him, that she had had enough of his manipulations and the war. That the bombing in Wick and the work she did there had become a true calling and that she would leave him as her mother did. In case the latter was true, he knew he needed to strike.

He took her hands in his. "Millie, of course you got back to work. There is no shame in wanting to help destroy the people who took your beloved's life if that is indeed what has happened. In fact, it may be the only rational response. No harm has been done. You simply did what you had to do by going back to work. I, too, find it easier to cope with an occupation. Trayfords aren't built for wallowing. Peter let me know about Elliot. I have already reached out, and if Elliot is alive in France, we will find him and bring him home."

The words *bring him home* hit her like ice water. Her heart began to race so loudly she worried her father might hear. She sat up and wiped the tears falling from her face. She had to pull herself together, so her father wouldn't piece it all together.

Her tears were not tears for Elliot, as her father thought, but for herself. The tears began to fall when she finally accepted that those three words were why she hadn't wanted to come to see her father. They fell when she admitted that she wasn't sure if she wanted Elliot to come back. When it finally sank in that that day, four days ago, when she heard the news, she had collapsed on the tarmac because of a different three words, *Elliot is missing*. The words had sounded like a declaration of freedom for her.

"Thank you." Millie popped up, thinking *this will never do*. She flicked the remains of the cigarette into the fireplace. "It really is a disgusting habit." Facing the mantle, she smoothed out her clothes in a frantic attempt at composing herself. What would her father think of all this? There was nothing left but to try to repair the damage.

She offered her father a hand. Now that she understood what had been paralyzing her, she was determined to keep it secret. She needed to pull herself together and show her father that she was simply bent, not broken. She needed time to sort things out.

She wished there was someone to talk with, some confidant. *If only Clara was here. But she isn't.* Millie was left alone to sort out why, having never felt trapped before, the idea of being decoupled from Elliot felt liberating.

"You're quite welcome." William noticed the shift in his daughter and was grateful that his consoling words helped. He smiled, seeing her animated again. He wrapped his arm around Millie and escorted her toward the door, treating her like a fragile flower for the first time in her life. "Now that we know the search is on, why don't you dry your tears and let's go down to the kitchen and see if Cook has left anything in the larder."

Millie took the handkerchief her father offered her and bent down to grab the copy of the *Groat* on the floor next to her father's briefcase. It was the perfect way to change the dreary and shame-filled subject. She hadn't the energy to discuss Elliot any longer. And she needed to convince her father that his pep talk had restored her.

As they made their way down the back stairs, she asked, "How did you get this so fast?"

"Peter sent it with the note telling me Elliot was missing. It is a great image. Seeing it would have made your mother proud."

Sitting at the kitchen table, Millie asked, "And what about you?" Millie pushed at the topic for the first time in years. She held up the paper. "Does it make you proud?"

"Of course," William said between bites.

*Then why have you stopped me pursuing it,* Millie thought, but didn't press. She needed her house of cards to stand, for now. The secrets on all sides were too many to count, and they were all in it too deep. The only way out for any of them was to keep digging.

# CHAPTER TWENTY-SIX

MI6 Station-Paris, France

September 10, 1943

269 days until D-Day

Bonnie Marie found William's dispatch among the other papers waiting for her when she returned to the station house in Paris. She slipped it into her pocket, recognizing his handwriting, wondering if anyone else had seen it.

Before removing her coat, she turned around and went straight to the cafe on the corner. Thank goodness the Germans had a taste for coffee and hadn't shut them down. She winced at the pain shooting down her left leg as she dragged it along with each step. William had called the bombing a good bit of luck. "No one will notice an aging woman with a crippled leg in Paris." It would make her invisible. *Yes, but who wants to be invisible forever?*

With what passed as an espresso these days now in front of her, she retrieved William's message and read the words, "Elliot Harrington didn't make it home from a recon flight. They lost him over France. Please find out what you can. If it's possible, get him home." The note was unsigned.

Her first thought was of Millie. *She must be aware by now that he is missing.* The news would be unmooring to her. *How was she going to navigate with another ghost in her life?* The trauma of losing her mother so young shaped so many of her choices, or rather how willing Millie was to go along with other people's choices for her. Bonnie Marie couldn't make out how this new loss might affect Millie. After all, they hadn't seen each other for years.

She pulled a cigarette from its case. Holding her silver lighter, she traced the monogram, MTA, and allowed herself to go back. She smiled, thinking of Millie and the boys battling with swords made of sticks. Margaret reading every adventure she could find aloud to them. Peter teaching Millie to be a boy. Millie emerging from her darkroom. And when she couldn't take any more, she went one step further into the past. She let herself think of her friend, lying cold in the ground, leaving behind her fledglings before they learned to fly.

*That's enough.*

She lit the lighter and, before igniting her cigarette, set William's note ablaze in the ashtray. She took out a small pad and scribbled out the code that would be broadcast over resistance radio tonight. If Elliot Harrington were alive in France, she would get him home safely. What happened after that would be up to Millie.

# CHAPTER TWENTY-SEVEN

RAF Medmenham-Central Intelligence Unit
Fall 1943

Traveling back to RAF Medmenham after her revelation in London, Millie decided she had better make the best of things for now. She had a talent for going along. Why not put it to use? Because of conscription, she had to serve or get married. She found comfort in the fact that this war was constraining everyone's choices.

Her consolation was her camera. She promised herself she would use it. The work here at the Central Intelligence Unit might be secret, but they all did shift work. And when they weren't working, they looked after each other and played. She would take photos of that. She started with a dance at the YWCA canteen after her first shift back. While the staff of *Evidence in Camera*, a publication put together at RAF Medmenham with the blessing of the Ministry of Information, took photos of the young people dancing, she pointed her lens in the direction of the matrons of the county who tended to the service folks' needs. Things felt better. Not great, but better.

Millie got back to her assigned work with gusto, letting the unprocessed film collect in her top bureau drawer. The British needed to stay a step ahead of the Germans, and she could help with that. They were calling her little crew's mission Bodyline these days, and they still hunted for rockets *and* flying bombs. By now, Millie had scrutinized tens of thousands of photographs.

Throwing herself back into the mystery of whether the bombs were a threat and how they might work, Millie pored over new photographic cover every shift. All of the new intelligence suggested that Peenemunde was being rebuilt. Day after day, she scanned images, hoping to find a hint of a bomb with wings and how it might take flight, or the concrete works necessary for the existence of another heavy site.

The second week of September, Millie received a letter from Callum. She left it unopened. It taunted her as Peter might. Every time she saw it, she could hear it blowing a raspberry at her. For four days, she ignored it. On the fifth, she gave in. *What the hell.*

> *Dear Millie,*
>
> *Peter told me you didn't want to see me. I can live with that, but I want to be sure you are all right. Please send word.*
>
> *Yours truly,*
> *Callum*

She tore it to shreds and tossed it in the wood stove. All that fuss over three puny sentences. She slid an old box of photographs from beneath her bed and dug until she found what she was looking for—an old man sat on a plinth thrusting two fingers in the air. He hadn't wanted her to take the photo. She flipped it over and, using a grease pencil, wrote, "I'm fine!"

Before she started her shift the next day, she asked the Duty Officer for an envelope. She slid in the photograph and, sealing it, said, "Take that."

"What's that, miss?" the duty officers asked.

"Nothing. Would you send this in the bag for RAF Benson?"

"Will do."

Upstairs she found a fresh stack of images from the northern coast of France. Situating a pair under her stereoscope, she wondered if Elliot was walking under the canopy of trees.

Red came in with Neil, carrying an extra cup of tea for her.

"You going to the dance tonight to dance or take pictures?" Red said.

"I'll be armed," she tapped her camera, "but I could make time for a spin around the floor." She wouldn't dance with Callum, she had to punish herself somehow, but a dance with her married colleague would be harmless.

"Glad to hear it."

By the middle of October, they had confirmed the existence of three more heavy sites like the one in Watten and worked with the plotters to mark target areas for Bomber Command. They hadn't found any concrete evidence that the pilotless bombs existed, but they kept at it—rockets were real, so why not an unmanned guided flying bomb? The search was long and tiring. But in the early days of November, they got a break.

When Millie arrived for her shift, Red, who should have been on his way to bed, held back. Wg. Cmd. Thomas was with him, making a snack of the end of his cigar. His thumb flipped the lid of his lighter like a percussion instrument, creating a steady beat of clicks.

"Why don't you light the damn thing?" Millie said.

"The smoke burns my eyes."

"Then why have it at all?"

"Helps calm the nerves." The tone of his voice made her think of W.C. Fields. The only difference was that instead of waving his cigar, he clenched it between his back teeth.

"Does it?" Millie pointed to the frantic lighter in his hand. He immediately stopped playing.

"What's grabbed your attention there?" she said.

"A couple of things. We'll start with this." Ham handed her a copy of a report from Colonel Terence, director of technical development at the Ministry of Supply. "Basically, it says they don't believe the Peenemunde rocket is ready for large-scale production."

"So that means they acknowledge that it does, in fact, exist. That what we saw on the photos wasn't a decoy," Millie said.

Ham nodded and continued while Millie took a seat at her desk. "They believe the Germans are more likely to try the lighter projectile first, using a launching system formed with two rails that incline at a steep angle."

Red walked over and took the report from Millie. "So, they aren't talking about rockets here. They are describing something light enough that it wouldn't have to be served by a rail system as the earlier brief suggested."

Neil had returned in time to hear most of the discussion and added, "Some of the images coming from Rowell's section had these qualities. I put them aside because they didn't match the heavy sites we found in the Pas-de-Calais region."

"Do you still have the photos, or did you send them back to the library?" Ham sat on the edge of a desk, crossing his feet at the ankles.

"I have them. They are over there." He pointed to the stack of boxes beneath one of the windows.

"Good. The most interesting item is this." Ham extended a requesting hand to Red, who gave him the report. He flipped to the exhibits in the back and showed them a drawing of a building with the distinctive shape of a ski lying on its side. "They suspect it might be a firing installation and want us to report directly to them whenever we see one."

"Will do," Millie said, taking a box from the tower Neil had pointed to. "I'll give these a look. You said *things* before. Is there anything else?"

"New cover of Peenemunde." He had a fresh set of prints carefully positioned under his stereoscope.

"Out of commission yet?" Millie cleared her throat. She knew better. They had received intelligence from Whitehall explaining that most scientists survived the bombings and were moving production and experimentation underground. She put down the box of images in her hand and eased around Ham's desk to have a look for herself.

"You can see smoke and fresh tracks of all sorts." Millie looked up at her boss. "They're back to work—did you notice the scorched earth? We had a note saying those little flying monsters might have a pulse jet engine. Like the little Messerschmitt that gal Constance in Hazel's group found this summer."

"Could be. Why don't you jump into your stack, and Neil, you join her? Red, you can continue with Peenemunde when you are back on shift. Lord Cherwell is convinced those rascals are going to be the nuisance. Constance and her team are looking over the shots of Peenemunde for the little bugger itself. I'll leave it to the three of you to find the damn launchers. Let's find them and blow them up too," Ham said.

Neil spent most of his time with his head down, concentrating on France and the infrastructure necessary for the Germans to launch their menacing weapons. He was quiet and kept to himself, not rowdy like the crew of guys who worked in Hazel's section helping find the rockets. He had a friendly smile.

He and Millie put their heads together, and he described the kinds of evidence he had seen in Rowell's images: unidentified activity, felled trees, materiel dumps, and new railway spurs. The stack of photographs in front of him read Pas-de-Calais—a name familiar from Millie's notes. And her father's, for that matter.

Millie put an image of Peenemunde under the scope and concentrated on shape, size, shadow, and tone. She wanted to know what associated things to look for in the Rowell photos. The burn marks seemed new, but she might have missed them before if the tonal quality of the image wasn't as good as the one Ham received today. She put the photos on Red's desk. He would need to memorize them before he began combing through old cover of Peenemunde again.

She and Neil pored over photos of places with names like Mimoyecques, Cap Gris-Nez, and Cherbourg. To Millie, everything looked sinister. The images were mostly of treetops, making it nearly impossible to see what was going on below. They looked for clearings, new and old, hoping to find scorch marks that matched the Peenemunde shot. Unfortunately, the minuscule changes in the cover from month to month told them very little. Most days ended with a new idea or two, but nothing concrete.

"Anything worth reporting to Sandy?" Ham said, days later. He ran his fingers through what was left of his hair and joined Millie and Neil at the large table at the back of the room they commandeered.

"Small pieces here and there. It seems like the puzzle should have come together by now." Millie rubbed her eyes. "There's just one problem: we are working with two or three different puzzles poured out on the table at once. We need a system for sorting out the pieces."

"Not to mention that most of this cover of France is at least four months old. So, who knows what they're up to now?" Neil pushed a stack of photos toward Ham and pointed to the dates. Most of the images in the bunch were taken on or before June 23.

"Lord Cherwell has always been convinced that the flying bombs represent the most imminent danger." Ham whacked the images on the table. "With a push, I can get you some new images."

# CHAPTER TWENTY-EIGHT



William had installed the placard on the year anniversary of Clara's death. The German bombs annihilated her flat, and the home guard never found a body, so he had it hung here on the garden wall next to one of her favorite camellia bushes. Millie picked at its blooms, wondering what excuse Peter and her father would offer for arriving so late.

While she waited, she meandered through her mother's rose garden. She had to give it to Gertrude. Her need to tame everything made for a beautiful garden: the pathways passable and the canes trimmed. Even the tendrils of her mother's favorite Royal Sunset climbing rose comported to the constraints Gertrude had the gardener install. Walking under the trellis arch, Millie remembered when this kind of order would never have been allowed.

Under Margaret's care, the rose garden ran wild. Millie giggled, thinking of Gertrude's disgust when her mother instructed the gardeners to let the roses snake through the path as they liked. It struck Millie as she reached out for a threatening thorn that her mother preferred things a little out of order. Even on the day Millie almost cut down her favorite rose bush trying to fetch her a vase full of bloom, her mother hadn't scolded her.

On her mother's birthday years before, Millie's brothers

all bragged over breakfast about the magnificent gifts they had made for Margaret: Michael, a bracelet made of twigs and stones; John, a crown made of blooms; and Peter, a wand made of a fallen branch he had whittled and decorated with ribbons he stole from her dressing table. Millie had nothing. The boys said she needn't worry; she was only four after all. Their mother didn't expect her to have a gift. But Millie didn't want to be left out.

Dressed in her nightgown and wellies, she ran to the gardener's shed and dug out a pair of gardening shears before making her way to her mother's favorite rose bush. A good bit of the climber lay on the ground, its tendrils slithering this way and that. Millie climbed over the thicket to reach the blushing peach blooms. She crept deeper and deeper into the canes, cutting every bloom she could find. When her arms could carry no more, she dropped the shears and ran to find her mother.

She ran into her mother's rooms and found her still in bed. Standing at the door flung wide, with her arms full of her harvest, Millie heard her mother let out a scream that could wake the dead. Margaret leapt from the bed, knocking her breakfast tray to the floor, and ran to her daughter. She slapped the roses from her arms, tore off her blood-stained gown, and began searching for the offending injury. But the blood didn't come from a single source, rather the thousands of small gashes made when the thorns found purchase.

Making her way to her daughter's face, Margaret began counting the tears on her darling girl's blood-stained face. Millie pushed out the words, "I wanted to give you a gift."

A relieved Margaret pulled her into her lap, wiping away her tears, and said, "Thank you, my love, these are my favorite." She picked up a bloom, put it behind her ear, and stood, Millie in her arms. "You must help me. I will be the prettiest girl in the county with these laced through my hair."

Sitting down at her dressing table, Millie now beside her,

Margaret braided her hair. It was black and full of curls that made Millie think of the offending trailing rose cane. Millie studied her mother's movements as she threaded her fingers in and out of her mane, taming it, just a bit.

"Now then, go collect the best blooms." Margaret whispered in Millie's ear.

As Millie placed the roses on the vanity, Margaret tucked them here and there in the folds of her braid. She was the picture of summer. And the fragrance—it intoxicated Millie.

"You should wear it that way all the time." Millie let the thought slip from her mouth. "You look like the queen of the fairies."

Margaret lifted her eyebrows and grinned ever so slightly as if to say, "What makes you think I'm not?"

"Let's go find the boys; the queen of the fairies needs subjects."

Millie hesitated just a moment as her mother swept out the double doors to her rooms, her linen nightgown and robe billowing in the breeze. Margaret looked back and said, "Are you coming, Princess?"

Millie reached up and touched the one scar on her face that hadn't faded. It was just above her left eyebrow.

"Does Elliot still tease you about that divot in your forehead?"

Millie turned to see Peter leaning on the wall. He had been watching her. She suddenly felt exposed—*how did he get so close without my hearing him?*—and marched over and punched her favorite brother on the right upper arm. "Where have you been?"

"What did I do?" Peter said, rubbing the now tender spot. "It was all Elliot. I seem to recall him once saying, but for that scar, you would have the perfect face."

"I don't recall you ever resisting the chance to tease me." They began to walk back to Clara's memorial.

"Yes, but never to tame you."

Millie stopped short. "Are you sure about that?"

A flash of guilt washed over Peter's face before he managed to turn away and nudge her along. Her long-forgotten assertiveness took him off guard. He hadn't seen this side of Millie since their grandmother Gertrude got her hands on her. He couldn't decide if he was pleased to catch a glimpse of her or not.

"Why do you suppose Father had that inscribed on the panel? I don't remember Clara ever speaking French to us outside of our lessons."

Millie read the words *impossible n'est pas français* aloud. "Though Clara's mother was French. She used to regale me with stories about her grandfather." *Come to think of it, he lived somewhere near Bayeux in the area I scour day after day.*

"Where is Father?" Peter said, taking a handkerchief from his pocket, polishing the placard.

"I sent him a note telling him we would be here." Millie looked at her watch, another reminder of her mother. She was wearing it the night she died in the car accident. William had given it to Millie on her sixteenth birthday. The sapphires surrounding the face were what gave Elliot the idea to get her the sapphire engagement ring.

"I have to get back soon, so we had better get to it." Peter was antsy. Off just a bit. He was anxious to be away from this place and all its memories and back to his beer and cards. He lived with the fact that he could die every time he left the ground in his specially outfitted Spitfire. All the photo-reconnaissance pilots did. Mingling with death seemed a poor choice when he had both feet on the ground.

They took hands and stood next to the marker. Bowing their heads, they stood quietly for some time. Peter had to will himself to be still. When the moment felt complete, Millie squeezed Peter's hands, and together they yelled, "Luck favors the brave!"

Peter noticed his sister's lips pull into a tight line. He knew she was holding back tears. He wanted to run, but they stood connected for just another moment before Peter cut through the tension with his usual dodging charm. "That'll do then. It's time for a drink. Join me?"

Millie walked side by side with her brother, wondering what went on in his head. He always knocked off before saying or doing anything real.

"Where is your engagement ring?"

Millie pulled the chain meant for her locket from beneath her blouse. Her engagement ring was dangling with the locket. "Since the weather turned cooler, I'm afraid it will fall off, so I'm keeping it here for safekeeping." She dropped the charms back into place and patted her heart.

"How sweet." Peter made the face of someone who just ate something bitter.

"What is your problem today?"

"Besides the fact that I was just made to stand beside the makeshift grave of the second mother I've lost in a single lifetime?" Peter snapped.

"Yes, besides that."

"Callum says you've been avoiding him," Peter spat. He needed to change the subject. He was partly to blame for the situation his sister was in. Envy is a powerful companion. But he simply refused to get into it. Doing his job was all he could manage at the moment.

"I sent him a letter."

"You sent him a message to fuck off." Peter shot two fingers in the air toward his sister. "Very lady-like."

"As I recall, you've never been too thrilled when I behave like a lady."

"Well, things have changed. You seem to have forgotten who you are and what you stand for." It bothered Peter that she was so willing to surrender to what others wanted from her, all in the name of being agreeable, but he would never admit to Millie the part he played in shaping the woman she was becoming. So, he doubled down. "You should be proud of the work you are doing, the way you are representing the Trayford name, and instead, you are wasting away." He pulled up her tunic and pointed to the safety pin holding up her skirt.

"How dare you!" She shoved Peter, causing him to lose his footing. "I'd be happily taking images for the Ministry of Information if you could have found a way to take my side instead of Father's. You made me feel selfish, ashamed of my work."

Peter walked off in a huff in the direction of their mother's grave. Millie followed close behind.

"Don't walk away from me!" she demanded.

Standing in front of the headstone, Millie continued laying into Peter. "Who do you think you are running away from? Pouting like we were kids again."

Peter held up both hands in surrender. He didn't have it in him to fight. It was hard enough coming home. "Don't you wish we were?" Peter took a seat on a bench nearby. "If we were kids, we could spend the days just as we liked, with anyone of our liking. Now there are too many rules. And the war only makes it worse. I want to follow along, but it's hard to see the point when every time I go up in the air, there is a reasonable chance I won't be coming back."

There, he said it. Every time he went in the air, there was a chance he could die. He simply couldn't fathom why Millie wanted him focusing on more death. Death from the past. There was plenty right here in the present.

Millie sat beside her crumpling brother, thinking of everything she had given up, even temporarily, including Elliot, and erupted. "You petulant child. You are the third son of an earl whose financial future was secured the moment our mother died. You can do anything, or at least more than most. For all we know, Elliot is dead, and you sit here next to me, taking stock of your limited options."

"You will never understand. There is so much I want that I can never have."

"Like what?" Millie asked, now on her feet towering over him.

"Lady Millicent," a voice called to Millie from the gate to the family cemetery. It was the butler. "I'm sorry to disturb you, but a note just arrived from your father."

Millie tore into the envelope, heart racing. She sat to read it, breathing deeply, trying to calm down. After reading the contents, Millie crumpled the handwritten note into her fist.

"He's not coming." Peter bolted up. He doubted he would. Their father was less interested in seeing the toll their choices for Millie were taking on her than Peter. Millie buried her face in her hands. All she had wanted was a quiet moment with the two men in her life she felt she could count on. "In that case, I think I will finally go get that drink."

"But Grandmother arranged a tea for us," Millie said to her brother's back.

"Enjoy it without me." Peter waved, without turning around, without saying goodbye.

Millie fidgeted in her seat, wondering if this was all there was, just her and the ghosts in her life. *If so, then perhaps I should start looking after myself for a change.*

The problem was, despite her mother's and Clara's pleas, she had forgotten how.

# CHAPTER TWENTY-NINE

Senate House-British Intelligence Headquarters
November 6, 1943
212 days until D-Day

William had lived too many years to be concerned that Duncan Sandy, Prime Minister Churchill's son-in-law and coordinator of all rocket investigations, had asked to come to see him. He was comfortable with silences in a way most men were not. He found they mostly liked to hear themselves talk. They also got antsy when they didn't receive a bit of acknowledgement during their monologues. William could outlast the best of them, always gleaning some scrap of useful information. And put even the most confident of men on edge. Duncan Sandy was no exception. It did surprise him to find Sandy in his office when he arrived. William admired the move as he was rarely surprised.

Sandy hovered over his desk, handling a note card. William watched for a moment longer than would have been thought considerate before clearing his throat. Sandy dropped the card and turned around.

"So, your daughter is helping us with the rocket search." Sandy pointed to the card.

William noticed that catching him snooping had Sandy a bit off balance. That will teach him to arrive too early.

"Has she met Sarah?" Sandy asked, stepping to the proper side of William's desk.

"I couldn't say." William never relaxed his cards from his chest. It wasn't Sandy's concern if Millie and the Prime Minister's daughter had met before or if they spent time together at RAF Medmenham. He was here to discuss rockets.

William rearranged the objects on his desk, setting Sandy squirming again. He picked up Millie's invitation and discarded it in the waste bin. *She will just have to understand that I couldn't come.* After four years of keeping secrets and telling lies, he wouldn't risk blowing his cover. He would make up an excuse the next time he saw his daughter. His plans depended on the fact that she would believe him.

"How can I help you?" William asked Sandy.

"Lord Cherwell keeps planting seeds of doubt in Churchill's head. How do we put an end to the question of whether or not these hideous German weapons exist? Resources have to be committed to destroying them, or we may lose this war."

"I agree." William opened his top right-hand drawer and pulled out a red folder. Opening it, he pulled out the latest bits of communication from Bonnie Marie. "I've been giving these ramp drawings and the fact that the construction is inconsistent with the heavy sites some thought." Next, he handed over a copy of the report out of Denmark about the winged rocket. "It seems to me that these fragments of intelligence may relate to each other. We need to connect the activities at Peenemunde to what they are building on the northern coast of France. If we do that, we will be much closer to putting the question of whether these things on the ground in Germany are decoys or not to rest."

"Agreed. I'm glad to know we are on the same page." Sandy pulled on his coat and donned his hat.

"Was that all?"

"It was indeed. I'm off to RAF Medmenham to hear what Ham thinks."

William watched Sandy leave Senate House from his office

window. He got into his car, and it pulled off, heading north. *He is collecting allies. This morning's meeting was nothing but a test. I guess I passed.*

# CHAPTER THIRTY

RAF Medmenham-Central Intelligence Unit
November 7, 1943
211 days until D-Day

Whatever Ham said to Sandy, it worked. In the days that followed, the photographic interpreters had more cover than they could handle. With the preparation for the invasion of France underway, Millie's boss, Wg. Cmd. Hugh Hamshaw Thomas, must have painted quite a picture to convince the War Office to divert reconnaissance pilots away from the shores of Normandy. Of course, it didn't hurt that Duncan Sandy was backing him up.

Every in-box overflowed with freshly printed images still curling from the fix. Sandy ultimately ordered the Photographic Reconnaissance Units to photograph the entire Pas-de-Calais area again. It took hundreds of sorties and produced thousands of images. He also insisted the PIs review every image taken of Peenemunde again. If there was a connection between the German activity in northern France and the Germans' esteemed research center, he wanted it found.

Millie, Neil, and Red hunted for new roads, railway spurs, clearings, and construction every day, looking for some link between research and operations. And with every set of images they slid under their stereoscopes, the PIs asked the question, "Could this have anything to do with a flying bomb?"

Millie looked up from her work, twisting her neck this way

and that. *I'm never going to get to all of these.* Her stacks of images had grown so tall. She moved them to the floor rather than work in the fort created by the towers. She worried that the very image they needed languished, unseen, at the bottom of one of her stacks. From what Ham and her father said, all of their lives depended on finding the rockets and flying bombs so they could be destroyed. *Maybe I should flip the stacks over?*

The door to their cell burst open, followed by Ham, hands full of boxes of new photographs. Millie dropped her head. *You must be kidding me.*

"And that would be..." Millie had developed a bad habit of throwing thoughts in the air rather than ask the real questions. *Will there ever be enough evidence to satisfy Lord Cherwell? If they manage to accumulate enough proof, will resources be committed to bombing? And how will the three of them ever get to all these images?*

"Images of eight different sites taken because of a tip from the French resistance. The spies informed MI6 that unexplained groundworks were under construction. They expect us to figure out what they are."

"Do they suspect rocket activity?" Red asked. He hadn't taken a day off in over a week. None of them had.

"There's nothing new in these images." Neil's tired eyes squinted as he slapped the photo down on his desk. "And nothing in them suggests that they could get a winged bomb to the site effectively. There're no railway spurs leading to the sites. I don't see tracks anywhere in the vicinity."

"Let me take a look." Millie reached for the images. In her months at RAF Medmenham, it had become clear that Millie was the one for the job if there was a needle to be found.

They kept searching. There were days when it took all of Millie's strength not to open the window and send her stack flying on the wind. Details of Bodyline's meeting with Terrence made their way around the sections, fueling rumors that the mass production of German rockets was underway, and they would be catapulted at London with some sort of ramp. PIs whispered in the mess about a manifest stolen by Polish slave laborers, suggesting that the Germans planned to launch two thousand flying rockets a day. One could feel the fear growing. So many plans were underway, and these sorts of weapons could ruin them all.

"Why can't I figure out how they mean to launch their prized little fiends at us?" Millie threw a pencil across the room.

"Watch it!" Red said.

"Sorry." Millie shrugged her shoulders.

"Good thing your aim stinks." Neil's attempt at humor didn't lift her funk.

"I can work on that," Millie shot back.

"All right. Talk me through it then."

"All I can say for certain is that the Germans are building structures to the same specification in multiple locations, though it appears that the construction schedules vary. Each site has nine standard buildings. The shape of three of them is odd. It must mean something, but what?" Millie pushed back from her desk, offering the stereoscope to Neil.

"What do you mean the buildings have an odd shape?" Ham asked, chewing his damn cigar again.

"They look like skis for a giant if you ask me," Neil said.

Ham walked over to Millie's desk. "Wasn't something like that mentioned in Colonel Terence's report? Show me." He pulled a stereoscope from his breast pocket. He looked up, nodding. "Neil, you check every clearing, pit, dump of material, and partially complete building. Trayford, you take the roads and paths. Before we leave this room, I want a working theory about whether these things are for flying bombs or something more hideous that we have yet to consider."

By the end of their shift, they had convinced themselves that the Germans designed these eight sites as some kind of offensive measure, because they were too far from the shore to be defensive works. Each site was the same, except for the placement of the buildings. Millie looked up to see that Douglas Kendall had joined them. He was working with Ham to write up a report to take to London for a meeting Kendall had that evening with Duncan Sandy.

Neil, Red, and Millie pushed onward, tackling their respective stacks, two images at a time. Before Kendall's report was complete, they identified nineteen identical sites in the older pictures sent up from the photo library.

Kendall's one order as he put on his coat to make for London was, "Keep looking for sites. There is something there."

Millie reached for a stack of images four inches thick, feeling lighter, sitting up a bit straighter. It was just the spark she needed to continue down the dark tunnel.

# CHAPTER THIRTY-ONE

## Hare and Hound Pub
## November 7, 1943
211 days until D-Day

Millie faced stacks everywhere. At her billet, the stack of letters stood five deep. Fiona, Gertrude, Aggie, and two from Callum. *When is he going to give it a rest?* Millie tossed Callum's letters in the trash bin. She didn't need to open them. He had been writing the same six words for weeks. "I hope you are doing well." *At least he isn't still insisting on seeing me.* She slid a finger under a loose crack in Aggie's envelope and read about all her adventures at RAF Wick and her adventures at home with her little brother and sisters. Millie would have been hard pressed to say which sounded more juvenile. The last paragraph concerned the topic on everyone's mind—Elliot. The one topic Millie found she didn't want to think or talk about. She skipped over the words that were meant to be reassuring, going straight to the words she prized—your friend, Aggie.

She sat down at the small desk in the room she shared with Hazel, determined to write an upbeat letter. Millie knew she couldn't give Aggie any actual details. Chances were Aggie wouldn't believe them if she had, but she could tell her about some of the light-hearted moments she's shared with Neil and Red and Wg. Cmd. Thomas. After all, they did more than just work. And though she had lost sight of her goal to take more pictures, or any at all come to think of it, there were some lovely anecdotes she could offer as proof to Aggie that all was well. All except the looming reality that they could all die any day now if those rockets made it across the channel.

As she wrote, the other letters kept demanding her attention, so she tore into them. It was the only way to quiet them. The opening lines of each yelled an inquiry, "Have you had any news about Elliot?" Gertrude speculated about the worst possible outcomes and whether or not they needed to make other marriage preparations. Millie balled the letters tightly into her fist. *Why does everyone always feel the need to make plans for my life?* She let out a grunt of disgust.

"Is it all that bad?" Hazel said, entering the room. "If so, thanks for the warning." She eased back out of the room.

"Get back here." Millie pushed away from the desk; her heaviness returned. "Everyone is asking about Elliot. If I think they will find him? If I should be making other plans?"

"That was Gertrude, right?"

"Yes, and in some ways Fiona, too, though she is campaigning for my becoming a woman of independent means." Millie reached for her coat. "All of their planning is infuriating. And I was having such a good day."

"A bit of progress, then?" Hazel said.

"Indeed, and now a drink."

Millie marched down the stairs.

"You're not going anywhere without me." Hazel followed closely behind.

Peter sat in the back corner of the main room of the Hare and Hound. His sister's arrival surprised him. He had never seen her there. Or out much at all, now that he thought of it. With Elliot missing, she had chosen to live the life of a nun. *All work and no play, as they say.*

He sat watching her for a while. She and Hazel each ordered a beer, and Millie topped it off with a shot of whiskey. The bartender seemed dubious at first, but she convinced him after slamming back her second drink. He kept pouring. She kept drinking. When Peter saw her bobble on her stool, he decided to intervene.

He held up a pausing hand as the bartender lifted his bottle to pour. Hazel gave him a nod of thanks.

"Maybe we should be getting back to Boyton House?" Hazel tried to get Millie back into her coat.

"No. We're drinking with..." She pointed at the bartender and searched her mind for his name. *Did I ever get his name?* Hazel touched her arm. Millie jerked back. "No! I'm drinking!"

Peter leaned on the bar. "Make that two shots."

The bartender set up the glasses in front of Peter. When Millie reached for one, he slapped her hand away.

"Now, now. That isn't for you. It's for your dear friend and roommate Hazel here. She's the one who deserves it. Keeping you on that stool has been quite a job." He offered the drink to Hazel. She waved it off, so he dangled it in front of Millie's face before drinking it down himself.

"I need to get some sleep. I'm back on shift in ten hours." Hazel's eyes pleaded with Peter to take over the watch.

"I've got this in hand."

He escorted a fighting Millie by the shoulders to his quiet table.

"What's all this about?"

"Plans. Plans. And more plans." Millie swayed as she spoke. "We make plans at RAF Medmenham so the bombers can make plans. Then we send you fellows out to see if the plans worked, and the cycle starts all over again. It's a game of cat and mouse, really. And then there are the family plans. Plans on who I should marry, how I should spend my time." She pointed a finger in Peter's direction. "You're not married, and I never hear anyone making plans for you."

"Then you aren't listening, my darling."

"Just once, I'd like..." Her thought was interrupted by the sight of Callum walking into the bar carrying a book. *Who brings a book into a pub?* "Did you send for him?" Millie's eyes accused Peter.

"I did not. He comes here because you never do. From what he tells me, you want nothing to do with him. What was his crime? Helping you have a lovely day away from all of this."

"You know nothing about it." Her swinging hands knocked over her empty pint, sending it crashing to the floor.

"Well, so much for hiding quietly in the corner."

Peter tipped his head in Callum's direction. Callum returned the gesture and took a seat at a booth on the opposite side of the room.

"What, is he afraid to face me?"

"No, you fool. He doesn't want to upset you." Peter stood up and offered a hand to Millie. "It's time to put you to bed before you say something you don't mean, or worse yet, share state secrets."

Millie knocked his hand away. "I'm a grown woman and am perfectly capable of making plans for myself. I'll decide when I'm going home."

Peter fought the urge to punch the wall. He wanted to have sympathy for her but found that he was furious instead. The idea that any of them had free will was absurd. The Trayford allegiance to duty dictated all of their lives. *Why should things be different for her?* The price for living by a different code meant risking their entire way of life and perhaps everyone they loved. *Neither of us has the courage for that.*

Callum watched the two of them battling. Nothing had changed since they were kids. Peter pulled her braids. She reached to shove him to the ground. He bobbed and weaved until he exhausted her. *She gives in too soon. She is so much stronger than they are. She just doesn't see it.* He returned to his book—actually, Peter's book—confident Peter would win the fight.

"We are going now." Peter hoisted Millie up by her upper arm.

Millie stood her ground. "I am going nowhere!"

"Have it your way."

Peter walked to Callum's booth, with Millie standing, fists

clenched, by her table. "Don't let anything happen to her, mate. I can't take another minute of her self-pitying babble.

"Will do," Callum said.

"I don't need a nanny," Millie called after the retreating Peter.

She may not have needed one, but at that moment, she wanted Clara desperately. She would know what Millie should do, how to help her dig out of this hole that just seemed to be getting deeper by the day. She scowled in Callum's direction. The sight of him made her so angry. He made her want to make bold moves, and she hated him for that.

The bartender walked over to Callum when he and Millie were the last two in the pub. He hated to ask anyone in uniform to leave but wanted to close up. He wanted Callum to get Millie to go. He wanted him to do it now.

"It's time to go now, Millie." Callum stood over her. Her head was resting on her arms crossed on the table.

"I'll decide when I leave," she mumbled.

"No, the barman has decided. Let me help you get home."

"I don't want your help."

"Well, you managed to run everyone else off."

"I'll leave, but I don't need your help." She didn't look at him as she stood up. She didn't want him to see that she had been weeping.

She took her bike by the handlebars and began pushing. The world was spinning around her. Balancing on the seat seemed impossible. She could hear Callum's footsteps behind her, but she refused to turn around.

When they arrived at Boyton House, having walked the entire way in silence, Millie dropped her bike on the ground and sat down beside it. Callum reached to pick up the bike to store it properly. *Millie will be sad to find it wrecked when she wakes from her haze.*

"Leave it."

"Don't be silly. Someone might hit it, lying in the drive like this."

"I said, leave it." She got to her feet and propped the bike up on a stone wall.

"When is this going to stop?" Callum asked her.

"When is what going to stop?" She knew she sounded like a ten-year-old, but she found she didn't care.

"You believing that the world is against you and thinking that I am the world."

Millie's jaw clenched, and her nostrils flared. All that was missing from this bull fight was the stomping of her foot. She walked straight up to Callum, looked up at him, and said, "Why do you care if I talk to you or not?"

Callum stood his ground, sure she wouldn't notice his slight quivering, and said nothing.

Millie felt pulled to him. She refused to give in. When she did what she wanted, even the smallest thing she wanted, the floor always seemed to drop away, sending her falling. She wanted him to take a step back. She didn't want to fall.

"What do you want from me?" Millie whispered.

Callum didn't answer. He stood his ground.

"What do you want from me?" Millie repeated.

Callum whispered, "I want you to tell me what you want."

Millie looked up into his eyes. It would be so easy to lean into him. Maybe she would enjoy falling.

She stiffened at the thought, and she lowered her head.

Callum moved his hand slowly, not wanting to frighten her, and lifted her chin.

She put her hands on his chest. His heart beat too fast. She pushed him ever so slightly. He took a half step back. "I want you to stay." Her words were barely audible.

"I am not going anywhere." Callum stood still. Millie wanted him to close the gap between them. He wanted to take her in his arms and make everything right for her. But deep inside, he knew if there was ever going to be a "them," she had to find a way to do the wanting. He didn't want to be another thing she accepted in her life because someone else advised it or decided it for her.

"What were you reading back at the pub?"

Callum could feel the edge of the hardbound book he borrowed from Peter digging into his back. Peter treasured it, so he had tucked it safely in his trousers' waistband. "*Peter Pan.*"

Millie's eyes widened. She had loved Peter's adventures as a child. As a grown woman, she empathized with Wendy. Leaving the nursery is hell. "Which lost boy do you suppose I would be?"

"Nibs, no question."

"Why Nibs?"

"Because he is the most courageous."

As the words soaked in, Millie took a half step forward and laced her fingers into Callum's. Then, she stood up on her toes and brushed her lips against his. The kiss electrified every nerve in her body. She put her feet back firmly on the ground, she waited to fall. The earth didn't open and swallow her whole, but she held tight to Callum's hand just in case. She looked up into Callum's eyes, searching for reassurance. Something to tell her he wanted the kiss as much as she did. Unsure still, she began to loosen her grip on his hands, but he held tight.

Up on her toes again, she dropped Callum's hands and wrapped her arms around his neck and kissed him. All of the tension she had been carrying around melted away. He pulled her in tightly, and the two of them fell. The kiss took their breath away, but they didn't stop. Millie found the feeling of complete surrender intoxicating. Callum held her tightly, fearing it was a dream.

The front door light flickered on, rousing them from their moment of bliss. Millie broke the seal between them and spied Mrs. Clerie, watching them from a window.

"I have to go," Millie said, opening enough room for light to pass between them.

"What happens next?"

"I don't know." Millie pulled away and floated toward the door.

"Millie," Callum cried out. She turned to look at him. "Don't take too long deciding."

Millie could see the desperation in his eyes. She recognized it. Wanting something you can't have took a toll. She nodded before turning away. He's right. It's time I learn my mind.

# CHAPTER THIRTY-TWO

RAF Medmenham-Central Intelligence Unit

November 21, 1943

198 days until D-Day

Two weeks later, the count for ski sites stood at ninety-six. The only thing the Bodyline team knew about them for sure was that most of the buildings were within launching distance of London. Kendall had a map hung on the largest wall in the room. Neil marked the sites and the expected trajectory of the bombs with pins and red string. Watching him work, Millie thought he would have made an excellent plotter, if they let men do that kind of work.

"We've got to figure out what these damn buildings are for and how they work!" Ham slammed his forearm into the wall. "Neil, Trayford—get over here. I need to talk it out."

"These ski sites must be for storage—right?" Ham said through clenched teeth. Neil and Millie nodded. The buildings had no windows, so storage was the most likely purpose. "Trayford, what is the radius of curvature at the entrance?"

"My figures vary based on the site, but a thirty-eight-foot-tall rocket like the ones found at Peenemunde would just fit if they removed the base fins."

"They wouldn't go to that kind of trouble for one rocket," Neil said.

Millie cut her eyes toward Neil. "I'm just trying to give him every fact."

"You think the smaller building is for the fins?" Ham said.

"It could be, but—" Millie closed her eyes tight.

"But what, Trayford?" Ham got in her face. She pulled back at the smell of wet tobacco.

"But we don't think so?" Millie said, looking to Neil for support.

"Bollocks, girl, speak up!" Ham was out of patience.

"We think they're for catapulting the flying bombs, not launching rockets." Millie pointed out the concrete pylon pairs laid out like the rivets on a pair of leather shoes, each one a little higher as it traveled up the foot, based on the shadows.

Ham's eyes widened, and he took a step back, crossing his arms. "Explain."

"If you were trying to get a flying bomb in the air, you would need lift and thrust." Millie checked in with Neil to confirm and continued with their theory. "We think they're using the pulse jet engine Terrence mentioned for the thrust based on the scorch marks at Peenemunde. Lord Cherwell and his gang of scientists say it's possible to use a magnet for navigation. These ramp-like structures may be all the lift they need."

"The two of you think the Germans have nearly one hundred ramps aimed at London because they intend to fling pilotless flying bombs at us." Ham ran his fingers through his hair. "Wouldn't they need wings for that?"

"That's why we didn't mention it before. Something with wings couldn't get into the ski-shaped buildings. But when you mentioned taking the fins off, I thought maybe the wings are attached to the missiles on-site," Millie said.

Neil made a few calculations. "And if they use these square buildings to construct them, the wingspan must be twenty-two feet or smaller."

Their banter continued until they settled on a workable theory from the available intelligence—magnetic navigation with a pulse engine. They wrote a report asserting that the ski sites were for Lord Cherwell's flying bombs and sent it to London.

Two days later, Wg. Cmd. Thomas told them the War Cabinet *still* wasn't convinced, and a little more air seeped out of Millie's soul.

# CHAPTER THIRTY-THREE

RAF Medmenham-Central Intelligence Unit
November 24, 1943
194 days until D-Day

The flying rockets were an imminent threat to future operations and to the civilian population of Britain—the photographic interpreters at RAF Medmenham didn't doubt it. They had already discovered almost one hundred ramps in France, ready to pepper the British coast and its nearby cities with explosives. Within Bodyline, they generally believed that they would have to connect the ramps on France's northern coast to Peenemunde to persuade the War Cabinet to destroy them, but with every day that passed, Millie lost faith that they would ever be convinced. With thinning resources and preparations ratcheting up for the invasion of France, it seemed to her they didn't want to acknowledge the looming threat. They weren't going to accept the existence of flying bombs until one hit London—she was sure of it.

Still, Wg. Cmd. Thomas urged them all to keep at the search. He agreed the Germans had the technology. Critically, he believed their bombers must destroy the French sites before they interfered with the forthcoming Normandy invasion. The found ramps pointed right at the heart of the Army and Navy's efforts for Operation Overlord—the boat launch sites. If the Germans managed to catapult the flying torpedoes in England's direction, it would mean losing over six months of planning and an extension of the war for...no one could say how long.

The rockets might have been hiding in plain sight. When you look for something you have never seen before, you could be staring straight at it and not even know it. The team in Bodyline had years' worth of images of Peenemunde. Now they needed fresh eyes. Douglas Kendall, Wg. Cmd. Thomas's commanding officer, nominated Hazel's section, led by Constance Babington Smith. The bombs were built to fly on their own, and they were the aircraft specialists.

Douglas Kendall asked Millie to bring the images he asked her to procure from the Photography Library and follow him to Section L—aircraft and aircraft factories. They found Constance bent over a stereoscope in an old servants' bedroom on the other side of the manor. Three other PIs were working with her, including Hazel.

"Sorry to disturb you, but we need you to look for something," Millie whispered to Constance, pointing in Kendall's direction.

"We have been looking for your *hypothetical* flying bomb and haven't seen anything that even resembles such a thing." Constance twisted around in her wooden desk chair so she could see Millie. As they walked toward Kendall, she added, "It's a waste of time. We need to be searching for new airstrips and airplane production plants, so the Germans don't have new planes when we invade France."

"The rockets were real. Why not flying bombs?" Millie insisted.

"Hello, Constance," Kendall greeted her. She had found a small jet plane not long ago in photographs of Peenemunde, and he hoped she could repeat her good fortune in their search for the smaller rockets. "I'd like you and a few folks from your team to help out Bodyline. This is Millicent Trayford."

"We've met. She billets with one of the members of my section."

Kendall looked to Millie. "Yes," she pointed to Hazel. "We live together at Boyton House."

"I hear Mrs. Clerie can be quite strict," Kendall said.

Millie nodded, remembering how she interrupted her and Callum's first kiss. *I wonder how he is.* He told her not to take too long, but she still didn't know what to say. With Elliot missing, not dead or alive, just missing, Millie found it impossible to admit she didn't want him anymore. *How do you call it off with a missing person?*

"I trust I can leave you two to it?" He checked in with both women. "Millie, tell her anything she needs to know. Constance, I hope it goes without saying that this intelligence is for your eyes only."

"What have you brought me?" Constance cleared a space for Millie's photos under her stereoscope after signaling that Hazel should join them. *It will be nice to be able to talk to Hazel about all this for a change.* Keeping secrets was part of the burden she carried around.

With Constance at one side and Hazel at the other, Millie began filling in the blanks. "The evidence suggests the Germans plan to launch the flying rockets from ramps built on these pylons." Millie indicated the proper position on the images under her glasses. "They will be smaller than a fighter plane and have a wingspan of less than twenty-two feet. Our best guess is that some type of magnetically directed autopilot will guide them."

"It sounds like you are writing science fiction," Constance said. "First rockets that could reach the stratosphere, now unmanned flying rockets. Unbelievable." Millie watched them both shaking their heads, coming to grips with the hideous nature of what they were dealing with.

"They could launch a full-scale attack on London and never lose a single pilot," Hazel said.

"Some of the intelligence hints at something like two thousand rockets a day if we do nothing," Millie added.

Hazel took a deep breath. "My family lives in London. Is there any chance we can create a warning system, like during the Blitz?"

Millie reached a consoling hand to Hazel's shoulder. "Perhaps, but we have to persuade the War Cabinet to order the destruction of the ramps first."

"Will do."

Millie started to leave when Constance asked another question. "How many ramps have you found on the northern coast of France?"

"We've found ninety-six." Millie watched as both women knit their brows. "Most of which are pointed directly at London."

Constance jammed her hands into her hair and rested her elbows on the desks. Millie was familiar with the impulse. Millie waited for what felt like hours for a response.

When Constance looked up, Millie saw determination. She had a plan.

"If we're going to find something that small, we're going to need clear photographs." She shoved her chair back and got to her feet.

"Where are you going?" Millie said.

"To the library to pull the back cover of Peenemunde; you might have missed something," Constance said. "Hazel, can you take these and split them up? We need to connect what's happening in France to Peenemunde." She put on her tunic and buckled her belt. "Millie, you get back to the cover of France. I will let you know if I find anything in Germany."

What a brilliant thinker she was, Millie thought. It had taken her only seconds to come to the same conclusion she and the others in Bodyline had taken weeks to reach.

# CHAPTER THIRTY-FOUR

RAF Medmenham-Central Intelligence Unit

November 28, 1943

190 days until D-Day

Hazel took a deep cleansing breath past her lips to clear her mind. Days had passed, and they still hadn't found anything definitive. However, they had discovered a new small aircraft, which Constance named Peenemunde 20 because of its wing-span. It piqued Kendall's interest, but he pushed it aside. They needed to connect the ramps in France to Peenemunde. There had been a few metal frames that matched the design in some much earlier photographic cover of the research center in Germany. And yet, they had no images of a pilotless bomb and nothing to link a flying bomb to the ramps in France. *If only we knew what we were looking for,* Hazel thought, fighting the urge to clear her desk with a single sweep of her arm.

Millie had a new habit of stopping in on her way to and from Boyton House to check on Section L's progress. From the looks of Hazel's hair when she shuffled in early that November morning, she was going off shift.

"Are things really that bad?" Millie's eyes floated up to Hazel's tangles.

"We haven't found anything new in the last twelve hours. How about you?" Hazel said, combing her hair back with her fingers.

"A few new ramp sites in the beginning phase and a note

from Callum." Millie waved the note in Hazel's direction.

Millie had filled Hazel in on the kiss, or rather kisses, as she helped nurse her hangover the morning after. Hazel didn't know how to advise her friend, but she listened. She thought the kiss sounded amazing and was stunned that it was so much more magical than times with Elliot but had no idea how one would navigate breaking off an engagement with a missing person.

"What did it say?"

"It was very polite." Millie unfolded the note, summarizing it as she went. "He thanked me for my last letter and apologized for having to cancel our dinner plans last week. I suspect he's been busy taking roll after roll of film for the invasion." Millie collapsed into the chair next to Hazel's desk. "I guess I should be grateful he canceled. I would have probably ended up in bed with him this time. How would I ever have explained that?"

"So, it's to be Callum, then?" Constance asked. She had overheard Hazel and Millie discussing Millie's romantic woes often. She found she was rooting for Callum despite the obvious hurdles. She came from a family of means as well and understood that decisions about marriage were complicated at best. But Elliot sounded like an ass. It seemed horrible to wish Elliot wouldn't come back, though it would solve a lot of Millie's problems. *I hope she finds the courage to follow her heart.*

Millie sat up red-faced, wondering how much Constance had overheard in their weeks together. "I don't know—it all just seems impossible."

"Constance, take a look at this." Hazel jumped back on her stereoscope.

"What is it?" Millie stood up straight, grateful to end the line of questioning concerning her love life, letting all thoughts of boys fly out of her mind.

"I'm not sure. That's why I called for Constance." Hazel and Millie acted more like sisters every day.

"Tell me what I'm looking at?" Constance peered through the stereoscope.

"Those crane-looking metal structures." Hazel pointed in the general direction with her pencil.

"Have you seen them before?" she said.

"Yes. The industry section thinks they are for excavation. But look here—just to the right. The ramps built up with dirt. Don't the shadows suggest an incline pointing to the sea?"

Millie took a turn at the stereoscope, forcing herself to push down any spark of hope bubbling in her chest—they'd had one too many close calls.

"Well." Constance was back at the glasses. "You might have something here," she said. "Millie, can you find Ham or Kendall?"

"They're in London."

Millie spent most days working to keep Wg. Cmd. Thomas from looking over her shoulder and she had nothing to offer. Now, just when they might have found the break they needed, they were nowhere near.

She slumped back down in her chair.

"We'll see what they think when they get back." Constance went back to her desk. "Hazel, keep at it. Maybe the pilot got a better shot later in the roll."

Millie removed the portable stereoscope from her tunic's breast pocket, jumping in to help. She had to do something with all her anxiety. They pored over the brothers and sisters of Hazel's first image, trying to find the missing piece of the puzzle they needed. A pair of PIs returned with hot cups of tea, whispering that new cover of Peenemunde had arrived. Constance sent Hazel looking. She wanted Section L to be the first to get a look at the photographs. Within the hour, Hazel returned, waving the images like a victory flag. Getting the photos had been a fight, one she had been determined to win.

"Millie! Constance! Come here." Hazel was either excited or panicked. These days it was impossible to tell which.

"What is it?" She shoved a single image and a magnifying glass Millie's way.

"There's no pair," Millie said, crestfallen.

"Nope." She shrugged her shoulders and stepped back, chewing on a ragged cuticle.

Under the glass, Millie saw a small object shaped like a "t." It rested on the end of the earthenwork ramp. *Am I seeing things, or is this real?* Her eyes had been giving her some trouble lately. She had put it down to no sleep. Between the Callum and Elliot mess, never getting to take pictures, and having no idea what she might do after the war, she found sleep elusive.

She flung the single photograph toward Constance. Constance held the image up to the light and examined it with her magnifying glass.

"We've got it." She looked at them, smiling.

"Are you sure?" Millie asked afraid to believe it.

"Yes! I'm sure." Constance pulled Millie and Hazel into a bear hug.

Then they were on the move. They raced down the old servants' stairs to the main hallway and back up the grand staircase to reach the Bodyline unit. Wg. Cmd. Thomas and Douglas Kendall were just back from London and taking off their overcoats as they burst into the room.

"What on earth?" Ham said.

"We've found it." Constance waved the image in the air.

"Found what?" He collapsed in his chair. He looked to Millie to explain the commotion.

"Constance and her team have found the flying bomb!" Millie said, as if she were calling a reel.

Millie pushed three images under his nose and built their case—a ramp near Peenemunde on one image, a tiny aircraft on a trailer on another, and finally a tiny aircraft in launching position on the ramp. In every shot, the small cross that was their pilotless bomb was clear.

"Trayford, I appreciate this has been a long search, but you must compose yourself." Kendall looked at Millie with dark-circled eyes. He envied her exuberance but found it as annoying as a gnat at times. Taking a seat at the communal table in the middle of the room, he waited for her to return to her senses and join him. Constance and Hazel got the message and sat straight-backed in the chair next to Wg. Cmd. Thomas, pretty pleased with themselves. "Neil has something to add to the mix." Ham took off his glasses and stroked his mustache.

"We found these ramps in images taken of the Zinnowitz radar station." Neil handed Millie the pair of images first. She gave him a slight nod in appreciation.

Then, Ham took all of the images and analyzed them under his stereoscope.

"Do they match the ski sites?" He leaned back in his chair, fingers laced behind his head.

"The earthen ramps at Peenemunde do." Millie looked to Neil.

"And the ones in Zinnowitz?" Kendall asked. Neil nodded yes.

Millie held her breath as Ham lifted his magnifying glass to his left eye. He moved the image of the small crucifix on the ramp under the light and continued staring through the looking glass. He put the photograph and the glass on the table, slowly stood up, and proclaimed, "You've done it!" His fist slammed against the oak tabletop, punctuating the news. "You've *all* done it. And, now Trayford, it's time to celebrate."

A chorus of cheers filled the room. After months of searching, years for some, they had finally proven the existence of two of Hitler's promised vengeance weapons, and they could demonstrate the Germans' plan to launch thousands of pilotless missiles to London. The word *London* ping-ponged in Millie's head. She was reminded of Hazel's early words, "Everyone I love is in London." She imagined her father walking past the victory gardens in Kensington Park. All she could see were vegetables laid to ruin by German bombs. *We shouldn't be celebrating. Why are we celebrating? The bombs are real. They're real! We need to find a way to warn the people of London.* A lump swelled in her throat; all she could see was Nanna Clara's flat razed to the ground.

"We have to warn them." Millie let the words slip past her lips. Hazel gave her a questioning glance. Millie simply looked to the ground, images playing like a slide show in her mind. Her girl from the bookstore. The people taking shelter in the tube. The boys at surrounding bases—they all deserved a chance to protect themselves, to prepare. She repeated with more force this time, "We have to warn London."

"What's that, Trayford?" Ham said. Millie hadn't realized she said the thought aloud.

"Those sites are all but operational, sir. I am glad we found them and hope we can destroy them before they launch a rocket—but we need to warn the people living in London, sir. Just in case." Her voice was strained, judgmental because she wanted to broadcast her words like a thirty-point headline.

The room grew hushed. "In time, Trayford. We will warn them in time if it becomes necessary. But, for now, we can't show our hand to the Germans." Ham walked over to the typewriter and sat down. "For now, we're going to write a report and inform the gentlemen at Whitehall about what we have confirmed. They will decide the next best step. If I had to guess, we'll be bombing the hell out of the northern coast of France within days, and the people of London will be none the wiser. But that isn't my decision." His eyes fixed on her. "It definitely isn't yours."

Ham saw a woman worn with the search. An expression he recognized because he saw the same look of exhaustion when he looked in the mirror. He would share his news with Red, Neil, and Millie soon enough. And then they would all have a well-deserved break. His eyes pleaded with her to keep it together for just a while longer.

Millie didn't get the message.

"Isn't it, sir?" She kept at it. "You can't just tell the War Cabinet and forget what you know. Don't you have family in London? Red, Neil. I know the two of you do." Millie rushed across the room to them. They stiffened. "We have information that might save them. Aren't we obligated to share it? Share the images, make people see the truth. For all we know, they may plan to start flinging those things at us tomorrow."

Ham got to his feet. He had seen the signs of fatigue in his entire team and had sent Red and Neil off for longer breaks. He should have insisted Millie do the same. She was just so damn good at her job. So dedicated. He nudged Millie gently into the hallway before lecturing her. "We took an oath to look into these activities and report what we find to the proper authorities. I'm sure I don't need to remind you that our military success depends on you keeping the vow you made when you signed the Official Secrecy Act. Don't go soft on me now, Trayford. Your contributions here are too valuable. Besides, they will act. Some of those new sites we found are pointing at the very ports we need to launch Operation Overlord."

"You think it's soft to warn people that bombs are coming?" Millie replied, staring down at her feet.

"What do you suggest? We call up the *Daily Telegraph* and announce that we have found the Germans' secret weapons?" He forced out a chuckle to diffuse the situation.

"When you say it that way, it does sound ridiculous." She started to tell him about losing Clara in the Blitz. How finding her bombed-out apartment had led Millie to this very room, but she found she couldn't. Everyone had lost someone by now. Her story was ordinary, so she simply said, "I lost someone in the Blitz."

"Many people did." Ham fought the urge to take her by the hand, hearing his sister's voice asking if he would coddle a man that way. "We will make sure they level every ramp out there. That I can guarantee." Kendall had joined them in the hallway and overheard Millie's last comment. "Duncan Sandy has been a believer for some time now. The bombings will happen." They both looked down on her, smiling and nodding. They meant for their words to reassure Millie, but it only made her feel small. She stiffened and threw her shoulders back. She didn't want to be the object of their condescension or concern.

Hazel and Constance sneaked into the hall, presumably on a rescue mission. They were all sure Millie was about to break, never entertaining the idea that she might be the only one thinking straight. "Millie, why don't we go for a cup of tea? You could use a break. You've been working around the clock for months." Hazel took Millie by the arm and gently tugged. Millie jerked her arm free but followed. It was time to drape herself in duty and obedience once again.

"If Kendall says they will bomb, you can count on it," Constance said.

Millie gave voice to her irritation. "Bombing won't do any good. This will end just like the attack on Peenemunde. We bomb them, our pilots and their people die. They rebuild or recalculate. We send recon pilots to get lost or worse, die, taking pictures, and then more pilots to bomb."

"You always say we simply need to stay one step ahead," Hazel said.

Millie stopped in her tracks and looked deep into Hazel's eyes. "My father says that." Hazel's eyes sprang wide open, and she looked to Constance for help. The look on Hazel's face stabbed Millie's pounding heart. She gently took Hazel's and then Constance's hands. None of this was their doing. Millie continued, her tone less accusing. "I'm not so sure anymore, but what else is there?" Millie thought of Callum and her cameras and all the women waiting for her to photograph them. That's what's waiting; that's what else there is. *Will I ever make it out of this dark tunnel?*

Wg. Cmd. Thomas caught up to the women before they climbed down the stairs. "Millie, after you've had a hot cup of tea, go to your billet. I don't want to see you back here for two days. That's an order!"

"Of course," Millie said. Just then, she didn't have any fight left in her.

They were all sure she was going to crack under the pressure. Millie knew they might be right, but not in the way they thought. Every day the voice deep within her telling her there was more, more to see, more to do was growing louder. If the crack in the veneer of duty and obedience grew too big, she just might listen to herself for a change.

He took her by the hand and slipped her a small brown paper bag. Millie felt the hard cubes within. He leaned in and whispered, "There's enough for the three of you. You all did great work."

# CHAPTER THIRTY-FIVE

RAF Medmenham-Central Intelligence Unit

**December 1, 1943**

188 days until D-Day

Millie sorted and straightened her piles back at her desk as if she were in her father's study. *How long before he hears the news about the ramps and bomb at Peenemunde? He will be so pleased.* Gathering from the clues Millie saw in his office, he had been looking for this kind of confirmation since the British declared war on Germany. Maybe longer.

Ham returned and asked Red, Neil, and Millie to join him at the communal table. He looked at Millie with a down-turned smile and soft eyes. "I've worked you too hard. What you all need, no deserve, is a bit of time off. I'd suggest a stiff drink and a cigar as well, if you think that'd help. I'm sending you all home for Christmas for a couple of weeks. In the meantime, I need you to take our newly assigned PIs in hand and train them."

"New PIs?" Millie was so tired. She had stayed away as ordered, but sleep eluded her. She had hoped for a moment with Callum. Why, she couldn't say. She didn't have any answers for him, but she convinced herself that no harm could come from holding his hand or perhaps even another kiss. She only knew that seeing him would set the world right, if only for a moment. And she hoped seeing him might clarify things in her personal life. But both he and Peter only had time to fly and sleep. *This invasion of France had better work.* Millie didn't know how much longer any of them could keep up the pace.

"New PIs indeed. Duncan Sandy has renamed our little group Operation Crossbow and is staffing us up. Much to your delight, Trayford, I have been informed that crews will begin bombing the ski sites immediately. Bomber Command needs to prioritize which sites to hit first, so they need us to stage the progress toward completion of each site."

"Makes sense. If that's all, sir." Red started to get to his feet.

Ham held up a hand. "There is one more thing. I will be retiring this month."

"Retiring, sir." Millie reached for his hand, unknowingly. She pulled it back quickly. This man wasn't her father. "What will we do without you?"

"You will all be fine. You three do all the work around here anyway. I just keep the trains running on time."

"You do more than that, sir," Neil said.

"In any case, I flew taking pictures in the Great War and have spent this one looking at the images blokes like Trayford's brother are taking. It's time I hang up my lens. We will have a bit of a send-off on December 22, after which we will all go home. You will have two weeks' leave. Be as good for the new bloke as you have been for me."

Wg. Cmd. Hugh Hamshaw Thomas poured out four glasses of whiskey, and they all shared a farewell drink.

# CHAPTER THIRTY-SIX



William found the routine nature of his current work tiresome. It wasn't as bad as spending your days in a prisoner of war camp as he had during the Great War, but his life in the interwar period was decidedly more interesting. He hadn't confirmed it, but he believed he was one of the last Britons out of Berlin in September of 1939.

Listening to Peter at dinner last night as he described flying solo at thirty-thousand feet, spying on the enemy with his cameras, he felt envy swell within him. And though he knew the chances of his boys returning after a bombing raid or recon sortie weren't good, he wished he could join them as they worked to destroy what the Germans were now calling their vengeance weapons in public speeches.

Instead, he marched toward his office from his requisite Friday morning meeting with Duncan Sandy in the War Rooms. Once in his office, he sat and sorted the dispatches from agents around the country and on the continent of Europe. Each note contained intrigue and danger, something William sorely missed. In the middle of the stack, he found a typed fragment of information of particular interest. Decoded, it read:

*I have received news from Amniarix that an RAF pilot believed to be Flt. Lt. Elliot Harrington is hiding in Bayeux with members of the Druid network. Should I confirm his identity in person or arrange for immediate extraction?*

He pulled his ashtray closer and set the note aflame. If Amniarix said it was Elliot, it probably was. She had sent the Wachtel report linking Peenemunde to the ramps in northern France. She told them there would be 108 sites, and so far, they had identified 103. William was certain the photographic interpreters at RAF Medmenham would find five more.

On the other hand, if by chance agent Amniarix had misidentified the pilot, it would be wiser to send him over the Pyrenees Mountains like so many of his mates. Sending a plane for a Flight Lieutenant, even one of Elliot's station, was highly unusual. William needed to know for sure before he made such drastic arrangements. He would have to risk sending Bonnie Marie to him.

The coded return said simply—*we need to be sure it is him.*

# CHAPTER THIRTY-SEVEN

RAF Medmenham-Central Intelligence Unit

December 12, 1943

176 days until D-Day

The memorandum from Col. Caldwell was marked top secret. Wg. Cmd. Thomas read it through for the second time. *I will not be sad to leave this part of the job behind.* Extracting VIP personnel out of occupied France had only gotten more dangerous now that Bomber Command had been directed to annihilate the ramp sites.

"Millie," Ham tapped Millie on the shoulder to get her attention. "Would you join me in my office?"

Millie followed behind him closely. She had only been to his basement office on a few occasions since coming to RAF Medmenham. It had been over a week since her so-called meltdown, and no one had mentioned it. *I hope he isn't planning to write me up. Or worse yet, rescind my time off. It was just a bit of necessary reality. They all spent too much time here living with theory. Someone had to remind them that they were talking about real people. Oh well. Let them believe what they what. Just let me go home.* Fiona and the others were expecting her in Wick.

"Have a seat, Trayford."

*Oh, no. He is going to reprimand me.* "Sir, I am feeling much better." It seemed better to go along with their understanding of her reaction to finding the winged bomb at Peenemunde rather than get into it again. "I am sorry for my—outburst, if that's what you would call it. I can assure you I am back at it, full steam ahead." She stood as tall as she could without lifting onto her toes, and she spoke loud and clear.

"That is all forgotten." Ham gestured to the chair. "I called you here because I have a different assignment for you." He took a seat as well. "My duties here at CIU include arranging VIP extractions from Axis territory—people like agents who may be in jeopardy, high-ranking officials who have escaped capture. You get my meaning, yes?"

"Yes, sir." Millie was nodding enthusiastically, too enthusiastically perhaps.

"You are not in trouble. I simply need your help. And I thought you would welcome a break from the rocket search. Unless, well with your fiancé missing..."

"A distraction would be nice." Millie grasped her own hands and laid them in her lap, pushing all thoughts of Elliot that threatened to flood in at the mention of him back into the box she kept them in inside her mind. She needed to show Ham she was up to the task.

"So, we need to get someone out of Germany?" she continued. She thought it must be an officer who escaped from a POW camp like her father had during World War I.

"No, France. Northern France. And because you know every rail line, street, river, and fence row in the area, I thought you would be the best person for the task."

"When will the rescue happen, sir? I should think that would be the most important detail."

"That's just it. The date seems to be up in the air. Because of that, I need you to identify three locations near Bayeux with a strip of land large enough for a small plane to land and take off. I will take it from there."

"That should be easy enough. Should I compare the current cover to the latest models and maps?"

Ham nodded. "Just so. I knew you were the one for the job. That will be all."

Millie took her leave. *Who could it be? Surely anyone of importance left France long ago.* They would be going to a lot of trouble and risking a lot of lives to rescue them. *I hope whoever it is deserves it.*

# CHAPTER THIRTY-EIGHT

Outskirts of Bayeux, France
December 17, 1943
171 days until D-Day

Bonnie Marie limped toward the farmhouse on the fringes of town. She kept her eyes down and walked on the tiniest streets to avoid the German occupiers. They were far crueler here than in Paris. Here there was no one to impress. The last thing she wanted was to find herself in an interrogation room at the Hotel Lutetia. The damp, cold sea air reached into the fields of this lovely town, making it all the harder to walk. After a rhythmic knock, a young boy opened the door and led her to the cellar door covered by a rag rug.

With the cellar opened wide, she dangled her feet over the edge and sat. *This will have to do.* She knew she would never make it back up the ladder. The boy handed her a lit candle, and she held it down into the cellar, illuminating the space. A face appeared beneath her. It was undeniably the face of Elliot Harrington.

She expected his look of surprise. For a moment, he stood frozen, jaw slacked. Then he asked in utter amazement, "What are you doing here?"

"I've come to get you home."

# CHAPTER THIRTY-NINE

Teaghlach

December 24, 1943

165 days until D-Day

Millie found Teaghlach alive. The staff and folks from town buzzed about as if her ancestral home was a beehive. Ferguson told her they had big plans for her return and a surprise on the drive from the train station. And as they made the curve in the drive, they almost smashed right into one. The men from town were hauling a massive Christmas tree down the road for the main hall. Millie smiled, seeing them put their hands to something so joyful. The last time she saw them, they were digging for their dead.

Fiona greeted her at the door, looking as regal as ever. "What an unexpected pleasure!" She was pleased Millie was there. From the looks of her, she needed a break. "Take a deep breath. This cold, crisp Scottish air is the cure for just about anything that ails a body."

Millie did as she was told. Breathing out and breathing in, she felt her spirit restore. Just to be hiding from the world for a moment was a relief.

"Now, what is this surprise Ferguson mentioned?"

"Come in, and I will show you." Kicking a ball in the main room, while some townsfolk rolled up the rugs, making way for the tree, were four children—three boys and a girl. The count of children in the house was now up to four. "The girl and boy lost their folks in the bombing, and I couldn't bear to send them away. The only thing I have to spare around here is space, and they know how to fill it up. I haven't heard so much shouting or laughter since your brood was their age."

"I think that's Peter's rugby ball. Too bad he isn't here to teach them how to play." With the invasion planning in full gear, Peter and Callum were spending more time flying and taking pictures than they were with their feet on the ground.

"I think your brothers are planning on sharing a pint with your father on Christmas in London." Fiona took Millie by the hand. "I'm delighted to have you all to myself." As the words left her mouth, Aggie and Mrs. Drummond rushed in and engulfed Millie with hugs and kisses. "Aggie, why don't you help Millie unpack? I will see you all at dinner tonight." With that, Fiona lifted onto her toes, gave Millie a peck on the cheek, and took her leave.

"How is she always so graceful?" Millie watched her favorite grandmother glide across the hardwood floors as if she were dancing a waltz.

"You have your moments," Aggie said. "Let's get you to your room so they can transform the hall."

Millie pulled a black silk gown from her trunk. She brought the trunk along so she would have room for everything she needed: clothes for dinner (Fiona never missed an opportunity to get dressed up), tweed trousers and wool jumpers for hiking, and her camera. Unpacking, she held the camera to her heart and swayed—the loose threads of her seams tightened by the minute.

"Lady Blair mentioned that Callum might surprise them with a visit. Did he mention anything to you?"

At the sound of his name, Millie could feel his fingers plunging into her hair as he pulled her into him, mouth searching, wanting. A quiver shot down her body. She put the camera down and sat on the edge of the bed.

"Oh, Aggie, I've made a mess of things."

Aggie joined her on the bed. "Spill it."

"I kissed him." She took in Aggie's round eyes. "I really kissed him."

Aggie twisted around facing Millie, understanding immediately she was talking about Callum. "How was it?"

"You don't think I'm horrible? I'm engaged." She lifted the ring dangling about her neck. "And my fiancé is missing, perhaps dead. What was I thinking?"

"You were thinking, 'I'm not married yet' and 'I've wanted to do that for years.'"

"You knew?" Millie walked over to the window, fiddling with the locket and the ring.

"Stop fidgeting." Aggie took her by the hand. "There is nothing to be embarrassed about. He is gorgeous and so kind. Everyone in the county has their fingers crossed that you will dump Elliot and marry our Callum. His father may have bought their titles, but he is grand."

"Even Fiona."

"Mrs. Drummond says Fiona thinks you're better off alone, but if you're going to marry, she'd take Callum over Elliot any day. That you're only with Elliot because your other grandmother bullied you into it." Aggie grabbed Millie's other hand too. "Fiona wants you to have your own life. She says your mother did. Not one in your husband's shadow. Says it takes quite a man to stand aside and allow that."

Millie thought of her father. *He may have let Mother live her own life, but he hasn't extended the courtesy to me.* Millie tightened. *Is Callum just another choice made for me by others?* She shook her head, dropped Aggie's hands, and picked up her camera. "I'll be back for dinner."

Aggie didn't close the gap between them. "Will you need help getting ready?"

"No, I've been managing on my own for years."

# CHAPTER FORTY



Millie depressed the cold metal shutter button, capturing the waves crashing against the cliffs. Turning around, she took a shot of Wick from above. The snaking River Wick drew her eye through the composition. In the frame, she also watched dark smoke rising from the chimneys mix with fog and was sure she would be able to smell the smoke every time she looked at the image. She walked toward town to take in the micro view with the wide view safely captured and trapped in its light-tight home. Two ancient headstones at the Old Parish Church, nets and cages left on the dock by the fishermen, the masts of three fishing boats docked in a row. When she took the last shot on the roll, she made her way to see Mr. Graham and Eldon at the paper.

The smell of fresh fried fish and chips tempted her as she passed Mrs. Layla's. Fiona would never forgive her lack of appetite, so she continued on her way. With one finger depressing a button on the bottom of her camera and the other rewinding the exposed film, Millie slipped through the front door of the *Groat*. Neither of the men looked up when she closed the door behind her.

"What took you so long?" Mr. Graham said.

"How do you mean? I only arrived this morning." Millie

grabbed a handful of quoins and carried them to Mr. Graham, helping him lock in the type. "Did Fiona tell you I was coming to town?"

Mr. Graham finally looked up from his work. "That grandmother of yours has told everyone in the county you were coming home for Christmas, but that's not why I was expecting you. I received a telegram from the Ministry of Information yesterday. I wasn't going to open it, thought it was a slap on the wrist, but Eldon convinced me it might be important." He went back to his work and pointed at the dreaded yellowish correspondence.

Millie froze. *Elliot is dead. Why tell the Wick paper. He never flew out of Wick. No one here knows anything about him other than we're engaged. The whole town knows we are engaged.* As the cruel thoughts settled in, Millie risked a question. "What did it say?"

"You know you have to speak up when Eldon is working on the Linotype."

"WHAT DID IT SAY?"

Mr. Graham pointed at his desk and said, "Why don't you read it and find out?"

*Dear Millie,*

*I had a lovely chat with your father over the Christmas punch bowl the other night stop He mentioned that you would be in Wick for the holidays stop There is a munitions plant nearby I need photographed stop If you are willing, please call stop*

She hadn't heard from her old boss since before she left Wick. Why now? It must have been father's idea. *Did Ham say something to him about her meltdown when they found a bomb and ramp at Peenemunde?*

Millie slipped the telegram into her camera bag, setting it aside. "Can I use the darkroom?"

"Are you going to do it?"

"What?"

"Don't be coy with me. It doesn't suit you. Are you going to photograph that munitions plant near Inverness for a new piece of propaganda?"

Millie shoved Graham out of the way and locked in the frame for the front page of the Christmas Day edition of the *John O'Groat*. A pain shot up her arm. Shaking off the sting of pinching herself, Millie answered with a shrug, feigning disinterest. "I guess." Inside, her stomach turned upside down. *Hell yes, I'm going to take the images.*

He snarled. "Don't go getting bashful on me now. You know as well as I do, they are looking for a shot as good as the one you took at the bookstore back in '40. Think you're up to the challenge?"

"You bet I am." Millie couldn't contain the smile that spread across her face.

"Try to take some real shots for yourself. Don't just concentrate on spreading their lies." Mr. Graham knew every image in the boxes under Millie's bed. She printed many of them in his darkroom. He considered publishing one or two of them back when Millie was stationed at RAF Wick, though he never told her that. He was drinking then and miserable, preferring to keep the people in his orbit miserable as well.

The flat woman who stood before him now had been so effervescent then. Perhaps if he had supported her ambitions, she wouldn't have gone back south. In Wick, she had the best of all worlds, fulfilling her duty to country, family, and most of all, herself.

"Spoken like a hardened newspaper man." Millie tried to coax a smile out of Mr. Graham, but he just grumbled.

"Joke all you like, but remember they will tell you where to point the camera if they can get away with it." He plucked the telegram out of the camera bag. "You could say no." But he had seen the color come back into her face as she read the request. She would do the propagandist's bidding in exchange for access to her beloved subjects—women, who she was convinced ran the world without notice.

"No, I'll do it."

"Then you had better call in for the details. You can use my telephone," he growled.

# CHAPTER FORTY-ONE

Teaghlach

**December 24, 1943**

165 days until D-Day

Standing just inside the front door, Millie felt the tension in her muscles fade away. She was surrounded by people who loved her, and she had a photography assignment in her pocket. *I'm grateful Wg. Cmd. Thomas sent me home.* The transformation happening to the main hall flabbergasted her. And the weight of her camera on her chest thrilled her. In the center of the room, seven women from town, two on ladders, decorated the Christmas tree. Millie headed straight to them.

She knelt on the ground a few feet from the women, making them appear to be in a circle. The wood floor was hard and cold, but the image was perfect. When they began to place candles on the branches, Millie scurried nearer to them, so their hands appeared in the pictures. One of the women abandoned the tree and reached for a bolt of fabric. As she unwound the bolt into a pile, the white folds looked like whipped cream, tasty. Little by little, the folds smoothed out as the youngest woman in the group tied one end of the fabric to the stair rail and wrapped it round and round. Millie couldn't resist the contrast between the dark wood and the white cotton. She got to her feet and took the stairs two at a time, all the while snapping away.

The workmen constructed tables for the buffet, and the

staff dressed them in elegant linens and fragile dinnerware. Mrs. Drummond was pulling out all the stops. Food might be scarce, but they had their belongings and traditions to remind them of happier times. The clinks and bangs blended in a symphony of hard work and exactitude. Before Millie finished her roll of film, Aggie and her mother walked into the hall, followed by Mrs. Drummond, the conductor of the entire affair.

Mrs. Drummond worked with precision and an ease Millie couldn't help but envy. She seemed a woman unafraid to ask for exactly what she needed. She crafted concise commands, and her troops worked in harmony with her desires. Millie couldn't help thinking that she was wasting her talents here. With her as its model, the military would be wise to swing wide its doors to remarkable and talented women—especially into its highest ranks. If Mrs. Drummond were the Prime Minister and her team of fearless mothers the generals, Britain would have won this war years ago.

She moved in Millie's direction, unaware of her presence on the stairs, unpacking the tree topper—a silver star. Millie composed a shot, remembering a Christmas long ago. Millie was hiding under the tree with Peter. They were already in their night clothes. Coming down the stairs and climbing one of the ladders, her mother placed the topper on the tree. Millie and Peter were transfixed as her shapely body moved with grace, hovering over the bare wood floors.

"Isn't she stunning?" They overheard their father say to a stranger standing next to him.

"She's the swan, indeed." The stranger's voice was laced with admiration and jealousy.

Hidden under their branches, the children watched as her raven hair, sheer white sleeves, and navy skirt blurred. *She was mesmerizing, damn it.* When she turned, her braid swung in unison with her skirt. She was Millie's ideal subject. *I wish I could have taken a portrait of her.*

"Your hair makes me think of a stallion's mane," Callum

said, pulling her back into the moment.

*Callum. Mrs. Blair had said he would do his best to be here.*

Holding her breath, Millie stood up and resisted the urge to fling her arms around him. She could feel hot red blotches spreading on her chest. "That's why I keep it tied up most of the time," she stammered while she braided the loose coils into one thick rope. "I've considered cutting it, but I can't bring myself to do it. It makes me feel strong, like Samson."

"I don't mind that." His voice was a whisper. It felt like he was looking right through her. "Did you take any good shots?"

"A few, perhaps. I won't know for sure until I get back into the darkroom."

"Millie," Aggie called from the top of the stairs. "Oh, hello, Callum. I'm glad you're here, but this one needs to get dressed. They've started to light the candles."

Sure enough, the crew of seven women each held a wick and were lighting the hundreds of candles on the tree. Millie took one last shot and bounded up the stairs. *I can't avoid him forever.* The truth was, she didn't want to. She simply couldn't see a way through.

After slipping her black silk dress on, Millie went to check on Fiona. When Millie entered the room, a bent-over, rumpled old woman in a simple twill dress and floor length wool cardigan emerged from the parlor door. She wasn't even five feet tall. When Millie was three, Fiona convinced her she was so small because she was a fairy. Over her shoulder hung a thick grey braid. It was a comforting sight. *I've never seen my grandmother wear her hair any other way.*

"Get in here!"

"Why aren't you dressed?" Millie said, closing the gap between them. When she reached her, Fiona pulled her into a hug. She'd always been comfortable with intimacy. *She must have taught that to Mother.*

She ushered Millie into a suite of rooms that were clearly her dominion. She had converted the parlors into a small apartment for herself. There were four chairs and two tables covered with books, mending, and knitting in the first room. Shelves crammed with books and memories lined the walls. Through an adjacent door, Millie saw the bedposts and more books. Clutter filled the rooms, but somehow it felt cozy instead of messy.

"Do you think I should cut my hair?" Millie asked, taking her grandmother's hand, frightfully aware of the tissue-like skin and the bulging blue veins.

With a squeeze, she said, "Absolutely not. I will show you how to twist and pin it like all of the smart girls. Those curls are your birthright, my love."

Leading Millie to the mirror, she sat her in a chair and began to work. Millie's hair bent to her will as she combed through it with her fingers. She sectioned black tendrils eight times and began twisting them together, spearing them expertly with the long pins she drew magically from her pocket. Fiona's frail hands worked like a master weaver as she mixed the warp and weft threads summoned from her hair. The rhythm hypnotized Millie. When she finished the work, Fiona rested a hand on each of Millie's shoulders to get her attention.

"Darling, you have my blood in you. You come to the world with a sense of purpose and honesty. Hold true to those things, keeping fear at bay, and you will be fine." She took Millie in her arms, and their tears fell like a steady spring rain.

"Enough of that." Fiona dabbed her damp face with a linen handkerchief and went behind a screen to change. She emerged in an emerald green velvet dress that reached for the floor. "Ready."

Hand in hand, they took the elegant staircase together. Making the last turn, Millie saw her family, blood and adopted, smiling and dancing. When they reach the landing, the opening phrases of Tchaikovsky's "Sleeping Beauty Waltz" popped and crackled on the long-forgotten piece of vinyl, inviting everyone to their feet. The group coupled off as best they could. Men were a scarcity in those days. Millie smiled at the sight of Mrs. Drummond and Aggie tiptoeing to the beat across the floor, Mrs. Drummond taking the lead. Watching Mr. Graham offer a hand to Fiona, Millie felt a tap on her shoulder.

"May I interest you in a dance?" It was Callum.

"Yes." She didn't dare to say too much for fear she might begin blaming him for her life again. Once in his arms, she risked talking. "I am sorry. I'm all over the place. I just can't see a way through the mess I've created."

Instead of responding, Callum tightened his frame, smiled broadly, and moved Millie skillfully around the room. *I won't fight with her tonight.* Millie got lost in the violins and flutes, floating on air, supported by Callum's strong arms. As they glided around tables covered with wine and brandy-stained linens, Callum closed his eyes and lost himself in the music until it stopped.

The needle scraping the record's edge ripped him from his dream—the two of them growing old in Wick or traveling the world so she could take her damn photos. "When this war is over, you are going to have to find the courage to stand up for what you want. The people who truly love you will stand by you, including me." Callum whispered in her ear.

Millie pushed him away and ran. She didn't stop running until she was in the rotting garden. The door to the shed was swung wide open. Inside she found a lamp and lit it. She sat, skin covered in bumps. She waited to hear the approaching footsteps of Callum or Aggie or Ferguson or anyone who could advise her on what to do next. She waited and waited. As seconds became minutes, it became clear to Millie that no one was coming.

She walked alone toward the cliffs. As she got closer, a shadow lengthened across her path. She held up the lamp to see that it was Callum.

"Are you playing with me, Millicent Trayford?"

"Millicent Trayford?" Millie set the lamp on the ground,

and Callum wrapped his jacket around her. He so wanted to hate her, but he just couldn't bring himself to do it.

"I'll call you whatever you like if you can explain why you insist on lingering in this purgatory. Don't you think it's time you pick something?"

"Don't you mean someone?" Millie walked closer to the cliff's edge.

"I mean something; who are you? A photographer? An agent of the war? I can't tell anymore. You've got a finger in every pot. Isn't it time you settle on something?"

"You don't understand. I can't just run off and do whatever I please like you can."

"Whatever I like?" He picked up a stone and hurled it into the sea.

"You know what I mean."

"That's rubbish. You have more choices than anyone I've ever met." *His face looked lovely in the moonlight.* "You just need to make one. It may cost you something, but that's how life works out here in the real world."

She picked a fight because she was not ready to commit to him on anything. She longed to explain her need to do something meaningful and how desperately she wanted it to be taking pictures, but the words refused to come.

"I would if the world would let me have what I want."

"Let you? Adulthood means making your own choices." He dug in.

So did Millie. She was dizzy with the possibilities. Never go back to RAF Medmenham. Do what everyone expects; marry and leave photography behind as a long-forgotten hobby. Break things off with Elliot.

"I'm not willing to disappoint everyone, especially with the war raging. No one will be free to do what they want until it is over." Millie watched as Callum took a step back toward Teaghlach. She followed. "You said while we were dancing 'when the war is over.'"

He took pity on her and replied, "That I did. But promise me one thing. Before you marry Elliot, find out if he loves you or the idea of you, and find out exactly what kind of man he is."

"What does that mean?"

"You will have to ask him that."

Callum walked away, past the house and to the car park. Millie let him go.

# CHAPTER FORTY-TWO

Munitions Plant-Near Inverness, Scotland
December 27, 1943
161 days until D-Day

Millie held the eight-by-ten portrait camera she borrowed from Mr. Graham on her lap as if it were a two-year-old child. She felt stiff after the three-hour ride to Lairg, but she didn't dare put it in the bed of the truck; after all, it was made almost entirely of glass and mirrors. She made Aggie ride in the middle. Before their fight three nights ago, Callum offered to take Millie on this errand, and Mr. Ferguson had heartily agreed. Millie didn't know if it was because Ferguson also wanted her to abandon her promise to Elliot and choose Callum, or because he didn't want to make the long journey. Regardless, Callum was taking Aggie and her to the munitions plant. Millie found that her heart was pleased with her chauffeur even though her head wanted her to be furious with him because he kept insisting her path forward was a simple one.

Smartly, Millie left the film loading for after they arrived because security at the plant was as tight as RAF Medmenham's. The guard at the Royal Ordnance Factory for Munitions insisted she take the entire camera apart, making sure it wasn't a bomb. To a novice's eye, the large polished wooden box with cranks, gears, and baffles that extended eighteen inches was a strange-looking object; to Millie, it was a marvelously conceived machine.

Once inside the gate, they fell out of the truck in front of a smartly dressed man with beads of sweat forming on his forehead and upper lip. After dabbing them with his handkerchief for the second time, he stepped forward.

"I'm the plant foreman." He crammed the now damp handkerchief into his pocket. "My orders say you should start by photographing the girls on the north side of the plant packing shells and then move to the other side to those loading fuses in the anti-tank mines." Like everyone Millie worked with, their guide walked briskly as he gave Millie and her assistants instructions. Arms full of film and flashbulbs, Millie smiled at Callum and Aggie, equally burdened with equipment, grateful they came to help. "The note said something about the light being best on the west side of the building this time of day," he said.

"That was my request," Millie said. "I have a few flashbulbs, but there was some concern that they might be dangerous. Something about the materials being highly explosive."

He dabbed his forehead again. "You can use them, if necessary. We've taken steps to make sure it will be safe." He stopped in front of the door that led to the plant. "You will only photograph approved areas. Are we clear?"

Every man Millie had met in the last three years had asked her that same question at least once. Are we clear? *Do they think I'm an idiot?* "Yes, sir."

He took them to a workstation at the top of the first column of workers. The smell of sulfur overwhelmed, but the scene was wondrous. The room was a rhapsody of repetition and lines—a photographer's dream for building dimension in a flat image. Two rows of seven I-beams supported perpendicular beams that ended at the exterior walls. The rafters looked like they could go on forever because they mirrored the long tables flanked by women on either side.

A set of twins with brown hair, tied in low buns accentuating their long necks, stood at the end of the first table, the icing on the cake of the dimensional scene. One of them wore a wedding ring. They looked right at Millie—clearly her models for the day.

Millie pushed past her guide, who hovered and gave Callum and Aggie, who were managing her gear, a wide-eyed look before she said to the girls, "As I'm sure you've been told, we are going to be taking images for the Ministry of Information. They want shots of you working, so if you can, do your best to pretend I'm not here."

The twins chattered away, telling Millie their names, Peggy and Polly, while she separated the tripod's legs, secured the camera, and slipped in the film. Every three feet or so, there was a window, so she didn't need a flash. She took a test shot, focusing on the reflection bouncing off the end of the conical tips of shells the size of a whiskey bottle and a girl in the distance wearing the same clothes as her models, grey coveralls with her hair tied up in a headscarf.

"Polly, when you're ready, I need you to take a seat and start loading the shells. And, Peggy, you can just stand over there."

"You got our names right," Polly said.

"Is that unusual?"

"We can still trick our parents," Peggy said.

"I guess I have a gift for details." Millie winked, trying to put them at ease. She needed to get to work before she lost the light.

She got what she needed with ten sheets of film and was ready to move to the next *designated area*. The foreman sent the models across the hall, and Millie sent Callum and Aggie out to the truck for more film. Locking down the baffles, Millie felt the pressure shift in her ears, and then...

Millie blinked away the dust from her eyes. Her shoulders pressed against the hard floor, making them ache. All the sounds around her muted, as if she'd been plunged underwater. Grabbing at her ears, Millie smelled heat mixed with sulfur. Sulfur? *Yes—I'm at the munitions plant, aren't I?* They needed sulfur to make the land mines. Land mines meant to explode with the slightest touch. She struggled to sit up and heard ringing. Grabbing her ears again, she made out a water truck approaching the building through the hole blown into the opposite side of the building. *My ears are fine, but those women are not.*

Before Millie could gather herself, she heard Aggie's screams. "Millie! Your face!"

Callum was next to her on his knees, steady as ever, picking pieces of glass and mirror out of her forehead, eyes welling up a bit. *Your beautiful face.* "You must have been packing the camera when the place blew," he said slowly and with care to keep Millie calm.

All around Millie, mixed with shell casings the size of a pint, were the remains of Mr. Graham's portrait camera. "Mr. Graham is going to have my hide." She picked up a shard of polished maple. *He didn't want me to take this assignment.* With trembling hands, she reached up and touched her cheek— it was sticky. Her lips tasted of iron.

Bewildered, Millie looked across the hall into the gallery where they made the anti-tank mines, through a gaping hole where the door she entered through once stood. The explosion had blown a hole in the ceiling, and electrical fittings swayed in the breeze. Millie let Callum tend the superficial wounds on her face with the handkerchief Aggie forced on him.

"Was the place bombed?" Millie asked Callum.

"I doubt it. This plant is a powder keg," he said.

"You think there's been some kind of accident?"

He nodded. "And I think it's time we go. Who knows when it will go up again?"

Millie let his words settle in, listening to the cries and moans all around her. She got to her feet and looked around— their chaperone was nowhere to be seen. She flipped open the latch on the metal box that held her 35mm camera and secured its strap about her neck.

"I can't miss this," she told Callum and Aggie.

She stumbled with her first step, but Callum was there to catch her. She gave him a reassuring glance, and they walked together, toward the worst of it, pushing past overturned tables and shell casings.

They found a room frozen in time, yellow dust covering every motionless soul like a net. Millie forced herself deeper into the catastrophe as Callum and Aggie checked on victims, awakening in a daze. At the far end of the once harmonious construction stood a tangle of metal and wood with what was once a girl on top. *At least, I think it was a girl.* Her skin was melted away from her face and shoulders, but Millie could still make out her hands.

How did this happen?

Two other girls, not disintegrated but dead just the same, were sprawled out beside Millie. The one closest to her was wearing an engagement ring. Polly. Millie's nose burned, and tears pooled in her eyes. She took a deep breath and pushed the shock and sorrow down, lifting her camera to her face.

She moved around the heap, trying to find just the right angle. Looking up from Polly's decorated hand, the shot emerged. Her outstretched arm drew Millie's eye to both Polly and Peggy's faces. They didn't look frightened at all. They hadn't seen it coming. Millie's fingers worked the rough lens edge until the sisters were in focus. She started shooting as fast as she could. She needed to capture these women's sacrifice for their country before someone stopped her.

Before she finished the first roll of film, her chaperone jerked at her camera, dragging her away from the sight.

"Hey, that's mine," she yelled, rubbing her neck. Mr. Graham had warned her they would tell her where to point her camera.

"I told you to only photograph in designated areas. This isn't one of them." His stern—correction, hostile—face told her he was not sorry for leading her away like a dog. "I'm going to need that film."

"I have every right to photograph. The people need to be told what happened here today. Those girls…"

"The film now, or I will take it with the camera."

"You can't take my camera!"

He leaned in, inches from her face, and hissed, "I assure you I can."

He took the camera in hand and searched for the latch to liberate the film. Jaws clenched and body quivering, Millie jerked the camera back.

"I'll do it myself."

Fumbling with the back of the camera, Millie walked away from the scene. "I need a dark corner to unload the film."

"I don't care how you do it. I just need the film."

Once in the corner, Millie rewound the film, slipped it into her pocket, and immediately unwrapped an un-shot roll. With the venerated images safe in her pocket, she handed the decoy roll of film to the plant manager. He dropped it to the floor and crushed it with the heel of his boot.

"You can't think you will keep this a secret," Millie said. "These women deserve to be remembered."

"I don't intend to keep anything a secret. But it will not be reported with pictures." He stood his ground. "It's time for you to go now."

Millie found she couldn't make herself move. The plant manager was back to dabbing his brow as perspiration spread on the fabric under his arms. Callum stepped up and whispered in Millie's ear, "You've done all you can here."

She flinched when he took hold of her arm, and she looked him dead in the eye, nostrils flaring.

"Millie." His words stretched out, pleading. "Aggie is waiting for us outside. She is ready to get home."

She did as he asked, certain the foreman would take her by the collar and forcibly toss her out if she didn't go of her own free will. Once outside, Millie broke away from Callum and embraced Aggie.

Without letting go of Millie, Aggie said, "Mr. Graham was right. They aren't interested in telling the truth; otherwise, they would never find workers."

"The girls here know what they're in for. They do it because it pays so well," Callum said.

"Is that true?" Millie asked Aggie.

"That and it's a way for them to help. Our troops need that ammunition."

"Then their sacrifice should be honored and remembered, not hidden away," Millie said.

"That may be, but no one has the stomach for looking at dead women on the front pages of our papers," Callum said.

"Why not—they see dead men often enough these days," Millie shot back.

"I don't know why, but somehow it's different." Aggie ended the conversation.

They drove the rest of the way home in silence.

# CHAPTER FORTY-THREE

Teaghlach
December 28, 1943
160 days until D-Day

The morning after the disaster at the munitions plant, before Millie had a chance to process her film, she sat alone at the kitchen table reading the papers. She came across three short sentences reporting the incident in Lairg. Three sentences. One for each girl who died. No explanation of the risks these women took every day. No gratitude for their service. No ribbons awarded for their sacrifice. Just three bland sentences from the nation's paper of record. But what else did she expect? If they had been men, it would have been front page news.

Setting the paper aside, she slid Callum's note out from beneath the newspaper spread out on the worn farm table.

"I'll write. But the next move is yours."

*What an ass. Why won't he acknowledge that I am in an impossible situation?* She couldn't decide anything until there was definitive news about Elliot. On the drive back from Lairg, he seemed to understand. Though, when he asked her if she had handed over her film to the plant manager, she wondered for just a moment if he knew her at all.

"Of course not." Millie pulled the film out from deep inside her trouser pockets.

"That's my girl." He punctuated the statement with a fist to the dashboard.

"Your girl."

"That is, if you will have me."

In the truck it sounded like he planned to wait for her decision. Now he wanted her to make the next move. *To hell with him.* She planned to make a move, but not toward Callum. She planned to make a move back to herself. *The next thing I'm doing is processing this film. Sorting out my love life will simply have to wait.* She packed up her things and headed to the *Groat*. She refused to think about anything else until she had new images to add to her collection. It had been stagnant for too long.

When she opened the back door, she found Callum lifting a fist, preparing to knock.

"What are you doing here?" Millie said, thinking of the eight words she just read.

"When I arrived at the base, they had news about Elliot."

Millie plunged out the door into the rain. Every single time. She bent over and yelled, fists pointing to the earth. *Will the universe never spare me a moment for myself without punishment?*

Callum put a hand on her back. "Are you all right? You didn't even give me a minute to tell you he—"

"He's dead, isn't he? And the last thing I did was stand him up to spend the day with you." She cut her eyes his way.

"And Aggie and Peter, and in case I need to remind you again, he was taking the flight either way." *I have never met a woman more infuriating.* He took a deep breath instead of just walking away, leaving her to think the worst. "Millie, it's too cold and wet to be out here. Let's go inside." He tried to pull her up, hoping she didn't begin to hyperventilate.

"Just tell me. Is he dead?" Millie turned around.

"No, Elliot isn't dead. He is in a hospital near London. If you like, I will fly you there."

"Why would you do that? You don't want me to be with him."

"I want you to be happy. If you think he will make you

happy and he is what you want, then you can have him." On the one hand, he knew it was complicated, they were engaged after all, but he had grown impatient with her delays. "I don't have any interest in being another one of your *duties*."

She stormed away from him, staring out to the sea. *How can he think he is a duty? I thought he knew me. He must know that with Elliot alive...What?*

Time had run out. Millie knew it, but let her mind wander to questions like, where had Elliot been all this time and why hadn't he gotten news to her? *What am I going to tell him—say to him? Surely I'll know once I see him.*

"I'll need a few minutes to get my things together. Will you wait?" Millie fought to hold herself together. *Elliot is alive. I am going to have to make a choice.* It was going to be the most awkward flight of her life, but a train would simply take too long.

"No," Callum pointed to a bicycle. That would have been his answer even if he brought a car. He needed a break from her. She didn't seem to have any trouble standing up to him. Most days, he liked that fact, but today it was just irritating. He rode the bike from the airbase in these gales so that she wouldn't have the shock of a telegram. Instead of being grateful, she tried to blame him and his invitation for Elliot's accident—again! "Have Ferguson bring you."

Millie watched as Callum rode away. She wanted to chase after him and tell him she was sorry. Of course, it wasn't his fault that Elliot's plane went down. *Why does he put up with me?*

"Lady Millicent, you have to get inside." Mrs. Drummond stood at the servant's door.

The moment Millie cleared the threshold, she fell into Mrs. Drummond's able arms, and they melted onto the floor. She rocked Millie as they sat, encouraging her tears. She cried in relief for Elliot. She cried because of the mess she'd made with Callum. But most of all, she cried because she was spent—worn raw by her efforts to fulfill her commitments to her father, to her country, to Clara. The weight of it all held her to the ground. The door unlatched behind them, and Ferguson came into focus.

Millie jumped up, wiped her face, and straightened out her wet clothes. "Will you take me to the airfield? Callum is going to fly me back to London to see Elliot in the hospital."

"I certainly will, my lady" Ferguson said.

# CHAPTER FORTY-FOUR

Hospital-Outskirts of London

December 28, 1943

160 days until D-Day

The gunmetal greys of the war painted the landscape outside the car window. It reminded Millie of the color she mixed by mistake as a child. Somehow when she added black to the other pigments, a putrid puddle emerged. The war doused everything in that color. It did little to lift her mood. She should have been excited to see Elliot, thrilled that he had been found. But after everything, she had little energy for shoulds. *I am a terrible, selfish person. Elliot deserves so much better.*

The sights inside the hospital were no better. The blinding white draping accentuated the devastation of war. Reds and yellows stained most surfaces, hinting at the injuries the crisp white sheets tried to hide. The smell of disinfectant, disease, and urine mixed in the air. Millie fought against gagging as she wandered down an alley flanked by the feet of white metal beds.

She stood at the foot of Elliot's bed at the far end of the main room. Picking up the clipboard hanging near his toes, she read, "exhaustion and minor frostbite on extremities." Returning the chart, she noticed his feet were uncovered but wrapped in white cotton gauze. Thank goodness there weren't stains. His face was relaxed in an angelic pose. Not the cad Callum hinted at just days ago. *Have I been naïve? Is it possible that—No! He isn't the bad guy here. I am.* She swept his bangs over to the right, and his eyes fluttered open. He seemed vulnerable, and it took Millie off guard. *How have I never seen this before?* Blinking rapidly, he focused on her face.

"Elliot, it's Millie," she said.

"I know that." He jerked back, sat up, and leaned back on his pillow. This was an Elliot Millie recognized. "You caught me dreaming."

"Was it a nightmare?"

"Why would you ask that?"

"You seem cross." Millie pulled a chair over and took a seat.

"You'd be cross too if you had been hiding in a series of barns and cellars for the past four months, eating only scraps and freezing your ass off for the lack of a good fire." He kept a straight face while spewing the nonsense. When they debriefed him on the plane ride home, they told him not to share any information about his involvement with the French Resistance. The truth—he was cross. He had been having the time of his life. The people, and more specifically the women, well, one woman. Why couldn't Millie be as determined and self-assured as she was?

And now he was back, staring the rest of his well-mannered life in the face. He knew he was only home because of Millie and her father's connections. No pilot gets a VIP airlift out of France. She had ended his adventures.

"I didn't realize." It wasn't the reunion Millie imagined. His hostility was unexpected and off-putting. She felt less guilty by the second. "Do your fingers and toes hurt?" she said to fill the gap between them. She ran a finger down his bandaged hands. The loose weave scratched her fingertips.

He forced himself to stay perfectly still, which he found challenging. Her touch made his skin crawl. *What happened to her?* She had become weak, compliant. *How could I have ever wanted someone like that?*

"They have slathered me with all kinds of salves. They

say I will be just fine. Keeping me here is the procedure. I am going home tomorrow."

"I have a few more days off. I'd be happy to come with you. Help you get settled in?"

"That would be fine. Good even. That way you and Mother can discuss the wedding. Could you get me a glass of water?"

Millie crossed the room, dazed. Did he say wedding? She poured the chilled water from the clear pitcher into a small glass and returned to Elliot's side. As she put the glass to his lips so he could take a sip, she asked, "Why would we plan the wedding now, before the war is over?"

"Because it is over for us. Oh, they will put me on some desk where they can keep an eye on me, but from this point on, we will just be watching from the cheap seats." He sipped the water again and nodded that he was finished. Millie put the glass on the table next to his bed.

"They are expecting me back at RAF Medmenham." Millie's back was board straight.

"Not after we are married. Then you will be expected to look after me."

Millie lifted her hands to the locket, and Elliot didn't notice. There was a time when he would have told her to stop fidgeting. There was a time when she would have cared what he said.

"And why aren't you going to return to RAF Benson?"

"Once a pilot goes down in enemy territory, he's done. Just in case the Germans managed to turn me." Elliot lifted his eyebrows as if he had made a joke.

Callum was right. *I don't know this man at all.* Millie groped for what to say next, but a nurse rescued her.

"You ready for me to take off those bandages?" She was pushing a cart with scissors and a jar of salve.

"Certainly." Elliot offered her his mittened hands.

"I'll give you a moment," Millie said.

"Shouldn't you stay in case you need to wrap them later?"

Elliot called after her, but Millie continued until she was standing in the corridor outside the hospital ward.

Pacing like a caged animal, Millie felt the cocoon of her engagement transforming into a straitjacket. How could someone who was known to see things clearly have been so blind? Her job, her cameras, her boxes of photographs, Callum. Elliot meant for her to put them all aside in favor of his needs. She had spent a lifetime pleasing her father, and now she was expected to continue doing it for Elliot. *He was never going to let me pursue my passions.* By his side, she would never become the activist her mother was, the activist she was only beginning to understand she wanted to be.

By the time the nurse returned to inform her she had finished her work, Millie was resolved. Walking back to Elliot's bedside, she recalled the faces of the courageous women she had met who didn't shy away from explosions: her mother, Clara, the girl at the bookshop, the Red Cross workers, the townsfolk of Wick, Polly, Peggy, and the others at the munitions plant. She was finally ready to join their ranks.

Elliot pointed to the water with his chin as she settled into her seat. Millie could see only traces of injury. *He doesn't need my help.* She ignored his request. Taking a seat on the edge of the chair, Millie pulled the pin out of her life.

"Elliot, I'm not ready to leave RAF Medmenham." It was a lie, she was ready, but she wasn't going to marry him to get out of it. "We have to get this war behind us, see who we are once we make it through this grey place." This was also a lie. She had never been more clear on what she wanted in her life.

Elliot swung his feet to the floor. They sat knee to knee. "Is that your way of saying you don't want to get married before the war is over?" *Why can't she just say what she means?*

"I'm saying this war has changed me." She could hear her heart drumming. "I'm not sure I expect to marry anyone."

Elliot rose to his feet and sent the half-empty glass of water flying across the room. "Then why did you have them fetch me back?" Elliot towered over her. Millie looked up at him, barely moving her head, and remembered sword fighting with her brothers. She took up an imaginary stick and stood, pointing it directly at his heart.

"You have mistaken me for someone else." When she was a child, she would have added, *I am the descendant of great Viking warriors.*

They now stood toe to toe. The entire ward of men, those healing and those dying, had their eyes fixed on them. Two nurses had come to see about the shattered glass. Elliot took note of his surroundings, took a step back, and said, "You didn't have me rescued?"

"I assure you I did not." *What kind of power does he think I have?* "Since you can obviously walk, will you join me outside?"

"I will not." He got back in bed.

"Suit yourself. Surely, it is as plain to you as it is to me that we are no longer suited to each other." Millie unclasped the chain about her neck and slid the sapphire ring off, thinking of where she might find Callum. She set it on the bedside table. If she touched him, she might hurt him. *All that time wasted.* She shook her head. "I will write and make apologies to your family."

Millie turned and started to leave. Elliot called after her again. His words stabbed, stopping her in her tracks. "Your precious Nanna Clara is alive." She turned around to see a smile bloom on Elliot's face. "She is the one who arranged for my escape from northern France." Elliot watched Millie's face go ghost white. *She had no idea.* He had blamed her but had been wrong. *She may be the only honest one in the bunch.* He smirked as she wilted around the edges in front of him, delighted to be the one to tell her.

Millie steeled herself, refusing to let him see any more of her pain. Millie would find no consolation here. She made haste to the door. *It can't be true. It can't be true.* All she could think was *It can't be true.* Elliot had proven Callum right, but this must have been an act of retaliation or even cruelty. *Clara can't be alive, can she?*

# CHAPTER FORTY-FIVE

---

**RAF Benson**

**December 29, 1943**

159 days until D-Day

Millie spent the night at the Belgravia house, barely sleeping. While she waited for her father's return, she combed through every scrap of paper in her father's study, looking for proof of Elliot's claims that Clara was alive and well in France. Words like Calais, Bayeux, and Normandy taunted her from the bits of papers, making Millie think of the extraction she had arranged for Wg. Cmd. Thomas. *Did I arrange for Elliot's escape after all?*

As the early morning light crept into the wood-paneled room, Millie woke in her father's favorite chair alone. He hadn't come home, and she was no closer to the truth. At breakfast, Cook told Millie that her father was as likely as not to sleep at work. Not to be defeated, Millie headed to Paddington Station and boarded a train to RAF Benson to interrogate Peter. Or was it Callum she was searching for?

Millie stepped onto the path that led to the main building at RAF Benson. Something shiny caught her eye. Studying the southern horizon, she saw them; Dornier bombers flying straight for the airfields. Millie squinted and tried to make out the model to determine their payload—a trick she learned from Hazel. If she were looking through a stereoscope, she would have known everything about them.

First came the whistles of the guard stationed at the entrance.

Then the blasting screeches of the air raid sirens insisted she take shelter. She looked and saw the airman she had hitched a ride with from the train station driving to the opposite side of the base, far from the hangars and airstrip, to keep out of harm's way. Millie ran toward the fleeing car, arms waving to get the driver's attention. She wanted out of there.

The first plane flew over her, dropping its payload on the airstrip and hurling two parked planes into the sky. The earth quaked, knocking her off balance, but she managed to keep her footing. The next bomb hit the hangar. She kept running. She was not alone. Pilots, mechanics, clerks, and aides streamed to the bomb shelters outside the offices and hangars. Millie tried to find Peter or Callum in the mayhem, but everything was a blur.

Then two bombs fell on top of the main building, knocking Millie off her feet. She looked back to see the damage. Any pilot being briefed for an upcoming sortie would have been in that building. Millie cried, "Callum! Peter!" and watched as mammoth plumes of dust and concrete flew toward the sky. She got to her feet, reversing course, and ran toward the blast. *Please let them be all right.*

She ran toward the mayhem, watching the tail fins of the bombers as they turned to take another run at them. The boys operating the anti-aircraft guns spun around and started firing but didn't hit a thing. There was too much confusion. The day was too cloudy and windy for this kind of attack. It took them by surprise. Millie couldn't catch her breath, the heat and dust were suffocating her, but she pushed ever forward. *They could be in there.* She needed to get them before the bombers returned.

One step. Two steps. Three. Almost there. Millie took a sharp turn at the corner of the wrecked building and began digging. Hands pulled at her, begging her to stay back, but they didn't deter her. She reached for a scrap piece of steel, and when she stuck it under the large rock next to her, she took flight.

Heat enveloped her as she soared through the air. She crashed in a heap on top of the wing of a crippled Mosquito. Her legs wouldn't move. Her eyes saw only darkness. Her fingers searched for answers and found only hot, sticky liquid. Her nose filled with the smell of burning flesh, and her mouth tasted of iron. The world faded.

# CHAPTER FORTY-SIX



Millie woke to the maudlin sound of a voice singing. It was familiar, like a distant memory. The sweet smell of pine needles mixed with a hint of Shalimar and its bouquet of lemon, leather, and vanilla. Shalimar was her mother's perfume.

Darkness enveloped her.

"Hello, is anybody there?" Silence wrapped around her. The hairs on the back of her neck stood. Something wasn't right. *Where is everyone? Where am I?* She tried to open her eyes, and nothing. *I CANNOT SEE!* She reached out, but her hands didn't find purchase. She couldn't see her hands, but it felt like she was wearing mittens. Wiggling her toes, she realized they were snuggled into a pair of heavy winter socks. Determined to get up, to find someone, anyone to explain why she looked out and only saw darkness, she bent at the waist and tried to swing her feet to the floor. Her legs were stiff, but she bullied on, determined to succeed. With great effort, she stood. Agony twisted through her body. She crumbled to the ground.

Someone began to scream. A smoldering fear stabbed her. *Who is that?* She couldn't make out any words, just a high-pitched alarm of distress. The noise pealed on and on. *Why can't I see them?* She struggled in vain to get to her feet. The offending sound continued. She clapped her hands to her ears, desperate to block the wailing. It did no good. The cries grew louder and louder.

"Millie! Oh, Millie!" Someone was wrapping her arms around her. *There is the smell of Shalimar again. It's Mother.* The screaming continued. "Please, darling, calm down."

Millie's mind raced. *Please stop them screaming, Mother.* She rocked her back and forth, back and forth, back and forth. *Make the screaming stop!*

*Mother.* A hand covered Millie's mouth. The screaming muffled. "William, thank goodness. Help me get her back into bed. She won't stop screaming."

*Me? Screaming?*

"I just stepped away to get a drink of water, and when I came back, I found her like this. The doctor said the medicine should help her sleep. We have to help her, please. She thinks I'm Margaret." With Fiona's hand still over Millie's mouth, she and William lifted her back into bed. *William. I know that name. William is Father's name. Father is here too?*

They placed Millie back in bed. The darkness settled in, and Millie tried to pull herself into a ball, but her leg wouldn't bend. The world began to spin. She needed something to hold on to. *Please, God, let me see! How can I be a photographer if I can't see?* She waved her arms frantically, but there was nothing within arm's reach. She found no relief outside herself, so she dug deep for the lovely song she heard as she awoke. As it washed over her, Millie saw images of the grass blowing on the glen. Her heartbeat slowed. Her throat relaxed. A hand brushed up and down her back. "Mother, you came back for me," Millie whispered.

"It's Fiona, love. Your father and I are here, darling. There is no reason to be afraid."

Millie's mind flooded with questions. *Where am I? What is happening?* She started to have bits of memories, like being on the train headed to RAF Benson. But the answers didn't come, and she needed them. She especially needed to know why she couldn't see. Every inch of her rippled with dread.

"Mother, why can't I see you?" Millie said.

"Darling, it's Fiona." Fiona scowled at William, worried that Millie's confusion was lasting too long. This wasn't the first time she had mistaken her for Margaret. "You can't see right now because the doctor had to bandage your eyes."

Instinctually, Millie's hands reached for her face. She pulled at the mittens so she could feel her eyes. The mittens wouldn't budge.

"Help me take off these mittens. Why am I wearing them inside?" She kept tugging. Her voice was raspy, and her breath shallow.

"Millie, your hands and feet are bandaged, too." Fiona pushed the words out over muffled gasps. William felt the pleas in Fiona's voice but didn't know how to help.

"The flames from the explosion did quite a number on you," her father said calmly—too calmly.

"Explosion?" Millie's mind turned in again, searching for memories—only people were there: Elliot, Callum, and Peter. She tried to open her eyes, but the lids wouldn't budge.

"The day after you left Wick, you visited RAF Benson, and it was bombed. From what I have been told, you were outside. First, you tried to run away but turned back when you thought the bombers had retreated. The Dorniers dropped incendiaries that started massive fires and explosions when the flames reached the fuel storage. Then they came back to finish things off. It tossed you around a bit. You broke your right leg, burned your hands and ankles badly, and your eyes and throat were exposed to too much heat and smoke." William spoke like he was giving a report in one of his War Cabinet meetings.

"My eyes were burned?" Millie began to hyperventilate.

Fiona gripped a black handkerchief in her hands, a remnant from Peter's memorial service, and reached for her granddaughter in the hopes of consoling her. "No, darling, they were exposed to too much heat and smoke. You also hit your head badly. You just need time." She stroked Millie's hair. "Your eyes just need time."

Millie swatted Fiona's hand away. "How could this have happened? Who am I if I can't see?"

William ignored the comment, turning his efforts toward pulling Millie into the present. "What do you remember?"

Millie turned her back to his voice. He was to blame. She shook her head no. None of it mattered if she couldn't see.

William gave her a minute, then asked again, "Millie, what do you remember?"

Millie's breathing settled. She patted her hands on her eyes. She could feel the padding between her fingers and her eyelashes, but she couldn't open them.

"Why can't I open my eyes?"

William crossed the room and sat on the bed. Millie was beginning to make sense, ask productive questions. "They are taped shut and covered in layers of cotton and gauze. You just have to give them time. Now, tell me, what do you remember?"

Millie let out a deep sigh and forced herself to think.

"I keep seeing Elliot, Peter, and Callum." Millie reached out her hand, thinking she would find her father's. William took hold of it and let out a sigh of his own. "Were they there, at RAF Benson, I mean, when it was bombed? Are they okay?"

"Elliot wasn't there. He is all right as far as I know," her father said.

The image of her turning her back on Elliot came better into focus in Millie's memory.

"You left Wick early to see him in the hospital when you found out he had been rescued. Don't you remember?"

Millie couldn't tell if it was her mother's or Fiona's voice, but the concern was undeniable. *It has to be Fiona. Mother is dead.*

"It's coming back in bits. Elliot made it out of France. He insisted we get married right away because they won't let him back in the air." She paused, expecting a reaction. When none came, she continued telling them the bits and bobs she remembered. "I called off the engagement." Then the worst of it fell into place. The reason she had gone to RAF Benson.

She started breathing quickly, rage building, teeth clenching.

"What is it, Millie?" William said.

Jerking her hand back and looking in the direction of her father, she said accusingly, "He told me Clara is alive. That she got him out of France. He thought I knew. That I had made the arrangements myself."

Fiona picked up her hand and patted it gently. "That is absurd and cruel. I am thrilled he is out of your life."

William said nothing. The air thickened with tension.

"Father, I need you to say something. I can't see your face." Millie's body and spirit were a matched set—broken. She rolled over with her back to him and waited, forcing herself to stay in control.

"Millie?" Fiona rested a hand on her side. "Tell her it's a cruel lie, William."

"He can't." Millie's voice was muffled. She had heard the truth in what Elliot said the minute the words assaulted her ears. The two people she had given way to her entire life had betrayed her. She might have expected it from her father. Duty to king and country meant everything to him. But Clara. Clara was meant to be her ally. Her entire life felt like a lie. "You need to leave—now." Millie knew the words would sting, but she didn't expect a fight.

"Of course," William said.

Fiona shook her head no to him. "I'm not leaving her like this."

"Yes, you are. She asked us to leave. I can at least give her that."

Millie heard them leave the room and cringed as she rolled onto her back. She took deep breaths, trying to quell her rage. Crisp, cool air filled her lungs, and she began to relax. *A window must be cracked.* The chaffinches' song broke the silence.

She wasn't alone after all. They seemed to be cheering her on as if they were anxious to remind her that flying was a solitary adventure. The bright smell of the Douglas firs floated in on the wind, confirming that she was home at Stellan Hall. With each deep breath, she returned to herself. *Fiona said my eyes are injured, not broken—I can believe her.* She pushed the fear into a tiny box and tried to sleep, but it began to take root. She was back playing a waiting game.

*Two weeks. How is that possible?* Millie touched her bandaged head with her bound hands. *And what about Peter? Callum? Clara?* There was much to sort out. Too much.

Her wiggling fingers caught on their gauze sheath, hard evidence that the explosion happened, but the memories still tangled in her mind. When the cold settled on her ears and nose, she thought of the days she spent exploring the estate, taking photographs.

"I'll be back soon," she whispered to the encouraging birds. "Please, God. Let me be back soon."

# CHAPTER FORTY-SEVEN

Stellan Hall

**February 1944**

107 days until D-Day

Millie was running into a wall of flames. Something exploded to her right, sending her rocketing into the air. She plummeted to the ground. Heart racing, she tried to get up but couldn't stand. She hauled herself through the wreckage. Someone reached out of the debris and grabbed her hand. Millie bolted upright. A blood-curdling scream flooded her ears. There was only darkness.

"Millie, darling, you're dreaming again. Take a deep breath and try to relax. Was it the fire again?" Fiona's soft voice and gentle embrace brought her back to reality.

"Yes, and the explosion. I was trying to get to Peter." She moved her arm too quickly, and a sharp pain ravaged her skin. Through gritted teeth, she pushed out the question, "When am I going to see him? Were he or Callum on base when the bombs fell?" She left the question that frightened her the most unsaid. *When am I going to see anything again?* If she couldn't see, she couldn't take pictures. *Why have I wasted so much time with what others wanted for me?*

"You need to concentrate on getting yourself well, darling." The words felt like a pat on the head. *Doesn't she understand that not answering me only makes it worse?* "Would you like a cup of tea?"

Always—questions dismissed with a cup of tea. Millie's breathing steadied. *There is no point. Maybe when Father visits again.* Though she wasn't sure she would ever believe a word he said again.

For days now, Gertrude or Fiona had been pouring tea and feeding Millie stale biscuits, with forced cheerfulness in their voices. Her wardens each took turns reading in upbeat tones and telling only happy stories that did nothing to cover up the sorrow shrouding the house. Gertrude finally broke one day when Millie asked about Callum. She suggested that with the right introductions, he might make a proper husband, yet. Millie's heart leapt from her chest. *He is alive.* Then a more treacherous form of depression sunk in. *Callum is alive and hasn't come to see me.*

Millie was lonely, even though she was never alone. Aggie, Hazel, and Constance wrote letters that they knew Millie's grandmothers read out to her, limiting their contents. Aggie told tales of the base in Wick and of the antics of her younger siblings. Her fellow PIs regaled her with stories of their social lives at RAF Medmenham and dropped hints about the ramps, wishing her a full recovery and speedy return.

From what Millie puzzled out, they were bombing the ramp sites on a regular schedule. It sounded like the Germans attempted to rebuild, but Bomber Command showed no signs of letting up. Millie understood that Operation Overlord's D-Day depended on their success.

Her grandmothers worked in shifts. The on-duty warden sat patiently and kept busy with handwork. Millie couldn't see them, but the constant clicking of the knitting needles never let her forget one of them hovered nearby.

The doctor came every other day to check her injuries. Things were healing, especially her leg, but her vision remained blurry, so the bandages remained.

They told her when she hit the ground, her head collided with a plane wing. They blamed her limited eyesight on swelling and said that in time her eyes should heal. Every time they removed the bandages, she blinked furiously, trying to wash away the film that obscured her view. *If I can't see, I can't take pictures. I've wasted so much time.*

Someone put her treasured cameras, the 35mm Leica and the Minox, on the bedside table. She felt them as she searched for a glass of water late one afternoon when she was allowed a rare moment alone. They sat there still collecting dust. *Useless, like me, without my eyes.*

Her father came into the room, weeks into her convalescence, while the doctor wrapped fresh bandages over her eyes.

"Millie, as soon as you get those bandages off for good, we need to talk about your returning to RAF Medmenham," he said.

"You can't be serious," she shuddered. *Unbelievable.* They were the first words her father had uttered to her since she revealed to him she knew about Clara. For the past few weeks, when he crept into her room, he sat wordlessly. He may have been an excellent spy, but the sweet smell of his tobacco announced his presence every time.

She never spoke to him. She wasn't ready. But his audacity broke the ice. She turned her back to him and said, "I'm not the same girl who came to you for help when I thought Clara had been killed. I won't be so quick to give up on my dreams this time."

"As I said then, the battle at hand is for everyone's freedom."

"Are you sure about that? Or will we all be sent back to the kitchen and the nursery when the fighting is over?"

The doctor tucked the end of the gauze strip into place. "I'll see you in two days." He clamped his bag shut and scurried out of the room.

With the doctor gone, William towered over Millie. Through gritted teeth, he said, "I came here in hopes of having a reasonable conversation about your future."

"Fine! But first, I need you to explain why you let me believe Clara was dead." Millie threw gasoline on their chat, trying to take control.

The words flew at William like a fist to his chin. He took a step back. His sense of urgency had clouded his judgment. He had persuaded himself he could appeal to their shared sense of duty and avoid the topic of Clara for now. *Perhaps, after all she's been through, she sees her duty differently.* It was time for retreat.

"Yes, but I want you at fighting weight." William knew he deserved it, but he wasn't ready for an accounting of his sins. "I know I have it coming to me, but please keep in mind that we're putting the finishing touches on the plans for the French invasion, and you're one of the best phase three interpreters on the Crossbow team. The war will end. You will heal. You will have ample time to do everything you are called to do."

The strike had taken all the energy she had. Plus, she wanted to look him in the eyes when they finally discussed Clara. She decided to change tack, scratch her curiosity itch, and turn the temperature down a bit. "Did they bomb the ski sites?" The facts from Hazel and Constance had been cryptic to get past the censors.

"All ninety-five of the catapults were hit. It's a great victory, and it wouldn't have happened without you."

The fact that she cared about his agenda pissed her off. "I appreciate the pep talk, Father, but if my eyes don't recover, I'm out of the photography business, and you know it—analyzing them and taking them. I may have given up my one chance by following your dream rather than mine." When she said the words aloud, her voice cracked, the truth of them settling in her bones, breaking her heart along its old scars.

He walked over to the bed and took her into his arms. "They will heal. On my life, they will heal."

Millie jerked back. "I am not going back."

# CHAPTER FORTY-EIGHT

Stellan Hall

March 1, 1944

96 days until D-Day

Eight weeks in and the drama that was Millie's life had a fixed cast of characters. Fiona became the entertainment. Her routine began by reading Millie the latest edition of the *Groat* sent by Mr. Graham while the ink was still damp. Next, she told stories of days gone by, including her Margaret's adventures. Millie wished she could have known her. When things got a bit too sad, Fiona downshifted to small talk. She could spend an hour rambling on about the weather and her garden plans for the spring.

Gertrude spent less time confessing the past and more on encouraging Millie to take on the most significant role of her life—being a wife and mother. She encouraged her to knit, an occupation Millie despised, and so, she declined, blaming her bandaged eyes. Gertrude also filled the role of nursemaid. She fed, dressed, and bathed Millie, leaving only the brushing of her hair to Fiona. Having her hair washed and brushed had become the highlight of Millie's week.

Every day Millie thought about Peter but never asked after him. If he were well, he would be by her side reading their beloved *Peter Pan*. Deep down, Millie suspected he had left her too. *But maybe he is alive. Clara is.* Either way, she didn't confess what she believed. Saying it would make it real. She wasn't ready.

She didn't ask about Callum either. Holding herself together took all the energy she had. Her tangle with the bombs at RAF Benson felt like the universe's way of demanding she put herself first. Healing would take every ounce of strength she could muster.

On advice from Fiona, the gardener delivered a bouquet of early crocus the day the doctor came to cut the plaster off Millie's leg. When the doctor arrived, he insisted that Fiona take a break from her babysitting duties, and then he started unwrapping the bandages on Millie's hands, ankle, and eyes. She blinked her eyes, taking in as much of the view as she could, and pulled at the tightness of her healing skin, wiggling her fingers and toes. The bandages would go back on soon; she wanted to enjoy her freedom.

"Tell me what you see."

Millie scanned the room and noticed the blue of the fire flame. "I can see color!" Until that moment, she hadn't noticed its absence.

"Let me have a look." The doctor peered into Millie's eye with a small light. After a few "hums" and "well, well then," he asked how she felt about a pair of eyeglasses.

"Anything to keep those bandages off my face."

He slid a pair of glasses with tinted lenses wrapped in thick brass wire on her face, resting them on her nose and ears. Then he walked over to the window and pulled the curtains back.

"Now, what do you see?"

"It's a bit dark but pretty clear and colorful."

"If you promise to keep on the glasses, I will keep the gauze in my bag."

"How long will I need them?" Millie's eyes shifted to the Leica and Minox on the table beside her.

"Not long. I'd say until late spring-early summer. Your

eyes are healing well, but I would wager too much use may cause headaches."

She reached for the Leica, but he slapped her hand away.

"I know you are ready to get back to it, and I would be happy to see your photos. Fiona tells me they are phenomenal, but your eyes are not ready for that kind of work, not yet." He gave her a wink.

She lay back in frustration and relief. The rage that began to grow the day of Elliot's revelation still smoldered deep in her gut. She had no interest in quenching it. She was depending on it to keep her on her true path. The doctor said, "not yet," which meant eventually. She could feel her spirit flapping its wings like a fledgling starling. "What about my hands and ankle?"

"Take a look for yourself." She saw fresh pink skin growing on her hands. No scabs meant no scrubbing. Gertrude will be so disappointed. Torturing Millie seemed to be the highlight of her day. Every day for the past two months, Gertrude had unwrapped her wounds and scrubbed them until they bled. "The doctor said it was the only way to keep infection at bay." She completed the routine by slathering them in ointment before covering them back up. For the past months, there had only been ointment, new bandages, and Gertrude's unfamiliar hands.

"You're leaving the bandages off?" Millie said.

"Yes. Your grandmother is the best nurse I've ever seen."

She had been unusually attentive. At times, Millie wondered if she should talk with her more, but she didn't know what to say. Gertrude thrived with an occupation, and she knew her limitations. Every time Millie woke screaming, she stepped aside, letting Fiona hold Millie's hand, all the while humming the song about the glen.

"Here she is now." The doctor flashed a bashful grin.

"Neither of them is ever too far away." When her words reached their ears, Millie saw both of her grandmothers smile for the first time in months. They both had beautiful smiles. Millie smiled back, hoping to convey her gratitude.

"That's the nicest thing you've ever said about me," Gertrude said. Millie hardly recognized her without her typical sternness tensing her face.

Fiona gave Millie a sideways glance that yelled *shame on you.*

They had stuck, even though she had dropped everything: Elliot, her work at RAF Medmenham. Millie knew Gertrude was disappointed that her engagement to Elliot was no more, but she had proven her loyalty. The one time they discussed it, she spoke of how inappropriately Elliot had behaved when Millie visited him in the hospital. "Who would have imagined a man of his breeding yelling after you as you left?" Gertrude had said, patting her hand. "You are better off without him." Gertrude's defense of her surprised Millie. She should have had more faith. Even her father kept his own kind of vigil.

"Did you bring a cup for Dr. Long?" Millie tucked her chin sheepishly. "We need to celebrate. Today I am bandage free."

"Well, that is indeed a reason to celebrate. How do you take your tea, Dr. Long?" Gertrude asked.

"I'll have cream if you have it. I've learned to take my tea without sugar. It's a wonder what war can teach you."

"Millie and I do without it, but we would prefer a lump or two if we were honest." She offered Millie her smile again. Millie flashed one back for the moment of rare camaraderie.

"Could you wait on the pouring? I may have more good news." He took a small saw out of his bag and started cutting the cast off Millie's leg. After making a rut, he pried the cast open to get a view of her leg. Millie smelled the rank odor before she noticed how skinny her calf was. After weeks spent in plaster, her leg was ripe. "Can you stand up for me, Millie?" the doctor said.

With a cane for support, she pressed up and put some weight on the once-encased leg. No pain. No dizziness. "Okay, that's enough," he said. She sat down. "How did the leg feel?"

"Weak, but okay," Millie said.

"Try standing with this." He handed her a pair of crutches.

"Should I walk?"

"Yes, but only to the chair for now." The walk was wobbly, but successful. A smile bloomed on her face. No bandages and no cast. Time was taking care of things—well, time was taking care of her body.

# CHAPTER FORTY-NINE

Stellan Hall

April 1944

51 days until D-Day

Free from her bondage, Millie took baby steps toward independence. By April, she was photographing flowers on the terraces out back, her eyes getting stronger every day, and the fear that had taken root began to wither. She asked about processing photographs, but her doctor didn't like the idea of her working with the amber light and chemical fumes just yet. Moving and seeing again would have to be enough, for now.

Everyone smiled and cheered her on, but she felt them tiptoeing around her. The names Peter, Callum, and Clara went unmentioned. She didn't ask questions because she didn't want to face the answers. Her father only visited when she slept. The stronger she got, the more he dreaded having to face his crimes. She had trusted him completely. He missed her but didn't know how to repent, so he stayed away. Taking the coward's path, he convinced himself that she would come to him when she was ready to forgive him.

New routines emerged. Daily walks narrated by Gertrude relaying all of the news Millie had already heard on the radio. People married. Sons died. Children were born. The war waged on. Millie got a bit of gossip from Hazel and Aggie. Hearts broke. Love kindled. Adventures succeeded and failed. The bombing persisted, as did the aerial photography. And Millie healed—inside and out.

She listened attentively to any details about bombing assaults on Great Britain, searching the announcer's words for hints of the kind of bomb. If a pilotless bomb had made it to their shores, the radio wasn't reporting it. *How long will it take the Germans to find a new way to put them in the air?* Ham had been right when he said she hated putting down a puzzle once she had picked it up. But what she missed most about being at RAF Medmenham was knowing about things before they were reported.

Millie picked at the greens and corned beef on her lunch tray.

"Do you ever miss working on all of that secret information at Medmenham?" Gertrude's question surprised her because they usually ate in silence.

"As a matter of fact, I was wishing I had more information about what was going on out in the world. They censor the information on the radio too much," Millie said.

"Your father and Peter were so proud you agreed to help." She slapped her hand to her mouth, regret written all over her face. No one had dared to utter Peter's name since Millie woke up from the bombing. Her comment sparked Millie's courage, giving her permission to ask the one thing she dreaded most, now that her eyesight was on the mend.

"Grandmother, is Peter dead?"

"Yes, my darling, he is." Gertrude didn't move to hug Millie. She just sat and made room for whatever she needed. They sat in their customary silence as Millie let the truth soak into her bones. She began to weep. Still, Gertrude sat. Millie's shoulders shuddered as the tears streamed, and Millie fought to breathe. She saw his face, smiling just so, and she became hollow, missing him. She began to wail. Within minutes, Fiona busted into the room and indicted Gertrude. "Why aren't you helping her?"

"Oh, but I am." Gertrude blocked Fiona's path. Gertrude

knew the tears would come and that the only way to deal with this kind of grief was to move through it. "You need to let her feel this." They had made a mistake when Millie was a child, and her mother died. They told her to be strong. But there would be time for strength later. "We need to let her miss her brother."

"She knows, then." Fiona surrendered to Gertrude's blockade.

Millie let herself fall into the abyss of sorrow. Peter was her favorite person. It was impossible to imagine the world without his crooked smile, a conversation without his sarcasm, a family reunion without his infectious laugh. Her breathing came easier as she remembered him. Her tears began to dry up. She needed to be near him. "Will you take me to see his grave tomorrow? I need him to know he isn't alone."

"Of course," Gertrude answered before Fiona could say no. Millie found comfort in Gertrude's nature. She had always taught her it was best to deal with things as they came, and her resolve in this matter gave Millie strength.

# CHAPTER FIFTY

Senate House-British Intelligence Headquarters

May 3, 1944

33 days until D-Day

The memo said simply that twenty Belhamelin sites had been identified, and the search for the updated, now portable, ramp sites was on again. William picked up a glass paperweight from his desk and threw it against the wall. Back in March, they believed the V1 bomb threat was neutralized. Plans for Operation Overlord were in full swing. Every minute of every day, one of theirs was taking a photograph of the northern French coast. It had been four and a half years of this bullshit. And Gertrude had to go and tell Millie about Peter. He needed her back at RAF Medmenham more than ever, but he didn't know how much more she could take—how much more any of them could take.

# CHAPTER FIFTY-ONE

Stellan Hall

May 3, 1944

33 days until D-Day

Rain spattered against her window, flinging clicks and tinks around the room. It was a lovely way to wake up, but a little sunshine might have made this day easier. Fiona slipped into the room, loaded down with sweaters, coats, and a couple of umbrellas. She had wanted to cancel because of the weather, but at Stellan Hall, Gertrude gave the orders, and Fiona carried them out. Gertrude didn't plan on going with her only granddaughter to her grandson's graveside. That was a job for Fiona.

"Do you think you can manage with your cane and an umbrella? The rain is unrelenting." Fiona spread Millie's coat and rain hat on the bed.

"I wish I had my copy of *Peter Pan*. Father needs to get my things from Boyton House. I'm sure they need the billet for someone else."

"Are you up to this?" Fiona looked overly concerned.

"I'm just afraid I won't know what to say, and I'm still so mad at Father."

Fiona had no interest in going over the Clara matter, so she stuck with the safer subject. "Would you like me to find a copy of the book for your visit? Your mother used to have one in every nook and cranny around here." Fiona cringed inside at the mention of her daughter. *Today is going to be filled with land mines.*

"No, it's all right."

Fiona wrapped an arm around Millie. "Don't worry. You'll know what to say when we get there."

"You talk like we may actually see him," Millie said.

"Won't we?" She seemed sure. Millie expected a cold, rough headstone with his name chiseled into it forever, not a friendly ghost. All the while praying that somehow Peter would know she was there. "Millie, this visit is bound to be difficult, but in time I suspect you will grow to find comfort in the spot where Peter rests."

"He isn't resting. He's dead."

She waved Millie off. "Do you want a camera?" She offered her the Leica.

Taking it, Millie heard whistling coming from the hall, and the cook popped the door open with her toe. Her tray carried the basics: a pot of tea, biscuits, and a small bowl of canned peaches. "So, you're going to visit our Peter today? He'll be glad of it. I bet he's been wondering where you are—if you're okay."

How strange. For months, no one dared mutter Peter's name. Millie's acknowledgment of his death lifted a pall. Without the wall of a secret, the mood shifted. Soft smiles and words of understanding replaced the whispers and stoic faces.

Millie appreciated everyone waiting for her.

Once outside the main entrance, she opened her umbrella with a poof. Squeezing its curved wooden handle with one hand and the top of her cane with the other, she went out onto the drive.

The cemetery had been transformed by attention. Shoots of new life reached in every direction, pulling Millie's attention this way and that. The thorny canes of climbing roses had been liberated from their binding constraints, just as Margaret would have wanted it. As a matter of fact, the wildness Millie found here told her that Gertrude had finally given way to

Margaret's desires, at least here where her youngest son was buried. The smells brought back memories, but the sight overwhelmed Millie. Tangles of ivy trimmed the pathway and on the low gate that connected the waist-high stone wall hung a canister filled with bluebonnets. She thought to lift her camera and take an image as she moved among her dead family members, but of what? Finding a single point of focus, a place for her newly seeing eyes to rest, felt impossible. Until she saw Peter's headstone. It was brighter than the others in the family cemetery and clean. No moss or lichen or dark patina that works its aging magic. His was the newest death. This is what she was here to see.

Peter's freshly covered grave demanded Millie's attention. Peter Louis Trayford. November 17, 1914. December 29, 1943. Twenty-nine years old. *What a waste. He never got to have his adventure.* Millie stood, leaning against the gate, her anger growing. *He always said I had more freedom than he did.* No matter the truth of it, she would undoubtedly have more chances now. "It's not fair."

"That's what thousands of families are feeling."

Looking at the stone again, Millie read the inscription aloud: "Luck favors the brave." Closing her eyes, she remembered standing hand-in-hand with Peter on every anniversary of their mother's and Clara's death. *He will be looking for Clara, I bet.* She couldn't help thinking that perhaps he was the lucky one—dying before learning of their father's betrayal. She felt guilty for ever believing he might have known about the secret. *He would never have kept that from me.*

"Did Father have that saying engraved?"

Fiona nodded, tight lipped. William was another land mine she wanted to avoid.

"What right did he have? That was ours. Mine and Peter's." Millie pulsed with rage and sorrow. *He shouldn't have done it.*

Fiona risked speaking. "He wanted to do it for you. He remembered you both saying it." She took a step closer to Millie. "Do remember he buried a son that day, no matter what else has happened."

Millie's heart exploded. "I will not. He took everything from me."

Before Fiona faded into the background, she answered, "He did not. He isn't that powerful."

Millie lifted her cane to take a step and stumbled. She reached for Fiona, but she stayed back. Millie needed to work this out on her own. She got back on her feet and took a seat next to her mother's grave.

Looking at her headstone, Millie saw new details take shape. She traced the intricate carving of a bird surrounded by dancing flowers and vines with her eyes. Her mother's name, Margaret Abberly Trayford, filled the center. Millie dropped her umbrella and knelt in front of the granite rock. She traced the letters and collapsed to the ground. Water from the drenched grass soaked her pants. Her body heaved, and the tears she thought she didn't have flowed again. She reached out for Peter's stone, next to his mother's. *I'm alone.* Peter and Margaret were gone. Millie had put up a wall between her and her father. And because she never dared to show Callum, tell him she loved him, he was gone too. She cried out into the nothingness, begging the universe to tell her why!

Fiona knelt beside Millie with some difficulty, moving like she was approaching a wild animal. Cautiously, she reached out to her.

"He was the first person who ever loved me for me." Millie's words broke the silent reverie.

"Not the first." Fiona held her tighter, willing Millie to understand that many people loved her no matter what.

"But Peter never believed I couldn't have everything I imagined. He wanted the world for me. He believed I would get it, eventually."

"That's the best kind of love. One given so freely," Fiona said. The rain stopped, but the stubborn clouds hovered. Fiona kept hold of Millie.

When their tears ran dry and Millie's fires died down, Fiona stood up and shook the mud from her skirt.

"You're a mess," Millie said, exactly the way Peter might.

"You wouldn't know it now, but this is how I spent most of my childhood, your mother too, traipsing around the gnarly glens around Teaghlach, covered in dirt. I never let a little rainstorm stop a day's discoveries."

She unpinned her wide-brimmed hat, unwrapping her braid, and leaned back on the nearby statue. "A magpie, indeed." Fiona pointed to the bird on her daughter's headstone. "Mrs. Drummond was the first person to call Margaret that." Millie heard a faint giggle on the wind. "It was a fitting name. She was made for the land, made to be alone exploring it. She was never afraid to go after what she needed. What about you, Millicent? Do you have what you *need*?" She gazed at the horizon into the wood.

Millie got to her feet, her hair blowing in the wind. She had never considered that she might *need* to take pictures. She could hear Gertrude insisting she not confuse her wants and needs. Everyone treated photography as a hobby, so Millie had put the occupation in the want column.

She found it embarrassing to say the answer aloud. "I can't honestly tell you what I *need*. It seems easier to do what pleases everyone else. It makes them all so happy." Looking back on it, Millie was astounded by the lengths she had gone to so no one would ever be disappointed in her. "It kept you nearer..." she stroked her mane absently, "until now." She thought of her mother, Elliot, and now Peter. She looked to Fiona. "I suppose I thought I needed to please you all more than I needed to have something for myself." She smiled a thin smile, lifting her eyebrows and shoulders. "I've been trapped in the middle of that old Charles Lamb quote, 'Contented with little, but wishing for more.'"

Fiona's eyebrows arched up, and her smirk turned down. "Perhaps it's time you figure it out. Better to be happy alone than miserable in a crowd."

They sat together, with Margaret and Peter and the rest of Millie's paternal line enjoying the quiet. Eventually, a sweet note reached Millie's ear. It was the tune about the glen. Fiona was singing it. "What is that song?" Millie said.

"It's something Callum's mother sang to him when he was just a boy." The mention of his name loosened a longing inside of Millie. *Perhaps Callum is what I need. I'm sure I could bear the pain if he were here.*

"Did she sing it to you too?"

"Of course not. I grew up singing it as a child."

"Have you been singing the song to me?"

"I have." She twisted behind Millie and began braiding her hair. Her touch took Millie to a long-lost memory of spending easy time together with her mother and brothers.

"Why?" Millie looked back at her.

"Callum thought it would help."

Millie knocked her hands away.

"Callum was here?" Millie instantly regretted she sounded so surprised. It felt like a confession—like his absence was her fault. *It was too much to expect—asking him to take me to Elliot.*

Fiona took Millie's face into her hands. "Of course, he was here. I don't think we could have kept him away. Don't you remember?"

"No."

"The day after the explosion, your father requested that Callum fly the two of us here."

Millie didn't know what to say. *The fact that Callum helped Father doesn't mean he might not hate me for asking for too much—waiting too long.* She simply wasn't convinced he would want her—the real Millie, whoever that was. There were moments. Moments when she began to lean into a future with him, but she couldn't bring herself to choose, not while Elliot was missing. To disappoint everyone seemed too high a price. And now? Elliot was out of her life, but Callum was nowhere to be found.

The growing tension made Fiona nervous, and she began to ramble.

"You have to understand, Millie. Everything was a blur. The morning after the raid on RAF Benson. We knew you had been injured badly, and there was news from Elliot about the engagement, and then they contacted your father and told him about finding Peter's...." She put her hand to her mouth and began shaking her head back and forth. "Just like before with your mother, we didn't know if you would—"

"I'm here, Fiona." Millie touched her hand. "I'm fine."

"We were desperate to get to you, and finally, your father thought to call Callum." The wildness in her eyes gone, Fiona continued with brevity. "Callum knew about the bombing of RAF Benson. He was diverted to a different airfield when he completed his sortie that night. When your father reached him, he was desperately searching for you. You were supposed to be in Wick.

"Thank goodness you were wearing your identification. We might still be looking for you if you hadn't. Everyone who saw you that day on base said you ran back to the base to help rather than save yourself. What concerned the doctor most were your lungs and eyes. We took shifts soaking your eyes with cold compresses and holding you as you coughed up a grisly combination of blood and burnt flesh. Callum didn't leave your side for ten days."

Listening to the story, chills from some distant memory danced along Millie's skin. It was like a nightmare happening in a faraway time and place to someone else.

"You never told me all of this." Millie picked at blades of grass.

"You didn't ask, and I wasn't sure if I should bring it up unless you did." She took Millie's hand. "Those were painful days. Emotionally and physically. If you blocked them out, I thought there might be a reason. I have a few memories I would happily trade away." She kept shaking her head.

"Tell me now." Millie gripped her cane as if it might anchor her to the moment. *It's strange, losing bits of your past.*

"On the third night, you started having nightmares. Honestly, they were anytime-mares because you slept around the clock. We tried everything we could think of to calm you, but nothing worked. Your screams reached Callum in the bedrooms upstairs, and he came running. He swaddled you and began singing. At first, no one could hear him; your voice was so loud. He rocked and sang. You wailed. The entire household gathered in your room. It sounded like someone was torturing you. I had to explain to Gertrude that legend says the song keeps visions away. In time, you settled down." Fiona wiped away fresh tears.

"I tried to shoo everyone away, but Callum and your father refused to leave. Callum appropriated the seat beside you and sang the verses over and over and over. You rested. He stopped occasionally, but if he noticed even the slightest twitch, he would hum or sing." She began stroking Millie's hand in time, remembering. "Of course I knew the old tune and volunteered to take a shift, but Callum insisted on staying with you. Finally, the day came when your father couldn't arrange for any more time off for the boy, and he had to leave. He made me promise to keep singing. I tried, but it wasn't me you wanted." Her voice cracked, but she continued. "On our first day without him, you had the nightmare that brought you out of your trance."

Millie tried to take it all in. She licked her lips and tasted her tears. *When will I be cried out?* Everything felt too loose. She couldn't get a grip on it all: Peter's death, estrangement from her father, Clara alive in France, Callum looking after her, her life and body in shambles.

"Fiona? Will you help me to the darkroom?"

"But the doctor—"

She placed a finger on Fiona's lips, quieting her. "I need to find some solid ground. I think it's there."

# CHAPTER FIFTY-TWO

Stellan Hall

May 3, 1944

33 days until D-Day

Millie found her darkroom precisely as she left it. The stale, acrid odor calmed her. Standing in the middle of the room, she could reach an object in every direction: an enlarger, chemistry bottles, printing paper, unexposed film. She pulled four rolls of film from her pocket. Two had been shot here at Stellan Hall, and the others she found in some things Hazel sent her. She had taken one with her Minox. She arranged her tools, sat on the stool Gertrude had insisted she use, and turned off the lights. She could feel her equilibrium returning.

Working in complete darkness, Millie depended solely on her hands. After prying the tiny light-tight container open, she fed it on a reel. Millie settled into her work once one roll was completed and pushed tightly into the bottom of a metal canister. When she plopped the last reel of film into the canister and tightened the lid, she turned on the amber light. She slid the arms of her glasses over her ears and pushed them firmly to her face. *I can get used to this if I have to.* She poured and agitated the chemistry. Then she rinsed and hung the film to dry. The hours passed rhythmically, without notice.

She pulled the first mystery roll of grey film into the light and realized that it was from a birthday they threw for Fiona before Millie reported to her posting at RAF Medmenham. The negatives reflected ghosts of glasses, tables, and food. Fiona looked soft and open. Millie was grateful she had gone with her to see Peter's grave.

She pulled the next roll through her gloved hands. It was less than a half-inch thick. It only took a moment to realize she had taken it the day Callum took Aggie, Peter, and her to Old Wick Castle for a picnic. In the middle of the strip was a picture of Callum and her sitting on the ground with their arms around each other. She skipped down a few frames and saw her face cheek to cheek with Aggie's. They might have been ten again, making faces to keep Mrs. Drummond laughing. Next, she found Peter's smiling face. *This is how I want to remember him.* He had one arm draped around her and the other around Aggie. In the next frame, he was planting a wet kiss on Millie's face. He put a wet finger in her ear next, as Millie recalled.

Millie pulled out an envelope of photographic paper with a bittersweet smile and started printing—watching as her memories magically appeared in the developer one moment at a time.

The last image she printed was the one Aggie took of Callum and her. He smiled radiantly as ever, and his eyes—they were clear and content as he stood at her side. Millie's stomach flipped. In that instant, she admitted why she refused Elliot's proposal. She would rather spend the rest of her life being aggravated by Callum than go on a single adventure of Elliot's choosing. *Now I just need to find the courage to tell him I've made a choice, no matter the cost.*

Millie laughed at herself, feeling a twinge in her leg as she moved to put the image on the drying rack. *I can run toward a burning building, but the thought of talking to Callum scares me to death.*

# CHAPTER FIFTY-THREE

RAF Benson

May 10, 1944

26 days until D-Day

Callum took his time going to the makeshift briefing room. He had handed over his plots and was headed to bed when the duty officer told him that a Col. Caldwell was waiting to see him. He opened the door to find a familiar face alone in the usually crowded room.

"William, what are you doing here?" He told Callum to call him William in the weeks they spent at Millie's side. "Col. Caldwell ordered me to meet him here."

"You've found him."

Callum didn't understand the masquerade but understood that he shouldn't ask. It seemed that every citizen of Britain had signed the Official Secrecy Act by now. Asking someone in uniform a direct question only guaranteed they would lie to you.

"How can I help you?"

"I have a letter here from Peter to Millie." William held the letter like it was the crown jewels. "He gave it to me for her when he got his wings."

"So, she knows he is dead."

"I received word from my mother suggesting as much. I understand she has visited his grave."

"I bet she was pretty steamed that we buried him without her."

"Mother didn't say."

"You didn't go to the grave with her." Callum took a seat, stunned.

"Millie doesn't want to see me." William joined him at the table.

There was a knock on the door. "I understand you ordered some tea."

"Indeed, you can put it between us."

Callum couldn't believe it. He had never seen tea delivered at the base before. *Who are you around here?* He couldn't make out if William's social or military rank earned him such fine treatment. Either way, if he hadn't understood how important the name Trayford was before, it was clear now. William poured the tea and offered Callum both cream and sugar. *Unbelievable. No wonder Millie and Peter never told this man no.*

"I need you to take this to Millie."

Callum stirred the tea to cool it. "I'm not sure she wants to see me, either."

"Well, I am certain she doesn't want to see me. I've done something unforgivable." William paused and took a drink of the Earl Grey. "If I hold on to this too long, it will be added to my list of crimes."

"Millie wants to see you, sir. I'm sure of it. She values your opinion above all. I'm sure she has lots to decide. She will want your help." He put down the spoon, lest the clinking get on William's nerves. "Besides, don't you want to be with her when she reads the letter? It's bound to upset her."

"I assure you, you should take the letter." William grew anxious and got up to walk across the room.

"May I ask what you did that would stop Millie from seeing you?"

"You may ask, but I won't say."

Callum nodded. He had known better. "I would be happy to take the letter, but I only have ten hours for sleep before I have to get back into the air."

William drank down the tea. "If that's the only thing stopping you, I can make arrangements. Sending you to her is the least I can do."

Callum joined William at the door. "Should I go right away?" He hoped the answer was yes.

"Get some sleep first." William shook Callum's hand, grateful he had agreed. "If I can ever return the favor."

Callum walked William to the main entrance and held the door as Col. Caldwell left. Before William reached the end of the path, he turned around briefly. "Will you propose now that Elliot is out of the way for good?"

Callum started to answer but hesitated. He wasn't sure he wanted to tell William that he planned to ask her the moment he saw her again. He had wanted to since the day he found Millie in the cockpit of his plane at RAF Wick.

They hadn't bumped into each other since Millie arrived at the train station at Wick, but the locals who worked at RAF Wick buzzed about the future Duchess of Abberly coming to work with them. Callum kept an eye out, but they must have been on opposite shifts, and he had learned from Mrs. Layla that Millie billeted at Teaghlach. He had planned to ask his mother to finagle an invitation to the grand old manor house for them if they didn't bump into each other soon.

He watched from the edge of the hangar door as she poked her head in and announced her presence.

"Hello?" Her voice echoed. "Hello?"

Callum didn't answer her. He wanted to see what she would do next.

She rolled up the tracing paper and photos she carried and tucked them into her pocket before she stepped up on the wing of his plane. He wondered if the same adrenaline that coursed through his veins as he slipped into the cockpit ran through hers.

He came around the plane's tail once she planted herself in the tiny cockpit. He watched as she ran her fingers over the dashboard and then pulled something out of her breast pocket. She looked through the tiny rectangular metal box. She concentrated on the metal dials and instruments first, and then turned her attention to the floor. *She found my cameras.*

He heard the familiar clicking when she flipped on the camera's timing mechanism. It reminded Callum of a metronome keeping four/four time. Leaving the mechanism running, Millie stood. *She's going to see the lenses.* Callum dashed into the corner, knocking over a broom.

The sound of the sudden crash sent Millie slithering back into the cockpit, where she tried to make herself small. *Nice try. It's no bigger than a bathtub in there.* He decided to reveal himself, though he did wonder how long she would wait before popping her head up to see who might be there.

He climbed the ladder to the cockpit, peered over, and said, "What do we have here?"

Millie looked up into familiar eyes, relieved. "Hello, I was just having a look around." She lifted her eyebrows and shoulders simultaneously.

"What brings you out to the hangar? We don't see many photo interpreters out here. They're always too busy staring through those strange glasses."

"Stereoscopes," Millie said.

"What's that?"

"They're called stereoscopes. It's how we see things in three dimensions."

Callum knew that, but he liked the sound of her voice, so he tried to keep her talking. "And have you found anything interesting today?"

"Perhaps I need to verify it with the pilot." She suddenly remembered her errand. "I'm looking for pilot number 73B78."

"Well, it seems he's found you. And he's glad he did." He offered her a hand out of his plane. At that moment, she smiled a smile that set Callum's heart racing. There wasn't much to it, nothing to explain his physical reaction, but when she touched his hand, she smiled. She had hooked him when they were ten years old.

She kept her eyes down, hiding the blush in her cheeks, and fumbled to get the traces and photo out of her pocket. Straightening her blouse, she finally looked at him and said, "We need to get images to RAF Medmenham, but first, I need to verify some things."

"I get it, but before I agree to help, you have to promise to have a cup of coffee with me once we're off duty." He led Millie outside and headed toward the main offices.

"Do you usually have to coerce women into going out with you?" Millie asked, smirking.

Callum stopped in his tracks and turned around. He took a measured step toward her so that they stood toe to toe. Callum's stomach dropped, but he kept his cool. He leaned in slightly and whispered, "Not usually, but you are hard to track down."

Millie burst out laughing, a laugh so contagious Callum couldn't help but laugh along. She put a hand on his chest, pushing him back, and threw him a half-smile. "Do those lines work on anyone?" Callum stood, without a response, gobsmacked. She waited for another moment longer, but he couldn't get past the surprise, so she took over. "I'd be happy to have coffee anytime, or maybe some fish at Mrs. Layla's. Now, tell me about these traces so I can send them south."

William interrupted his memory. "I said, will you propose now that Elliot is out of the way for good?"

"I don't know," Callum lied. He wasn't sure it was any of William's business.

William nodded. He knew the boy was lying. He had watched him watching Millie for weeks. He had never seen someone more in love. He took a step toward his car and turned to say, "If you decide to, please know that I won't stand in your way."

# CHAPTER FIFTY-FOUR

Stellan Hall

May 16, 1944

20 days until D-Day


One morning in May, Fiona announced she would return to Teaghlach. The evacuees and orphans she had taken in were giving Mrs. Drummond fits, plus her people depended on her. Millie joined her in her room while she packed to go.

"It's time you make some plans too. You might want to consider going back to RAF Medmenham. Your father seems to believe it is important." Fiona took a stack of shawls from the dresser drawer.

"To Hell with him." Millie slapped a pair of gloves into a full trunk, slamming down the lid. "He has lost the right to do my thinking for me."

"I don't believe you should let anyone do your thinking for you, but you are going to have to find a way to forgive your father for the Clara mess." Fiona saw Millie take in a deep breath, preparing to interrupt, and put up a hand. "It may be unforgivable, but he is the only parent you have left. Decide what you want and insist he get it for you. Let him prove himself again."

"I don't think I can." Millie shook with anger.

"Would you like me to help you sort it out?" Fiona folded the shawl with care.

"NO! I'm not ready."

"That's a child's answer, but I will let it go for now. Why don't you leave this to me and get some fresh air." Fiona watched her youngest grandchild stomp across the room, sure of her next steps. "I said fresh air, not a dark room."

Millie stomped until she found herself at Peter's grave. That's where Callum found her.

"It seems a strange sort of portrait." His voice made her pulse race. He must have been standing there for a while. *He knows what I've been doing.*

"I want evidence of this. Somehow, it reassures me knowing he will be here waiting for me. He loved this place." Millie turned her head slightly to find Callum standing there out of the corner of her eye. The last weight dropped, and suddenly she was in balance.

"Yes, he did—in a way, I never quite understood until I spent some time here while you were... He was content to live out his days here, and so he will." Callum didn't share everything he knew. Peter's plans to write and tell the stories of their childhood, like Mr. Barrie himself, could wait.

"You talk about the dead as if they are still alive."

"Not alive, but with us still to be sure. True friends in this life are hard to come by. I'll take mine any way they come."

"I missed you." Millie wanted to stop the tears, but she couldn't.

"I know. I missed you too. I found the idea of you here without Peter to be too much. And with the invasion heating up, no one is getting leave. Can you forgive me for staying away so long?" His voice cracked.

"It gave me some time to get to know myself." Millie began wiping her damp face.

"You may want to wait on that." Callum stepped forward and extended a hand with Peter's letter. Millie immediately recognized her name written in Peter's hand.

Millie looked into his eyes for the first time in five months. He looked strong and capable in his uniform. His hair had grown. It brushed against his wool collar. A few stray black hairs clung to his forehead. He wiped tears from his face.

"You sure look better. How are the nightmares?" he said.

The sound of his clear tenor voice stirred Millie's memories. "*Though humble it may be, there my angel waits for me.*" Her eyes may have been bandaged then, but she could see him in her mind's eye singing to her hours on end. She walked to him, took the letter, and rested her head on his chest. She wanted desperately to tell him she loved him and didn't want to live without him, but she was afraid. She had very little practice asking for what she wanted. *What if he doesn't feel the same?*

"Still pretty bad. I don't scream anymore, so at least everyone else is getting some rest."

"How much powder are you using to cover up those dark circles?" Callum smudged the makeup under her eyes.

"Enough." She looked up at him and smiled. Her heart swelled with joy standing near him.

"Are you going back to RAF Medmenham? Your father says they need you."

"I won't go back." She knew he would accept her decision without question.

He nods. "It would have been nice to have you closer." He tangled his fingers up with hers. "I hear you turned Elliot down."

"It was pretty bad." She didn't tell him about Clara. She didn't want her father to steal this moment too. "But I couldn't say yes."

"And why is that?"

"I think you know." They locked eyes.

"Millicent!" Fiona called from the gate. They jerked apart instinctually. "I need to be on my way to the station." She looked at the ground, embarrassed she had interrupted them.

"Walk me back to the house," Millie said. A moment lost, again.

"Aren't you going to read the letter?"
"I'd rather do that alone. We can talk about it after?"
"All righty then. Let's get the Duchess to her train."

# CHAPTER FIFTY-FIVE

**Belgravia House**

**May 20, 1944**

16 days until D-Day

Millie gripped the satchel hung across her body, willing her photographs and Peter's letter to give her courage. She took the front steps fortified and feeling strong, having left her newly abandoned cane at Stellan Hall. She called ahead this time and knew her father was home. She paused at the front door, remembering better times.

She was eleven again and sitting in her father's plane, getting ready to take off for the first time in her life. It was the perfect birthday present.

Going to the aerodrome had always been a thrill, but until that day, she had kept her feet firmly on the ground. Once they got to the airfield, her father handed her a box. It held a luxurious leather jacket with a collar of thick yellow curled wool and a pair of matching boots. Unlacing her shoes and setting them aside, she pulled on the boots, tucking in the legs of her slacks. The luxurious lining cushioned her feet as she pressed them into the leather-made nest. She smiled up at her father. He lifted her chin and gave her an approving glance, adding, "It gets pretty cold up there."

The white wings of the Tiger Moth shot out from the bright red body of the biplane. The wing creaked a bit under their weight, but it didn't faze Millie. Nothing was going to deter her from taking her new rangefinder camera up and capturing the aerial sights.

"Millie, that camera cannot make an image from the sky. Unless, of course, I try to fly at an altitude of two feet," her father teased.

"Never mind, you," she said. "Look for the unusual. That is what you always say. And studying the world like a bird is a first for me."

*How could I have known that day was the beginning of my training? That Father knew precisely how to capture images at that height. Or that he would one day manipulate me into joining him in his work. I was naïve and just so damn thrilled to be invited into his world.*

At the top of the runway, the mechanic gave the prop a turn, and they sped ahead. Millie's body began to hum as they lifted off the ground. She felt gravity loosen its grip the moment the back wheels left the runway. Then they were riding the currents like a bird on the wind. As they flew, her father reached up and back to hold her hand—pure bliss. She had never felt so free in her life.

Three years later, she discovered that the inaugural flight had been Peter's doing. William confessed the day she began flying lessons that he never imagined she would be interested. The shared interest forged a bond between them, which William broke when he lied about Clara. *How am I supposed to forgive him?* She knew she had to find a way.

William sat alone in his study. Their cook kept her promise to Millie and let her visit be a surprise. Millie didn't want him running away. She wanted to get started with her new life and today's conversation blocked the way.

"Hello, Father," Millie said from just outside the door. She dreamt of barging in, making a scene with words that stabbed right at the jugular, but it simply wasn't her style.

William looked up and returned his fountain pen to its well with shaking hands. Flying fighter planes and then photo recon sorties hadn't ever set him so on edge. Before him stood his daughter, looking more like her mother, his beloved, than ever. He wanted to go to her on bended knee and beg for forgiveness for it all: for manipulating her to his cause, for bullying Peter into the Air Force, for indulging Clara, for lying to Millie about her death. She would have kept his secret, Clara had said so, but William insisted on his way. He couldn't risk her going her own way. He wanted her with him. Avenging Clara's death gave her reason to join him.

"There is a lot to discuss, I know, but I need to tell you something first." William made his way to his favorite chair, flanking the unlit fireplace. He gestured that Millie should join him.

"What else can there possibly be?" Millie spat out the words.

"Clara wanted to tell you about her assignment in France. She believed you could and would keep her secret. I insisted she go along with the lie when it presented itself." William found it hard to push out the confession. *How could I have doubted her loyalty? Put the government's rules over my daughter. I should have just asked her to help.*

Millie's heart broke as she watched her father shrinking in front of her. She clutched her satchel to her chest, sitting across from him, reminding herself that he had yet to begin his penance.

"Why was she sent at all?" Millie sucked at her teeth, seething. *Why did I take the bait? This is how he does it, isn't it? He pulls in a slightly different direction, fooling you into talking around a subject and thinking you reached a resolution when you haven't.* Today she wouldn't regret that they never got to the heart of the matter. Today she would hold tight to the thread.

William started to formulate a lie. Lies were less complicated than truth, but he hewed to the truth instead, hitting only the highlights. "She did some clandestine work for me between the wars. She speaks perfect German and French, as you know. She planned on working with the Red Cross this time around, but when they, and by them, I mean the Germans, killed her grandfather, she wanted, or perhaps it would be more accurate to say she needed, to do more."

Millie had never heard her father ramble so. He looked calm, collected, his typical self on the outside, but his stammering gave him away. *He is as nervous as I am.*

"That all sounds very heroic and protective of Clara, but is it true?" *It would be just like him to lie about the entire thing, so I wouldn't be estranged from them both.*

"It is," William leaned forward, trying to take her hand. "I promise."

The gesture set Millie off. She snapped her hands back and slid them under her legs. "You're not getting off so easily. You let me believe that my passions wouldn't help, couldn't help. You made my dreams seem selfish. You never..." Millie wasn't as well equipped to go for the jugular as Elliot, but her father needed to learn a lesson. "You never supported me the way you did Mother. You spent my entire life making my dreams out to be small, petty even, instead of lifting me up." Millie got to her feet, placed her hands on the arms of her father's chair, and leaned in until she could smell the tobacco on his breath. "Women need more than the vote. We deserve respect for all we do. She would be so ashamed of you." She pushed off and turned her back on him, hiding her tears, angry with herself for shedding them.

The truth was she had no idea what her mother would think of all of it. And Millie would have had to enlist one way or another once conscription for women started, but he took her photography from her by relegating it to a pastime, not something she needed to do. *The Ministry of Information understood the power of an image. Why didn't he?*

William flew out of his chair, lunging toward her. *How dare she invoke Margaret? What right did she have to use his precious wife as a weapon?* He opened his mouth to strike back, catching the photo of Margaret and Millie on the mantle out of the corner of his eye. The very picture that rested over Millie's heart in the locket Clara had left for her. *Why had he forged that letter? Why did he let Millie believe Clara, too, wanted her to work as a spy of sorts?*

He slowed to a creep. She was his daughter, for God's sake, not some double agent to level to the ground. She deserved a parent, not a superior. But William had never developed that skill. He turned around and slumped back into his chair, hiding his face in his hands.

Millie waited. She waited for the fury she had seen when William sparred with her brothers, who knew exactly where their father's soft spots were and didn't hesitate to take aim. She hoped for a tender word, an admission of guilt, or at the least some tacit attempt at accepting the blame and a promise to do whatever it took to mend things between them. But the clock on the mantle ticked away, and she got nothing. If she wanted a father in her life, she would have to do the work for them both.

"Father, go sit at your desk," Millie commanded.

William stopped chewing the inside of his cheek and asked, "Why on earth do you want me to do that?"

"Because it will make you more comfortable with the conversation we need to have." Millie understood now that there would be no rending of clothes or self-flagellation. Her father wasn't built for that. He needed something to do to make amends—a list he could check off that spelled out what was required for forgiveness. And ripping into her father wasn't going to make Millie any happier. Weeks of wallowing in anger and despair had taught her that.

William took a seat, sitting up straight. "Well, let's have it."

"Have what?" Millie asked.

"The list of my sins."

"I don't have one. I've only brought along your penance." Millie saw the relief in her father's face. He thrived with an occupation. The only question that remained was whether or not he could let go of his agenda and give way to her demands.

Millie opened her satchel and pulled out Peter's letter and a stack of her favorite photographs. She started with the letter. "First, did Peter write this?"

"Yes. I may be a practiced liar, but I am no forger."

"But you forged the letter from Clara." It was a guess, but Millie needed to know.

"I did, but if you recall, it was typed."

"How do you keep all the lies straight?" Millie shook her head.

"Years of practice."

"In this letter," Millie didn't open it. The folds were fragile from constant reading, and to date, she hadn't managed to read it without coming unraveled. "Peter told me to be easy on you if I found out about everything you have done for king and country. He claimed not to know much, but he said your work is dark and someone has to do it. Did he know about Clara?"

"No." William didn't elaborate. His worst crimes may have been against his son. He let Peter believe that Clara loved Millie more than him until the day he died. They had never understood each other, and Clara had been Peter's lifeline more times than William cared to admit. He took her from him the day he let them all believe Clara was dead and had written that letter. In a way, he used Millie when he persuaded Peter to participate in his plans to recruit her. Peter wanted to strike out on his own, and if William had allowed Millie to follow her dreams, Peter would have been unstoppable. Now he was dead. William would carry that particular crime to his grave. His daughter sat before him, now prepared to reconcile. He squirmed, preparing himself to pay the price, no matter the cost.

"If your work is as awful as Peter explains, king and country must owe you a favor or two?"

"As a matter of fact, they do, though I have had to cash in a few chips lately."

"Chips?"

William got up and poured them a drink, thinking how strange that it all began that way too. "I had Elliot flown out of France. I thought you would want that. But then, after two days by your bedside, I realized it was Callum all along. I arranged for him to stay for as long as I could. Planning for Operation Overlord was heating up." He handed a glass to Millie. "They needed the photo recon pilots."

"Don't try to distract me." Millie sipped her drink, wagging a finger at him.

"I want out." She began spreading her best images on the table in front of William. "The War Office will never give me credentials as a photographer to go to France after the invasion, so I want you to invent a way for me to go. I'll do whatever you ask as long as I am allowed to take my cameras. After that, I will find a way to show the world my work, the work of these extraordinary women."

William lifted the original image of the girl at the bookstore first. It was exceptional. No wonder the MOI papered the countryside with it. The rest he hadn't seen. There was one of the Red Cross workers tending to the woman killed during the Blitz. Another of a laundress in billowing white linen sleeves rolled up to her elbows, exposing the healed melted skin from regular encounters with scalding water. A stunning shot of a pair of plump, blemish-free hands—the left one wearing a thin golden band, with fingertips laced with whitening scars from the small collar irons. There was even one of a woman in uniform. It lacked much of the softness of the others, but it was there. Millie had taken it from behind. William's eyes were drawn to the seams of her hose and a dangling curl caught up in her epaulet. They showed women in their entirety—the soft and the tough. They were masterful.

Finally, he came to two of the images taken at the munitions plant. The definition of sacrifice in two shots. One taken before the explosion, perfectly composed, balanced, elegant. It put him at ease. The next taken after the blast, chaotic, off-center, every line pointing to despair like the painting—Picasso's painting of Guernica. It made his stomach turn. Looking at them side by side, William could see what happened in the intervening moments. She would make the world see how fierce women were, how essential—if someone would give her a chance.

But the invasion was far from a certainty. It should have happened this month. Things, lack of machinery, weather, moon phases, kept getting in the way. He put the images down, opened his center desk drawer, and removed a folder filled with images. Images taken at thirty thousand feet, making it clear that the Germans hadn't given up on their plans for the flying bombs.

"If I agree to this…" William was interrupted by Millie.

"I'm not asking. You owe me this." She moved to the edge of her seat, hissing at him. "I will not be your puppet on a string any longer. You can do this for me, and you will."

William fell back into form. "And if I don't?"

"I am ready to have that conversation." Millie got to her feet and picked up the image of her mother and her from the corner of his desk. She calmly said, "Are you?"

William leapt to his feet, fist planted on his desktop. "I don't like being pushed into a corner, young lady."

Millie waited for the shaking to come, for her heart to pound against her rib cage, for the heat to travel up to her face, but none of that happened. Months lying in a bed, thinking, formulating, and dreaming had reshaped her. Sure, he might refuse to help or stand in her way or, worst of all, abandon her, but she had seen the worst life had to throw at her and had made it through. She would make it through this too.

"It may come as a surprise to you, Father, but no one does. You have to ask yourself if it matters to you how I help. Isn't the important thing that I am doing my part?" Millie looked down at the framed portrait in her hand and tilted it for William to see. "Wouldn't she want you to help me find my own path instead of forcing me down yours?"

She had found a way to go for the jugular after all, and she didn't feel an ounce of shame.

William ground his teeth, fighting the urge to go after her like one of his subordinates. He looked down at his desk and the folder he had retrieved. His breathing came like a bull preparing to charge.

"Father, look at me." Millie walked around the desk and touched his left arm. He flinched, but she left her hand there. "Lots of people can read photographs. RAF Medmenham is filled with them." She pointed to her photos. "I'm the only person who sees the world like that. I need to take my chance. Look at me." She caressed his cheek. "I'm going to be taking pictures, with or without your help. I want you on my side."

The speech took William back to Margaret's early days in the suffragette movement and the first time he had to bail her out of jail. It stung, but Margaret pointed out to him she had done it, not him. She assured him she had done nothing to be ashamed of and reminded him that she had committed to this cause long before she committed to him. He couldn't blame her for being herself. She had never lied to him about who she was.

Millie stood before him now, finally coming into her own. He ought to be proud of her determination. He ought to move heaven and earth to help her show the world how important women were. He ought to, but...

William allowed himself to see his daughter, tall, beautiful, intelligent, and capable. He would miss having a common purpose with her. But he wouldn't miss her. Placing his hand over hers, he said, "Is there a deal to be made?"

Millie smiled. William wouldn't be William if he didn't try to get a little for himself. She sat on the edge of his desk. "What do you propose?"

William took up the folder full of images. He handed it and a stereoscope to his daughter.

"What am I looking for?" Millie took the offering.

"Ramps." His eyes bore into hers.

"You said we bombed all of the ramps."

"That was back in December," he said.

With the images under the glasses, Millie put a finger in the middle of each photo and slid them this way and that until she only saw one finger through the stereoscope. Magic. The images blended, transforming them from 2-D to 3-D. She scanned from corner to corner and back again to get her bearings. Pass after pass, she saw factories, cars, people, and tracks, but no ramps. She started from the bottom the next time. Halfway up the image, a metal inclined frame emerged between two buildings.

"It looks portable. It's not stable like the others. Have they tried to fire a missile?" She pointed to the ramp on the photograph.

"That's my girl," her father smirked.

"I hate disappointing you, Father, but it's just like I said months ago at RAF Medmenham. They build it. We find and destroy it. They build something new, and we're off, trying to puzzle it all out again. I won't do it anymore. I need to show the world what I see. What I know, so I can persuade them to stop limiting women and their choices. So women can finally get the credit they deserve." She pushed the photos and glasses into her father's hand.

"I could force you." It was a commanding officer speaking, not her father.

"But you won't." Millie wrapped her arm around him.

"How will you get the images published?"

"If you get me to France, I will find a way." Millie went back to her seat. Taking hold of her locket, she considered asking after Clara, but she stopped herself. One battle at a time.

# CHAPTER FIFTY-SIX

Senate House-British Intelligence Headquarters
June 6, 1944
D-Day

William held his breath as he slipped the top-secret document from its envelope. He had been awaiting its arrival since the wee hours of the morning when he got the call that there had been a break in the weather and the naval component of the French invasion was underway. The words Operation Overlord were underlined twice with a red pencil. Here are the words that followed:

> *Only Juno Beach and Gold Beach have been connected. Carentan, Saint-Lo, Caen and Bayeux remain in German hands. The search for the V1 and the V2 weapons must continue.*

The last sentence was written in all caps with the offending pencil.

# CHAPTER FIFTY-SEVEN

Grove Road, London

June 13, 1944

7 days after D-Day

The driver stopped in front of the destroyed railway bridge.

"Are you sure this is the right place, Miss?" the driver said.

The radio announcer had said air raid sirens sounded in Woolrich for the first time since the D-Day invasion at Normandy. The Ministry of Information informed the press that it was nothing but a solitary enemy raider and that it was shot down on Grove Road in the Mile End district.

"This is it. Do you mind waiting? You can keep the meter running," Millie said.

"Not at all," he said.

From the looks of it, the bomb fell on the railroad bridge. Both it and the surrounding tracks were demolished. The houses that once lined the tracks looked like a row of giant haystacks. The home guard was busy digging in every direction.

Millie waded through the debris and took a seat on a mound of bricks. She lifted her camera to her face and scanned the landscape. In the top right corner of her viewfinder, Millie saw a woman holding a child. She got up and crept toward her. She closed half the distance. That's when she saw it. A bounce of light reflected off a hunk of metal sticking out of the dusty terrain.

The Home Guard hauled out pieces of the bomb—the V1

bomb that took her so long to find under her stereoscope. One finally made it, but not before the Allies had a foothold in France. Six workers sifted through rubble to unearth a pulse-jet engine, large chunks of shrapnel, and an intact tail fin. The men loaded each piece they uncovered into an unmarked lorry driven by an RAF officer. Millie's finger twitched, anxious to snap a picture, so she allowed herself just one shot, and then she turned her attention back to the woman.

Millie knelt less than five feet away. The woman held a young boy, limp from death, in her arms, rocking him. Millie blinked away tears and began shooting. Her heart cracked into a thousand tiny pieces when the mother's lullaby hit her ears, unsettling her. It made her think of Callum singing her back to her life. Gratitude mixed with sorrow. After packing her feelings and ambitions away like items for the charity barrels for years, she welcomed the tears.

Two shots in, Millie heard a rustling behind her. She twisted and placed her finger on hushing lips. Callum stood two feet behind her as if she conjured him up with her memory.

She waved for him to join her.

"How did you know I was here?" Millie said.

"I went to your house, and your father said I could find you here. He seemed relieved that I was coming to check on you. I think he is nervous about you going into the fray." He took in the scene. *He isn't the only one.*

"What happened?"

"A pilotless bomb is what happened." Millie kept taking pictures of the mother. She moved a few steps closer. A female member of the Home Guard approached the mother and urged her to let go of the lifeless child. She snapped two more pictures. The mother gently laid the child down and leaned in to kiss him. Millie's shutter slapped as they lifted a blanket over his face. Millie stopped time once again, and a single burst of satisfaction spread through her veins.

"Shouldn't we do something to help?" Callum said.

"The Home Guard has the clean-up under control." Millie wiped away her tears with her shirttail. *We all have jobs to do.* "It is wretched work, and they've been at it for so long."

Millie turned and started toward the taxicab, anxious to be on her way. Her father had made arrangements for her to attach to a Red Cross unit going to the hospitals in Bayeux, France. She agreed to send him messages if she learned anything of particular interest in exchange for taking all the images she wanted. His colleagues had given her a basic training of sorts in the last few weeks. She had to admit it seemed thrilling. One of his agents in France would meet her in Bayeux. Millie walked faster, afraid that if she fell into Callum's arms, she would never want to leave.

"Millie, will you ever stop running?" Callum grabbed her hand.

She didn't turn around, but she relaxed her hand into his. He spun her around to face him.

"Are you ever going to slow down?" He laced his fingers into hers.

"Probably not. There are too many stories to tell."

"Then I'd better take my chance while I have it."

He pulled her into a kiss, tender and delicious. Melting into him, Millie stamped out the regret threatening to spread at the thought of wasting so much time with Elliot. She tightened her grip on Callum's hand when her tongue found his. When she was sure she would float away on the wind like a seed, she pushed him away. She wanted to see him. She wanted him to see her. She wanted him to know that she was his.

Their eyes locked, and Millie heard a hushed, "Finally."

Callum slipped his hand into her mane of hair and let out a satisfied moan before leaning in for more, but Millie placed her finger on his lips. It was the hardest thing she'd ever done.

"We have a lifetime for that." She swept a dark curl away from his eyes. "Right now, I need to get home. I have to finish packing. I leave in the morning for France."

"I bet I can persuade you to stay." He leaned in again with a dirty look in his eyes before jerking back. "Your father asked me to deliver this."

Millie grabbed it and tore it open, skimming the words.

"He's agreed. Callum! Mr. Graham agreed!" She took Callum's face in her hands and kissed him hard like she had been celebrating with him all her life.

Callum pulled away just enough to ask, "Agreed to what?"

"He will process and print my images. Father will get him the film, and my work will be published!" Millie knew it was a small outlet, but it felt right. "And if the images are good enough, one of the bigger papers will have to take notice."

"They'll notice." Callum kissed her ear lobe, her neck, and moved to her lips.

When they came up for air, Millie whispered in his ear, "When are you flying next?"

"Tomorrow afternoon." He pulled her into the cab.

Hands folded in her lap like a praying child, Millie looked up at him and said, "Would you like to come home with me? Father is bound to be out for the night with everything happening in France."

"I thought you'd never ask."

# CHAPTER FIFTY-EIGHT

**Bayeux, France**
**June 14, 1944**
8 days after D-Day

Kitted out with the basics, Millie stepped onto French soil. The last time she was in France was for the Paris World's Fair, where she had seen the painting by Picasso. She set down her pack, and it caught on the emerald ring Callum slipped on her finger that morning. He told her he would wait as long as she needed. He reminded her he would love and admire her for the rest of his life. He begged her to be careful. And then he humbly asked her to wear a token of his love until he slipped a golden band in its place on the day of their wedding.

Millie agreed to it all and gave him her locket in return, along with a copy of a photo of the two of them taken on the day of the picnic in Wick. Callum picked her up and spun her around, putting her down with a thud when Millie added that she didn't want him to come to the airfield with her. She had gotten lost in him that night, flooded by feelings, physical and emotional, that she wanted desperately. If he came with her, she might not get on the plane. Kissing his pouting face, all she could think was *yummy*.

William had come to the airfield. He implored her to stay on the proper side of the battle lines. He reviewed the procedure for sending messages and film and gave her the code name of the agent who would meet her in France—Bonnie

Marie. William found himself the coward once again. He couldn't bring himself to tell her the truth. He depended on the fact that his now self-assured daughter would manage the revelation with grace. He prayed he wasn't wrong.

Making her way down the grassy airstrip after landing in France, Millie saw a woman walking with the aid of a cane coming toward her on the makeshift tarmac. As they drew closer, the woman's face came into focus. It was misshapen, but familiar. It was the face of the woman who had read her an adventure and tucked her into bed every night after her mother died, until the day she left for boarding school. She wanted to be mad at her for leaving her, but she couldn't. She dropped her pack and began to run.

Flying into Clara's arms, Millie smiled through tears. Clara, back from the dead. "I missed you every day." She held Clara tight.

"And I you." Clara dropped her cane and wrapped both of her arms around Millie. "I'm so sorry."

"Don't. We are together. That's all that matters." Millie held tight, feeling restored, courageous. "Knowing I would see you again made me strong. It kept me from walking with one of those myself." Millie pulled back, running her fingers down Clara's fire-scarred face. "You were in the flat, then, when the bombs came?"

"I was." Clara found the only words she could speak without breaking down. She began to tremble.

Millie gathered her things and guided Clara to the jeep, helping her take a seat.

"You're not wearing the locket." Clara noticed.

"No, I left it with Callum." Millie smiled in spite of herself. "In exchange for this." She extended her hand, showing Clara the new emerald ring.

"So, no more Elliot?"

"No, when I told him I couldn't marry him, he immediately struck out and told me you helped him out of France. Telling me about the betrayal seemed to thrill him." Millie began shaking her head. "I don't know why I didn't see it before. Everyone else seemed to."

"Not Gertrude." Clara poked. They both broke out in laughter.

"I missed you." Millie hugged Clara again gratefully. She needed to come back to herself, and because of it all, she had. "And you are Bonnie Marie?"

"Indeed." Clara pushed Millie back so she could see her face and lifted her eyebrows. "Named for the flower."

Millie could see the plaque in the garden next to the Bonnie Marie camellia bush. *Impossible n'est pas français* to be sure.

"It's been a riveting few years, if not a bit challenging." She let Millie go, stepped back, and lifted her cane. "I'll be glad for the help. And glad to see you working with your cameras again. I was sorry to hear you had given them up."

"The war made navigating complicated. I couldn't find the right path. At least not at first."

"You just needed a push. You always have." Clara thought of Peter constantly needling her on. She didn't bring him up, though. They would have plenty of time to catch up on everything.

"It seems I needed a bomb to blow me out of my foxhole." Millie fiddled with the end of her braid.

"You ready for this?" Clara asked, taking hold of her hand.

"You bet I am!"

# EPILOGUE

---



Paris was alive. Reborn. Sitting with Millie in our favorite café, we enjoyed a cup of coffee while she caught up on dispatches from London. In her packet, she found a note from her father, a note from Mr. Graham, and a copy of the latest *John O'Groat*.

She opened the paper to see the headline *Humanity Victorious over Vengeances*. Under it, Mr. Graham inserted a photo of the French women of Bayeux, together with American and British Red Cross workers, tending to German soldiers' wounds. The headline came to Millie as she photographed the many who were once captive tend to the wounds of their captors. She told me it seemed miraculous to her, and she mused aloud, "Could I help the men who dropped the bomb that injured you or killed Peter?" She wasn't so sure she could. She hoped the image expressed to the world how magnificent these women were. She pushed the paper to me.

Taking a sip of her coffee, she handed me the freshly printed paper.

Reading it, I said, "He used your headline suggestion."

Millie nodded with a grin and moved on to the notes, handing them over as she finished them. Paris may have been liberated, but it still had big ears. Mr. Graham wrote to say he had shared three more photos with *The London Times* and

*The Daily Mirror. The Times* asked again for a way to contact Millie directly. I suggested she write back and ask Mr. Graham to act as her agent. She could give him first rights to printing. He had proven to be a loyal friend, after all. After that, they could be spread far and wide. I knew Millie intended to get the images in front of as many eyes as possible. The *Times* and the *Mirror* were just the ticket.

She read her father's note last. I took the note and read it next. His coded message told her the big rocket had finally made its way to London. Standing four stories high and carrying a ton of explosives, it killed three people and injured twenty-two. The contents didn't surprise me. I had received an identical message myself.

"He has been looking for that monster since before the war." I took a bite of a day-old piece of bread. "For a long time, he was the only one who believed they existed."

"It took a hell of a lot to convince the War Cabinet they were real." Millie skimmed the note again. "I'm sorry he was right."

I nodded and lit a cigarette. As the lid of the lighter slapped back into place, I noticed Millie turn the ring from Callum round her finger before picking up her camera and loading a new roll of film.

"What photo will you send next?" I asked.

# AUTHOR'S NOTE

A few years back, I came upon an episode of NOVA on PBS called "3D Spies of WWII" (season 39, episode 3). It described how the Allied forces used aerial reconnaissance and stereo photography to spy on the Nazis. The program emphasized the outsized role women had in the enterprise and for me, the hook was set. I spent a few years learning all I could about the program, reading books and visiting places of interest, and finally Millie's story was born.

The timelines and major events have been represented here as accurately as possible. Please forgive any small adjustments. As for the characters, most are the invention of my imagination, with a few exceptions.

For those of you who know your WW2 history, names like Churchill, Eisenhower, Hitler, and Goebbels will not be new. Others like Duncan Sandy, Hugh Hamshaw Thomas, Douglas Kendall, and Lord Cherwell may not be so familiar. While Millie and the others were concocted through the compilation of real people, a few, those listed above, Constance Babington Smith, and Amnianix (a.k.a. Jeannie Rousseau) are real people. I included them so you might know their names and contributions, especially the women. Constance Babington Smith is credited by some for discovering the V1 flying bomb while working closely with the Crossbow team. Amnianix worked for Allied intelligence as a member of the Druid network in France. They and many other women, most of whose contributions have been lost to history, helped stop the Nazis, including the work they were doing at Peenemunde. It is my hope that I have done their legacy justice on the pages of this book.

## Places of Interest

Danesfield House Hotel and Spa, Marlow, UK—Home to RAF Medmenham during WW2

National Collection of Aerial Photography, Edinburgh, Scotland

Peenemunde Historical Technical Museum, Peenemunde, Germany

La Coupole WW2, near Saint Omer, France

Battle of Britain Bunker, Uxbridge, England

Churchill War Rooms, London, England

British National Archives, Kew, Richmond, England

National Air and Space Museum, Washington, D.C., United States

## Books of Interest

*Women of Intelligence* by Christine Halsall

*Evidence in Camera* by Constance Babington Smith

*Operation Crossbow* by Allan Williams

*Spies in the Sky* by Taylor Downing

# ACKNOWLEDGEMENTS

Ten years in the making, this journey began with a short story and a NOVA special called *3D Spies of World War II*. I am indebted to the historians who have copiously recorded the details surrounding Operation Crossbow and the arduous work done by the folks who worked at RAF Medmenham. They inspired this work. Special thanks are owed to Peter Faarup at Danesfield House, once home to RAF Medmenham, and Kevin McLaren at the National Collection of Aerial Photography in Edinburgh. Walking the halls of that great home and looking through the stereoscope at a pair of images taken of Peenemunde made the past come to life for me. I am also grateful for the access to all sorts of documents stored at the British National Archives in Kew. It is a wonder holding papers and photographs made by the folks I spent so much time with on the page over these years.

I would never have gone digging but for my love of history, inherited from my dad, and of reading, inherited from my mom. I thank you both. These pages would not exist if not for all my early readers, especially Loriee Evans, Ann Matzke, Meredith Beau, Martha Ayers, Jenna Clark and Christi Loper. I thank you all. Special thanks to Trista Edwards, whose editorial eye improved my tale. And, but for the encouragement of Emily Roberson and my beloved, these pages would not have made it out into the world. Thank you both for making me brave.

# ABOUT ATMOSPHERE PRESS

Founded in 2015, Atmosphere Press was built on the principles of Honesty, Transparency, Professionalism, Kindness, and Making Your Book Awesome. As an ethical and author-friendly hybrid press, we stay true to that founding mission today.

If you're a reader, enter our giveaway for a free book here:

SCAN TO ENTER
BOOK GIVEAWAY

If you're a writer, submit your manuscript for consideration here:

SCAN TO SUBMIT
MANUSCRIPT

And always feel free to visit Atmosphere Press and our authors online at atmospherepress.com. See you there soon!

# ABOUT THE AUTHOR

**MELISSA CLARK BACON** was raised and stayed in Little Rock, Arkansas. By day, she works as a data analyst, and by night, she writes stories and makes photographs using historic and alternative printing processes. Her short story, "The Handkerchief," where her character Millie first appears, won Best in Show Adult Fiction Short Story at the Grand Prairie Festival of the Arts. Her current creative work focuses on revealing unnoticed women from the past through captivating stories and photographs that aspire to elevate their contributions and offer them up as role models to women today. *Through Her Lens* is her debut novel.

melissaclarkbacon.com

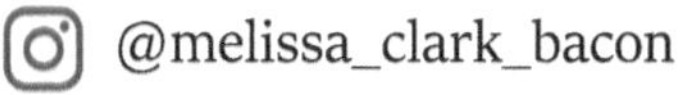
@melissa_clark_bacon